THE MAID OF THE WHISPERING HILLS

VINGIE E. ROE

1ST WORLD
LIBRARY
Literary Society

The Maid of the Whispering Hills

Vingie E. Roe

© 1st World Library, 2008
PO Box 2211
Fairfield, IA 52556
www.1stworldlibrary.com
First Edition

LCCN: 2007935415

Softcover ISBN: 978-1-4218-9366-2
Hardcover ISBN: 978-1-4218-9466-9
eBook ISBN: 978-1-4218-9266-5

Purchase *"The Maid of the Whispering Hills"*
as a traditional bound book at:
www.1stWorldLibrary.com/purchase.asp?ISBN=978-1-4218-9366-2

1st World Library is a literary, educational organization
dedicated to:

- Creating a free internet library of downloadable ebooks

- Hosting writing competitions and offering book publishing
scholarships.

Interested in more 1st World Library books? contact:
literacy@1stworldlibrary.com

Check us out at: www.1stworldlibrary.com

1st World Library Literary Society

Giving Back to the World

"If you want to work on the core problem, it's early school literacy."

- James Barksdale, former CEO of Netscape

"No skill is more crucial to the future of a child, or to a democratic and prosperous society, than literacy."

- Los Angeles Times

"Literacy... means far more than learning how to read and write... The aim is to transmit... knowledge and promote social participation."

- UNESCO

"Literacy is not a luxury, it is a right and a responsibility. If our world is to meet the challenges of the twenty-first century we must harness the energy and creativity of all our citizens."

- President Bill Clinton

"Parents should be encouraged to read to their children, and teachers should be equipped with all available techniques for teaching literacy, so the varying needs and capacities of individual kids can be taken into account."

- Hugh Mackay

To My Mother Who Has Been My Constant Help

My Father Who Was Proud Of Me

And My Little Brother,

These Two Long Asleep On The Hill At Carney—

This Book Is Lovingly Inscribed V. E. R.

CONTENTS

CHAPTER I

THE VENTURERS

"Mercy!" shrieked little Francette, her red-rose face aghast, "he will begin before I can bring the help!"

Like a flash of flame the maid in her crimson skirt shot up the main way of Fort de Seviere to where the factory lay asleep in the warm spring sun.

On its log step, pipe in mouth, young Anders McElroy leaned against the jamb and looked smilingly out upon his settlement. Peace lay softly upon it, from the waters of the small stream to the east where nine canoes lay bottom up upon the pebbly shore, to the great dark wall of the forest shouldering near on three sides. To him ran little Francette, light on her moccasined feet as the wind in the tender pine-tops, her eloquent small hands outstretched and clutching at his sleeve audaciously.

None other in all the post would have dared as much, for this smiling young man with the blue eyes was the Law at Fort de Seviere, factor of the Company and governor of the handful of humanity lost in the vast region of the Assiniboine. But to Francette he was Power and Help, and she thought of naught else, as it is not likely she would have done even at another time.

"Oh, M'sieu!" she cried, gasping from her run, "come at once beyond the great gate! Bois DesCaut,—Oh, brute of the world!—whips that great grey husky leader of his team, because it did but snap at his heel beneath an idle prod! Hasten, M'sieu! He drags it, glaring, along the shore to where lie those clubs brought for the kettles!"

In the dark eyes upraised to him there swam a mist of tears and the heart of the little maid tore at her breast in anguish.

The smile slipped swiftly from the factor's face, leaving it grave.

"Where, little one?" he asked.

"Beyond the palisade. But hurry, M'sieu,—for the love of God!"

At the great gate in the eastern wall he paused and looked either way. To the southward all was peaceful. An aged Indian of the Assiniboines squatted at the water's edge mending the broken bottom of a skin canoe, and two voyageurs, gay in the matter of sash and crimson cap, lay lazily beneath a drowsing tree.

To the northward there flashed into McElroy's vision one of those pictures a man sees but few times and never forgets, a picture startling in its clear-cut strength.

Against the mellow background of the weather-beaten stockade that surrounded the post there stood two figures, a man and a woman, and between the two there crouched with snarling lips and flaming eyes a huge grey dog.

Tall he was, that man, tall and broad of shoulder, but the head of the woman, shining like blue-black satin in the morning sun, was level with his brows.

She leaned a trifle forward and her eyes held fast to his passion-flooded face. It was evident that she had but just reached the spot from the fact that the club, arrested in its upward swing, still was poised in the air.

They faced each other and the factor stopped in his tracks.

"Quick, M'sieu!" begged Francette at his side, but he put out a commanding hand and ceased to breathe.

"Hold!" said the tall young woman at last, and her voice cut cold and clear in the sun-filled morning. "No more! You have whipped the dog enough."

The red face of the trapper flamed into purple and his lips opened for an oath. Quick as the heat lightning that flutters on the waters of Winipigoos in the hot summers the cruel club came down. McElroy heard its dull impact, and the husky crumpled like a broken reed.

With stern face the factor started forward, while the little maid covered her pretty eyes and whimpered.

But quicker than his stride retribution leaped to meet DesCaut.

He saw the woman's arm shoot out and her strong hand, smooth and tawny as finest tanned buckskin, double itself hard and leap in where the jaw turns downward into the curve of the throat.

The stroke of a man it was, clean and sharp and well

delivered, and DesCaut, catching his heel on a buried stone's sharp jut, went backward with his head in the young grass of the sloping shore.

For a moment she stood as it had left her, leaning forward, and there was a shine of satisfaction in her eyes.

Then as the man essayed to rise there was a mighty laughter from the two youths on the river bank and the spell was broken.

McElroy went forward.

"DesCaut," he said sharply, and his words cut like the lash of the long dog-whips, "you deserves death but you have been beaten by a woman. Go, and boast of your strength. It is sufficient."

DesCaut stood a moment swaying drunkenly with the force of passion within him, his lips snarling back from his teeth and his eyes measuring the factor unsteadily then he snatched off the little cap he wore and hurled it at him.

Turning on his heel he swung down toward the gate and the two voyageurs now standing and still laughing merrily.

One look at his bloodshot eyes sobered their mirth, and Pierre Garcon reached involuntarily for the knife in his sash.

But Bois DesCaut, savage to silence, swung past them into the fort.

McElroy watched him until he disappeared, fearing he knew not what.

Then he faced the little scene again.

Vingie E. Roe

Down on her knees little Francette had lifted the heavy head with its dull eyes and pitiful hanging tongue, lifted it to her breast, weeping and smoothing the short ears deaf to her soft words, and sat rocking to and fro in an ecstasy of grief. Beyond SHE stood, that tall woman, stood silent and frowning, looking down upon the two, and the factor saw with a strange thrill that the hand, yet doubled, was flecked with blood.

"Ma'amselle," he said, "is of the new people who arrived last night from Portage la Prairie?"

Then they were lifted for the first time to his face, those dark eyes smouldering like banked fires, and he saw their marvellous beauty.

"Of a surety," she said slowly, and there was a subtle tone in her deep-throated voice that made the blood stir vaguely within the factor's veins, "does M'sieu have so many strangers passing through his gates that he is at loss to place each one?"

And with that word she turned deliberately away, walked down toward the gate, and entered the stockade.

McElroy watched her go, until the last glint of her sober dress, plain and clinging easily to the magnificent shoulders that swung slightly with her free walk, had passed from view. And not alone he, for the two voyageurs alike gazed after her, this new-comer from the farther ways of civilisation who dared the brute DesCaut and struck like a man.

Then the factor bent above the little Francette.

"Sh!" he said gently, "little one, let go. The dog is dead, poor beast. Come away."

But the maid would not give up the battered body, and with the audacity of her beauty and life-long spoiling, besought the young factor for help.

"There is yet life, M'sieu. See! The breath lifts in his sides. Is there naught to be done when one sleeps, so? He is so strong at the sledges and he did not whimper,—no, not once,—when DesCaut was beating him to death. Is there nothing, M'sieu?"

Very pretty she was in her pleading, the little Francette, with her misty eyes and the frank tears on her cheeks; and McElroy went to the river and filled his cap with water. This he poured into the open jaws and sopped over the blood-clotted head, wetting the limp feet and watching for the life she so bravely proclaimed.

And presently it was there, twitching a battered muscle; lifting the side with its broken ribs, fluttering the lids over the fierce eyes; for this was Loup, the fiercest husky this side of the Athabasca.

With pity McElroy gathered up the great dog, staggering under the load, for it was that of a big-framed man, and entered the post, the little maid at has side. Near the gate a running crowd met them, for the tale had spread apace and wondering eyes looked on.

Down to the southern wall where lived the family of Francette they went, and the factor laid Loup in the shade of the cabin.

"If he lives, little one, he shall be yours," said he, "for he is worth a tender hand. We'll try its power."

Vingie E. Roe

And as he turned away he caught a glimpse of the tall stranger looking at them from a distance.

Small it was and crowded, this little trading post of the great Hudson's Bay Company in that year of 1796, and a goodly stream of beaver found its way through it to the mighty outside world.

Squatted alone on the shores of the Assiniboine, shouldering back the wilderness with the spirit of the conqueror, it faced the rising sun with its square stockade, strong and well built, log by log, its great, brass-studded gate in the eastern centre, its four bastions rising at its corners.

Here was a little world of itself, a small community of voyageurs, trappers, coureurs du bois, and all those that cast their lot in the wild places.

Adventurers from the Old World often passed through it on their way to the farther west, lured by the tales of dreamers who spoke of the Northwest Passage and the world that opened beyond the setting sun; renegades of the lakes and forest came for and found its ready hospitality, and into it came at all seasons those Indians whose skill and cunning accounted for so much of that great fur trade which made for wealth in the distant cities beyond the eastern sea.

Too small for a council, it gave allegiance wholly to its factor, young Anders McElroy, at whose right hand for sage advice and honest friendship stood that most admirable of men, Edmonton Ridgar, chief trader and anything else from accountant to armourer. Beneath them and in good command were some thirty able men whose families lived in the neat log cabins within the stockade.

With its back to the western wall there stood in the centre the factory itself, a good log building of somewhat spacious size; its big room, divided by a breast-high solid railing, with a small gate in the middle, serving as office and general receiving-place. Beyond the railing, in the smaller space toward the north, there stood the great wooden desk of the factor, its massive book of accounts always open on its face, its hand-made drawers filled with the documents of the Company. Here McElroy was wont to take account of the furs brought in, to distribute recompense, and to enforce the simple law. Attached to this room on the south was the great store-room, packed with those articles of merchandise most likely to seem of worth in savage eyes and brought, with such infinite labour by canoe and portage, from those favoured lower points whose waters admitted the yearly ships—namely, rifles and ammunition, knives of all sorts, bolts of bright cloth and beads of the colour of the rainbow, great iron kettles such as might hang most fittingly above an open fire, and bright woven garments made by hands across seas.

At the back of the big room was the small one where McElroy and Ridgar had their living, furnished scantily with a bed and table, an open fireplace and crane, some rude, hand-made chairs, and a shelf of books.

And to this post of De Seviere had come in the dusk of the previous night a little company of people.

They were tired and travel-stained, with their belongings in packs on the shoulders of the men, and the joy of the venturer in their eager faces.

From far down in the country below the Rainy River they had come, pushing to the west in that hope of gain and desire of travel which opens the wilderness of every land. They had met the factor at the great gate and entered in to rest and feast, as is the rule of every fire. By morning had come the leaders of the party to McElroy, and there had been talk that ended in an agreement, and the tired venturers had dropped their burden of progress.

When they had rested, there were to be three new cabins squeezed somehow into the already overcrowded stockade, and five more men and six women would belong to Fort de Seviere.

As he walked toward the factory the young man was thinking of all this. Of a surety the tall girl, had come with the strangers, yet he had not noticed her until that moment outside the stockade wall, when he had caught the striking picture in the morning sun.

Name? Most certainly it would be in that list which the leader of the party had promised him by noon. When he entered the big room the man was there before him, a picturesque figure of a man, big and graceful and dark of brow, with long black curls beneath his crimson cap. As McElroy went forward he straightened up from his lounging position against the railing and held out the paper he had promised.

"For enrollment, M'sieu," he said simply.

The factor took the proffered slip and read eagerly down its length, done neatly in a finished hand.

"Adventurers," he read, "from Grand Portage on Lake Superior, bound for the west,—agreed to stop for the length of one year at Fort de Seviere on the Assiniboine River,— Prix Laroux and wife Ninette, Pierre and Cif Bordoux and their wives Anon and Micene, Franz LeClede and wife Mora, Henri Baptiste and wife Marie, and Maren Le Moyne, an unmarried woman and sister to Marie Baptiste."

A sudden little light flamed for a moment in the young factor's blue eyes.

For some unknown reason it had pleased him, that last ingenious sentence.

"Prix Laroux," he said, turning to his new acquisition, "we will get to the work of our contract."

CHAPTER II

THE SPRING

Springtime lay over the vast region of lake and forest. Along the shores of the little rivers the new grass was springing, and in nook and sheltered corner of rock and depression shy white flowers lifted their pretty heads to the coaxing sun. Deep in the budding woods birds in flocks and bevies called across the wilderness of tender green, while at the post the youths sang snatches of wild French songs and all the world felt the thirst of the new life.

A somewhat hard winter it had been, long and cold, with crackling frost of nights and the snow piled deep around the stockade, and the gracious release was very welcome.

The somewhat fickle stream of the Assiniboine had loosed its locks of ice and rolled and gurgled, full to its low banks, as if the late summer would not see it shrunk to a lazy thread, refusing sometimes even the shallow canoes and barely licking the parched lips of the land.

In gay attire the maids of De Seviere ventured beyond the gates to stray a little way into the forest and come back laden with tiny green sprays of the golden trailer, with wee white blossoms and now and again a great swelling bud of the gorgeous purple flower of the death plant.

"Bien! It is of a drollness, mes cheries," laughed Tessa Bibye one day, stopping at the cabin by the south wall; "how Francette does but sit in the shade and nurse that half-dead wolf. Is it by chance because of the owner, or that hand which carried it here, Francette? Look for the man behind Francette's devotion ever!"

Whereat there was a laugh and crinkling of pretty dark eyes at the little maid's expense, but she sprang to her feet and faced her mates in anger.

"Begone, you Tessa Bibye!" she cried hotly; "'tis little you know beyond the thought of a man truly, and that because you have lacked one from the cradle!"

Tessa flushed and drew away, vanquished. Merry laughter, turned as readily upon her, wafted back on the golden wind. Francette, her eyes flaming with all too great a fire, set a pan of cool water beneath the fevered muzzle of the husky and glanced, scowling, across her shoulder toward the factory.

Five days had passed since the episode beside the stockade, and Bois DesCaut had said no word, of his property. In fact, the great dog was seemingly scarce worth a thought, much less a word. Helpless, bruised from tip to tip, one side flat under its broken ribs, he lay sullenly in the shade; of the cabin where McElroy had put him down, covered at night from the cool air by Francette's' own blanket of the gorgeous stripes, fed by her small loving hands bit by bit, submitting for the first time in his hard and eventful life to the touch of woman, thrilling in his savage heart to the word of tenderness.

Gently the little maid stroked the rough grey fur and scowled

Vingie E. Roe

toward the factory.

So intent was she with her thought that she did not hear the step beside her, springing quickly up when a voice spoke, cool and amused, behind. "Well said, little maid," it praised; "that was a neat turn."

The tall stranger, Maren Le Moyne, stood smiling down upon her.

Francette, sharpest of tongue in all the settlement, was at sudden loss before this woman. She looked up into her face and stood silent, searching it with the gaze of a child.

It was a wondrous face, dark as her own, its cheeks as dusky red, but in it was a baffling something that held her quick tongue mute, a look as of great depth, of wondrous strength, and yet of fitful tenderness,—the one playing through the other as flame about black marble, and with the rest a smile.

More than little Francette had beheld that baffling expression and squirmed beneath its strangeness. Francette looked, and the scowl drew deeper.

She saw again this woman leaning slightly forward, her eyes a-glitter on the prostrate DesCaut, her strong hand doubled and flecked with blood, with Loup at her feet,—and quick on the heels of it she saw the look in the factor's eyes as he had commanded her to silence with a motion.

"So?" she flamed at last, recovering her natural audacity, for the maid was spoiled to recklessness by reason of her beauty; "I meant it to be neat."

At the look which leaped into the eyes of the stranger her own began to waver, to shift from one to the other, and lastly dropped in confusion.

"But spoiled at the end by foolishness," said Maren Le Moyne, and all the pleasure had slipped from her deep voice, leaving it cold as steel.

Abruptly she turned away, her high head shining in the sun, her strong shoulders swinging slightly as she walked.

Francette looked after her, with small hands clinched and breast heaving with, anger, and there had the stranger made her second enemy in Fort de Seviere within the first fortnight.

Along the northern wall there was much bustle and scurry, the noise of voices and of preparation, for the men were busy with the raising of the first new cabin. As some whimsical fate would have it, there were the hewn logs that Bard McLellan had prepared a year back for his own new house when he should have married the pretty Lila of old McKenzie, who sickened suddenly in the early autumn when the leaves were dropping in the forest and fled from his eager arms. No heart had been left in the breast of the trapper after that and the logs lay where he had felled them.

Now McElroy, tactful of tongue and gentle, touched the sore spot, and Bard gave sad consent to their use.

"Take them, M'sieu," he said wearily; "my pain may save another's need."

So the first new cabin went up apace.

Anders McElroy looked over his settlement day by day and there was great satisfaction in his eyes. Fort de Seviere was none so strong that it could afford to look carelessly on the acquisition of five good men and hardy trappers, and, beside, somehow there was a pleasanter feeling to the warm spring air since they had arrived-a new sense of bustle and accomplishment.

Often he stood in the door of the factory and looked to where the women sang at their work or carried the shining pails full of water from the one deep well of the settlement, situated near the gate in the eastern wall, and the smiles were ever ready in his blue eyes.

A handsome man was this factor of Fort de Seviere, tall and well formed, with that grace of carriage which speaks of perfect manhood; his head, covered with a thick growth of sun-coloured hair curling lightly at the ends, tossed ever back, ready to laugh. Scottish blood, mingled with a strong Irish strain, ran riot in him, giving him at once both love of life and honour.

They had known what they were doing, those lords of the H. B. Company, when they had sent this young adventurer from Fenchurch Street to the new continent, and, after five years among the hardships of the trade, he found himself factor of Fort de Seviere,—lord of his little world, even though that world were but one tiny finger of the great system spreading itself like a stretching hand outward from the shores of the Bay to that interior whose fringed skirts alone had been explored.

A high station it was for so young a man, for his twenties were not yet behind him, and the pride of his heart, its holding.

Therefore, life was a living wine to Anders McElroy, and the small world of his post a kingdom. And into it, with that travel-tired band of venturers from Rainy Lake, had passed a princess.

Not yet did he know this,—not for many days, in which he looked from the factory door among the women, singling out one who wore no brilliant garment, yet whose shining head drew the eyes of the men like a magnet.

Slowly speech grew among them, very slowly, as if something held back the usual comment of the trappers, concerning this Maren Le Moyne.

"Look you, Pierre," ventured Marc Dupre to Pierre Garcon, as they beached their canoe one dusk after a short trip up the river; "yonder is the young woman of the strong arm. A high head, and eyes like a thunderous night,—Eh? Is there love, think you, asleep anywhere within her?"

Whereat Pierre glanced aside under his cap to where Maren hauled up the bucket from the well, hand over hand, with the muscles slipping under her tawny skin like whipcords.

"Nom de Dieu!" ejaculated Pierre under his breath; "if there is, I would not be the one to awaken it and not be found its master! It would be a thing of flame and fury."

"Ah!" laughed the other, "but I would. It would be, past all chance, a thing to remember, howe'er it went! But it is not like that you or I will be the one to wake it. Milady, though clad in seeming poverty, fixes those disdainful eyes upon the clouds."

CHAPTER III

NEW HOMES

The work of raising the new cabins went forward merrily. Every one lent a hand, and by the end of May the new families were installed and living happily. In that last house near the northeast corner of the post dwelt Henri and Marie Baptiste and Maren Le Moyne.

A goodly place it was, divided into two rooms and already the hands of the two sisters had fashioned of such scant things as they possessed and dared buy from the factory on the year's debt, a semblance of comfort.

In the other cabins the rest of the party managed to double, each family taking one of the two rooms in each, and the women at least drew a sigh of content that the long trail had at last found an end, however unstable of tenure.

"Ah, Maren," said Marie Baptiste, sitting on the shining new log step of her domicile, "what it is to have a home! Does it not clutch at your heart sometimes, ma cherie, the desire for a home, and that which goes with it, the love of a man?"

She raised her eyes to the face of Maren leaning above her against the lintel, and they were full of a puzzled question.

Maren answered the look with a swift smile, toying lightly with a fold of the faded sleeve rolled above her elbow.

"Home for me, Marie, is the wide blue sky above, the wind in the tossing trees, the ripple of soft waters on the bow of a canoe. For me,—I grieve that we have stopped. Not this year do we reach the Land of the Whispering Hills."

A swift change had fallen into the depth of her golden voice, a subtle wistfulness that sang with weird pathos, and the eyes raised toward the western rim of the forest were suddenly far and sombre.

"Forgive!" said her sister gently; "I had forgot. I know the dream, but is it not better that we rest and gain new strength for another season? Here might well be home, here on this pretty river. We have come a mighty length already. What could be fairer, cherie,—even though we leave another to win to the untracked West."

A small spasm drew across the features of Maren, a twitching of the full lips.

"Faint heart of you," she said sadly. "Oh, Marie, 'tis your voice has ever held us back. They would prod faster but for you. Is there no glory within you, no daring, no dreams of conquest? Bien! But I could go alone. This dallying stiffles the breath in me!"

She put up a hand and tore open the garment at her throat, taking a deep breath of the sunlit air.

"But it is poverty that must be reckoned with. By spring again we may be better equipped than ever."

So rode up the hope that was ever in her.

"Yes," sighed Marie, "as the good God wills."

But she glanced wistfully around the new cabin, to be her own for the length of the four seasons. And who should say what might not happen in four seasons?

She wondered fretfully what fate had fashioned the glorious creature beside her in the form of Love itself to put within the soul of the restless conqueror. Never had she known Maren, though they two had come from the same lap.

Presently Maren looked down at her, and the shimmering smile, like light across dark waters, had again returned.

"Nay," she said gently, "fret not. It is spring-and you have at last a home."

True, it was spring.

Did not each breath of the south wind tell it, each flute-like call from the budding forest without the post, each burst of song from some hot-blooded youth with his red cap perched on the back of his head, his gay sash knotted jauntily?

It stirred the heart in the breast of Maren Le Moyne, but not with the thought of love. It called to her as she stood at night alone under the stars, with her head lifted as if to drink the keen, sweet darkness; called to her from far-distant plains of blowing grass, virgin of man's foot; from rushing rivers, bare of canoe and raft; from high hills, smiling, sweet and fair, up to the cloudless sky—and always it called from the West.

Spring was here and cast its largess at her feet,—fate held back her eager hand.

A year she must wait, a year in which to win those

necessaries of the long trail, without which all would fail.

Travel, even by so primitive a method as canoe and foot, must demand its toll of salvage.

At Rainy Lake they had been held by thieving Indians and a great part of their provisions taken from them, leaving them to make their way in comparative poverty to the next post of De Seviere.

Further progress that year was impossible. Therefore, the contract of the trappers with the factor.

And Maren Le Moyne—venturer of the venturers, flame of fire among them, urger, inspirer, and moral leader, a living pillar before them in her eagerness—must needs curb her soul in bonds of patience and wait at Fort de Seviere for another spring.

Close beside her in her visions and her high hope, her courage and her eagerness, stood that leader of the little band, Prix Laroux. Fed by her fire, touched by her enthusiasm, the man was the mouth piece for the woman's force, the masculine expression of that undying hope of conquest which had drawn the small party together and set it forth on the perilous venture of pushing toward the unknown West to find for itself an ideal holding.

Back at Grand Portage the girl had listened from her late childhood to tales of the wilderness told at her father's cabin by voyageurs and trappers, by returning wanderers and stray Indians smoking the peace-pipe at his hearth. Long before she had reached the stature of woman she had sat on her stool beside that jovial old man, her father, grimy from his forge, and drunk the tales wide-eyed, to creep away and watch the stars, to dream of those dashing streams and to clinch her hands for that she was not born a man.

And then when she was fifteen had come the day when the tales had at last kindled to flame the parent fire of that wildness in her which slept unsuspected in the breast of the blacksmith, then old as the way of life runs, and he had closed his cabin and his forge, given his two motherless girls to the wife of Jacques Baptiste, joined a party going into the wilderness, and gone out of their lives.

Eleven years had passed with its varied life, at Grand Portage and he had never returned,—only vague rumors that had sunk in tears the head of gentle Marie, the younger of the two sisters, and lifted with sympathetic understanding that of Maren the elder.

Why not? She had asked herself in the starlit nights of those years, why not? All their lives he had been a good father to them, taking the place of the mother dead since she could just remember, speeding with tap and stroke of his humble craft those luckier ones who streamed through the stirring headquarters of Grand Portage at the mouth of Pigeon River each season, going into that untracked region of romance and dreams where the call of his still sturdy manhood had beckoned him,—how long none might know. And at last he had heeded, laid down the staid, the sane, and followed the will-o'-the-wisp of conquest and adventure that took the current by his door.

Never had Maren chided him,—never for one moment held against him the desertion of his children. For that, they were well provided for since he had left with Jacques Baptiste the savings of his life, not much, but enough to bring both of them to the marriage age.

And well and tenderly had old Jacques and his wife fulfilled the trust,—Maren's dark eyes were often misty as she recalled the parting at Grand Portage.

So tenderly had the two maids grown in the love of the family that Marie had, but at the start of the great journey, married young Henri Baptiste.

Marie was all for a home and some black-eyed babies, but she clung to Maren as she had ever done,—and now, in her twenty-sixth year, Maren had risen to the call as her father had done before her, and lifted her face, rapt as some pagan Priestess', toward that mystic West,—bound for the Land of the Whispering Hills, whence had come that old, vague rumour, lured alike by love of the unknown and shy, unspoken longing for the father whose heart must be the pattern of her own.

And in her train, swept together by that fire within her, touched into flame by her ever-mounting hope, her courage, and her magnetism, went that small band of men and women, all young, all of adventurous blood, all daring the odds that let reluctantly a woman into the wilderness.

Yet it has been ever women who have conquered the wilderness, for until they trod the trace the men had cut it still remained a wilderness.

So she leaned in the door of Marie's new home, this taut-strung Maren Le Moyne, and gazed away above the rim of the budding forest, and her spirit was as a chaffing steed held into quiet by a hand it knows its master.

For a year she must endure the strain,—then, as the good God willed, the leap forward, the wild breath in her nostrils, the forging into the unknown.

"Ah, yes!" she said again, "it is the spring."

"Bon jour," she nodded, unsmiling, as a slim youth swung jauntily up the hard-beaten way between the cabins.

"Eh!" said Marie, alert, "and who is that lord-high-mighty, with his red cheeks and his airs, Maren? You know, as it is always, every man in the post already. It is not so with the women, I'll wager. For instance, who lives in the tiny house there by the south bastion?"

"I know not," answered Maren, as though she humoured a child, and taking the last question first; "as for the youth, 'tis young Marc Dupre, and one of a sturdy nature. I like his spirit, though all I know of it is what sparkles from his roguish eyes. A fighter,—one to dare for love of chance."

Marie looked quickly up, ever ready to pounce on the first gleam of aught that might ripen into a love interest, but she saw Maren's eyes, cool and shining, watching the swaggering figure with a look that measured its slim strength, its suggestion of reserve, its gay joy of life, and naught else.

"A pretty fellow," she said, with a touch of disappointment.

Each and every man went by Maren just so,—eliciting only that interest which had to do apart from the personal.

But the black eyes of Marc Dupre had softened a bit under their daring as he approached the factory.

"Holy Mother!" he whispered to himself; "what a woman! No maid, but a WOMAN—for whose word one would fillip the face of Satan. She is fire—and, if I am sure, all men are tow."

CHAPTER IV

THE STRANGER FROM CIVILISATION

"How goes it, little one, with Loup?"

The factor stopped a moment in the sunshine before the cabin of old France Moline.

Clad in a red skirt, brilliant in its adornment of stained quills of the porcupine got from the Indians, Francette paced daintily here and there in the clean-swept yard, now snapping her small fingers, now coaxing with soft noises in her round throat, her sparkling eyes fixed on the gaunt grey skeleton that stood on its four feet braced wide apart, wavering dizzily.

For a time she did not answer, as if he who spoke was no more than any youth of the settlement, so exaggeratedly absorbed was she.

Then, pushing back the curls from her face, a pretty motion that always wakened a look of admiration in masculine eyes beholding,—

"If he would only try, M'sieu," she said, frowning, "but he does nothing save stand and look at me like that. The strength is gone from his legs."

It seemed even as the little maid protested. Massive, silent, contemptuous, his small eyes under the wolfish skull cold and alight with a look that sent shuddering from him the timid,—thus he had been in his hard-fought and hard-won supremacy, a great, mysterious beast brought full-grown from the snowbound wilderness of the forest one famine-time by old Aquamis and sold to Bois DesCaut for a tie of tobacco.

Now he stood, a pitiable shadow, and begged mutely of the only tender hand he had known for understanding of this strange weakness that took his limbs and sent the heavens whirling.

McElroy looked long upon him.

"'Tis a shame," he said, his straight brows drawing together, "the dog is a better brute than Bois."

"Aye," flashed Francette, talking as though it were no uncommon thing for the factor to stop at the cabin of the Molines, "and no more shall the one brute serve the other. You have said, M'sieu."

"Yes," laughed the factor, "I have said and it shall be so. I will buy the dog from Bois if he speaks of the matter. Take good care of him, little one," and McElroy turned down toward the gate. As he moved away, free of step and straight as an Indian, he filliped away a small budding twig of the saskatoon which one of the youths had brought in to show how the woods were answering the call of the warm sun, and which he had dandled in his fingers as he walked. It fell at the edge of the beaded skirt and quick as thought the hand of Francette shot out and covered it. A hot flush mounted under the silken black curls and she dropped her eyes, peering under their lashes to see if any observed. She drew the faded sprig toward her and hid it in her breast.

Before the cabin of the Baptistes, Jean Saville touched his cap and stopped.

"Yes?" said the factor; "what is it, Jean?"

"Assuredly, M'sieu, has the tide of the spring set in. Pierre but now reports the coming of a band of strangers down the river. They come in canoes, five of them, well manned and armed as if the country of the Assiniboine were bristling with dangers instead of being the abode of God's chosen. Within the hour they will arrive at the landing."

"Thank you, Jean," said McElroy; "I will prepare for the meeting."

The trapper touched his cap and passed.

"Ah," smiled the factor to himself, "I like this bustle of passage. It is good after the winter's housing, and who knows? There may be those among the strangers who bring word from Hudson Bay."

He turned briskly back and gave word to Jack de Lancy and his wife Rette to cook a great meal, also to see that the storeroom was cleared sufficiently by the more orderly packing back of the goods to allow of five canoe-loads of men sleeping upon the floor. Then he passed down the main way, out of the gate in the warm sun and took his place at the landing to look eagerly down stream for the first coming of the strangers. Not far from the enthusiasm of boyhood was this young factor of Fort de Seviere.

And within the hour, as Jean had said, they came, rounding the distant bend in an even distanced string, long narrow craft, each bearing the regular complement of five men, a bowman, a steersman, and three middlemen whose paddles shone like crystal as they sank and lifted evenly. Strangers they were in very truth, as McElroy saw at the first glance.

Never had they been bred in the wilderness, these men, unless it were the two guides in the first and fourth canoe, picked out readily by their swarthy skins, their crimson caps, and their rugged litheness. Fairer, all, were the rest, paler of skin, more loose of muscle, shown by the very way they bent to their work. Their garments, too, as they drew nearer brought a smile to the watcher's lips, a smile of memory. Those coats, brave in their gilt braid, had assuredly come across seas. Thus might one behold them on the Strand.

Ah! These were, without doubt, part of the fall ship's load of adventurers come to the new continent filled with the fire of achievement and excitement that brought so many youths over seas. They had, most like, come down from the great bay by way of God's Lake and the house there, traversed the length of Winnipeg, come along the river at the southern end, and at last turned westward into the Assiniboine. A long rest they would no doubt take at Fort de Seviere, and there would be news of the outside world.

McElroy was at the water's very edge as the first canoe of the string curved gracefully in and cut slimly up to the landing.

"Welcome, M'sieurs," called the factor of Fort de Seviere, using unconsciously the speech of the region, which had become his own in five years, "in to the right a bit,—so! Well done!"

The word was not so sincere as he would have made it, for

the bowman, jumping out into the knee-deep water to keep the boat from touching bottom, had floundered like an ox, thereby proving his newness at the business. On the face of the swarthy Canuck guide who sat in the stern there was a weary contempt.

"Friends, M'sieurs?" called McElroy tardily, scarcely deeming such precaution necessary, yet giving the hail from force of habit.

They looked for the most part Scottish, these men, save here and there among them one who might be anything of the motley that came across each year.

In the first canoe a figure had risen and stood tall and straight among the bales of goods with which the craft was seen to be close packed from bow to stern, a figure striking in its lack of kinship to its surroundings, yet commanding in its beauty. Garments of cloth, of a gay blue shade and much adorned with trimming of gold braid, fitted close to the slender form of the man. His limbs from the knee were encased in leggings made, most evidently, in some leather shop, while tilted on his splendid head he wore a hat of so wide a brim that no sunlight touched either face or throat, while from beneath this covering there fell to his shoulder long curls of hair that shone like silk. This, evidently, was the leader of the party.

"Friends," he said, "bound for the west and the country of the Saskatchewan."

For all his appearance he spoke with the accent of the French, and for a moment McElroy looked closely at him.

"Of the Company?" he asked sharply.

Vingie E. Roe

"Aye," said the other, with a little of wonder in voice and look, "of the Company, M'sieu most assuredly."

The momentary flicker of uneasiness that had gripped the factor with the stranger's speech died at his words.

So, of a surety, why not?

Had not he himself, born in the smoke of a London street, accepted with the ingenious adaptability of the Irish blood within him the very speech he now wondered at in the other?

As the young man sprang lightly to land he held out his hand, and it was gripped with a force that showed the spirit behind the beauty of this new guest.

"Welcome, M'sieu," said the factor, "to Fort de Seviere and all it contains."

"Bien!" laughed the other with a show of fine white teeth, "but it is good to behold neighbours in so deadly a wilderness as we have passed through for these many days. Naught but God-forgotten loneliness and never-ending forest. Yet it is for these that we barter the comforts of civilisation, eh, M'sieu, and waste ourselves on solitude and the savage?" He turned and waved his gloved hand over the five canoes, now curving one by one in to the landing, and shouted a few terse orders and commands.

"But I had nigh forgot, so unused am I to society and the usages thereof,"—he said, turning back with an engaging smile, "Alfred de Courtenay, known in that world across the water; and which my taste, or that of itself, more properly speaking, has caused me to forswear for some length of time, as Mad Alfred, I am, M'sieu—?"

"Anders McElroy," supplied the other, "and factor of Fort de Seviere."

"Monsieur le facteur, your servant, of French lineage, English nativity, and adventurous spirit."

With a motion indescribably graceful he swept off his wide hat and executed a bow which in itself was proof of his gentleness.

"And now, M'sieu, lead on to those delights of rest and converse which your hospitality hath so graciously promised."

Leaving his company to beach and store for the night the canoes with their loads of merchandise, under the direction of his aide or lieutenant whom he introduced to the factor as John Ivrey, a young man of fine presence, Alfred de Courtenay walked beside McElroy up the gentle slope of the river bank, entered the great eastern gate of the post, not without an appreciative glance at its massive strength and at the well-nigh impregnable thickness of the stockade, the well-placed surveillance of the towering bastions, and thus up the way between the cabins to the door of the factory, open and inviting.

"Mother of God, M'sieu!" he said with a copious sigh; "what it is to meet with white faces! For weeks I have beheld along the shores peering brown countenances that lifted my gorge, and I have well-nigh been tempted to turn back."

"It has been a long journey, then, to you?"

McElroy smiled, thinking of the first impressions and effect of the wilderness on such a man fresh from the ways of civilisation.

"Long? Though it is my initial journey, yet am I veteran frontiersman."

He turned upon the factor the brilliance of his smile, a combination of dazzling teeth and eyes that fairly danced with spirit, like bubbling wine, blue and swift in their changes from laughter to an exaggerated dolorousness, as when he spoke of these terrible hardships.

And if they were quick after this fashion they were no less so in roaming keenly over every corner of the enclosed space within the stockade.

Before they had reached the factory the stranger knew that there were three rows of cabins in the post, that the factory was a mighty fortress in its low solidity, and that the small log structure to the right of it with the barred window was the pot au beurre.

As they neared the factory the figure of a tall woman, young by the straightness of the back, the gracious yet taut beauty of line and curve, came from behind the cabin of the Savilles, and on her shoulder was perched a three-year-old child which laughed and gurgled with delight, holding tight to her widespread hands. The woman's face was hidden by the child's body, but her voice, deep-throated and rich with sliding minor tones, mingled with the high shrillness of the little one's shrieks.

"Hold fast, ma cherie," came its laughing caution, smothered by the flying folds of the baby's little cotton shift." See! The ship dips so, in the ocean,—and so,—and so!"

The strong arms, bare and brown and muscular, swayed backward, throwing up the milky whiteness of the little throat, the tiny feet flew heavenward and the baby's wee heart choked it, as witness the screams of irrepressible joy. As the child swayed back there came into view the face of Maren Le Moyne, flushed all over its rare darkness, glowing with tenderness, its great beauty transfigured divinely. The black braids, wrapped smoothly round her head, shone in the evening sun, and the faded garment, plain and uncompromising, but served to heighten the effect of her physical perfection.

Alfred de Courtenay stopped in his tracks, the smile fixed on his face, and drank in the pretty scene like one starved.

So long he looked that McElroy turned toward him and only then did he shift his glance, remembering himself, while a blush suffused his rather delicate features.

"Pardon!" he murmured; "truly do I forget myself, M'sieu; but not for a twelvemonth have I seen aught to match this moment. I pray you, of what station of life is the glorious young Madonna before you;—wife or widow or maid? By Saint Agnes, never have I beheld such beauty!"

"Maid," replied McElroy; "by name Maren Le Moyne, one of a party of venturers who came but a short while back from Rainy River, and who have cast in their lot with us for the matter of a year."

The woman and the child passed on their way, disappearing again behind the next cabin, unconscious of observation, still lost in their play of the tossing ship at sea, and the two men entered the great trading-room of Fort de Seviere, where Edmonton Ridgar, chief trader and accountant, came forward to meet the stranger.

The young factor went in search of Jack de Lancy and word of the meal he had ordered, and for some reason there was within him a vague vexation which had to do with the look he had seen in the merry eyes of Alfred de Courtenay,

He found the great kettles boiling over the fires and a ten-gallon pot of coffee Venting the evening air.

As he gave word for the feast to be spread on strips of cloth laid on the hard-beaten ground before the factory that many might sit round at once and partake, there came from the direction of the gate the voices of De Courtenay's men. The stranger and himself, with young Ivrey and Ridgar should be served in the little room off to the west where were the small table, the chairs, and the row of books.

Not often did Fort de Seviere have so illustrious a guest as must be this young adventurer.

CHAPTER V

NOR'WESTERS

"Merci, my friend, what extravagance is this! The savour of that pot does fairly turn my head!"

Alfred de Courtenay settled himself gracefully in one of McElroy's chairs and smiled across at his host with a twinkle in his laughing eyes.

A dozen candles, lit in his honour, where three were wont to suffice, shone mellowly in the little room, and Rette de Lancy, still comely despite her forty years and a certain lavishness in the matter of avoirdupois, set down in the midst of the table a steaming dish with a cover. There were a white cloth of bleached linen and cups of blue ware that had come with her and Jack from across seas, also a silver coffee-urn that had been her great-grandmother's. When the factor gave word for a meal to these two he knew well that all dignity would be observed. As for himself, his living of every day was scant and plain as regarded the manner of its serving.

"What is it, M'sieu, that so assails the nostrils with delicious aroma, if I may so far forget politeness? 'Tis not beef, assuredly,—there is too much of the scent of the wild about it."

"Moose," replied McElroy, and by this time the vague vexation had blown out of his heart as all ill-feelings were wont to do, "moose, killed in the snows and hung in the smoke of a little fire until the very heart of the wood is in the meat. And now, M'sieu, fall to. I would I had something better than Rette's strong coffee in which to pledge you, but, as you see, Fort de Seviere has no cantine salope. It is not the policy of the Great Company, as you doubtless know, to abet its trade with the Indians by the use of liquor."

De Courtenay looked quickly up.

"Why, I thought,—but then I have much to learn, in fact, all to learn, since I am but raw in the wilderness."

Like men hungry and athirst from the hardships of the trail and the stream, the camp and the portage, the guests did justice to the savoury viands, and at last leaned back in repletion, while Rette took off the plates and cups; the spoons and forks, and set in their stead a huge pot of crumbled tobacco with a tin box containing pipes.

"And now," said the factor, smiling, "let us have talk of that world of which I am hungering for news. You are of the fall ship's load of new arrivals, I take it?"

"No," said De Courtenay, "it was last spring, about this time, that I first saw the shores of the New World. Five of my men came with me from across seas and the rest I picked on starting into the wilderness. They are mostly Canadians of Scottish blood. I have a fancy that the strong blond peoples are best for the rigours of what one may find in this country. Though," he laughed as at some reminiscence, "I have found so far that my two swarthy guides are worth any three of the rest."

"You have found the way hard?"

"Mother of God! If the rest is like the first of it, I think you may find my bones bleaching beside some portage where I have given up the ghost. Truly do we pay for our whims of caprice, M'sieu."

"Whims?"

"Aye, what save a whim of the moment could have induced me to undertake so great a hardship as this winning to the Saskatchewan? What save the love of excitement sent me to be, like yourself, the head of a lost trading-post in this far north country?"

The merry blue eyes were full of gaiety and light.

"Truly,—and I pay."

A whim it might be, yet there was in the spirited face of Alfred de Courtenay that which told plainly that it would be followed to its end, be that what it might, as faithfully as though it were a deeper thing.

For a moment a little line appeared between the straight brows of the factor.

The word of so grave an office mentioned as a "whim," "a caprice," went down hard with him. There was nowhere in the heavens above nor the earth below so serious a thing as that same office, and he served it with his whole heart. Therefore he could not quite understand the other. Yet he thought in a moment of De Courtenay's newness and the frown cleared. Of a very wide tolerance was McElroy.

"And you came, I suppose, from York Factory, down by way

of God's Lake and the house there. What is the word of Anderson who presides there? A fine fellow,—I met him once at Churchill."

"York Factory? God's Lake?"

De Courtenay lowered his pipe and looked through the smoke.

"Nay," he said, "I know nothing of those places, M'sieu."

He turned to young Ivrey.

"It might be that these locations answer to different names. Heard you aught from the guides of these two posts?"

"We did not pass them, Sir Alfred," answered the young man soberly.

"Then, in Heaven's name, which way have you journeyed?" asked McElroy amazed.

"Why, by way of Lake Nipissing, across the straits below the Falls of St. Mary, by canoe along the shores of Lake Superior, into Pigeon River, and so on up the various streams to your own Assiniboine—from Montreal. How else, M'sieu?"

But the factor of Fort de Seviere had risen in his place, his face gone blank with consternation.

"From Montreal!" he cried, "but did you not answer to me as friends and of the Company"

"Aye," answered De Courtenay, also rising, the gaiety fading from his face and his eyes beginning to sparkle bodefully, "of the North-west Company, trading from Montreal into the fur country. I am sent of my uncle Elsworth McTavish, who is a shareholder and a most responsible man, to take charge of the post De Brisac on the south branch of the Saskatchewan. But I like not this sudden gravity, M'sieu. Wherein have I offended?"

"In naught, De Courtenay," said McElroy quite simply, "save that you are in the heart of the country belonging to the Hudson's Bay Company, as does this fort and all therein."

"Nom de Dieu!" cried the other, springing back and tossing up his head; "I knew it not! How is it, then, that at midday of this day we met on the river one who told us of this post of De Seviere, and that it served the Montreal merchants? That we should here find hospitality and friends?"

"Eh?" shot out McElroy sharply. "Of what like was such a person?"

"A big man, swarthy and dark, with sullen eyes, clad in garments of tanned hides and wearing a red cap and a knife in his belt. He bore on his left temple a pure white lock amid his black hair."

"Bois DesCaut!" said Edmonton Ridgar; "he has been these two days gone in his canoe."

"A traitorous trapper, M'sieu," said the factor, "one who has umbrage at me for a rebuke administered some time back and hopes by this sorry joke to win revenge. But what is done cannot be helped. We have met as friends,—the unfortunate fact that we find ourselves rivals,—that almost speaks the word 'foes,' I must inform you, M'sieu, since the strife between our companies has become so sharp,—should not cause us to forget the bread we have broken between us personally. I still offer you a night's rest."

But De Courtenay had drawn himself to his slender height, his hand at his hip, where, in other times, had dangled a sword.

"Nay, M'sieu," he said quickly, "a blunder found and unremedied becomes two. If I ay gather my men we will sleep outside an unfriendly fort,—and in the name of De Courtenay allow me to repay the cost of their entertainment."

Reckless, indeed, was this young cavalier, else he would not have made that speech.

Anders McElroy turned white beneath his tan and his fingers tapped the table.

"Not ungrateful am I, M'sieu, but I stick by the colours I choose. If our companies are rivals, then we are such, and I follow my master's lead. It is at present the North-west organisation. I am pledged in Montreal—and—I prove faithful."

The young man's face was fired with that spirit which ever lay so near the surface and he looked at his whilom host with a mighty hauteur.

"I thank you for your kindness, M'sieu, but I must decline it further. Come, Ivrey," and turning he picked up his wide hat, bowed first to McElroy and then to Ridgar, and strode toward the outer door. As he passed the lintel the not insignificant form of Rette blocked his exit, en route for a cup she had left behind. With an instant flourish the hat in his hand swept the logs of the floor, he seized the woman's toil-hard fingers and bore them to his lips.

"Excellent, Madame, was that meal," he murmured, "and never to be forgot so long as one unused to hardship faces privation. I thank you."

Comely Rette flushed to her sleek hair and some flicker of a girlhood that had its modicum of grace, flared up in the swift curtsy with which she acknowledged the compliment.

And with a last flash of his blue coat Alfred de Courtenay was gone.

McElroy ran his fingers helplessly through his tousled light hair and faced his friend.

"Now, by all the Saints!" he said with a strange mixture of regret and relief, "what an unhapy ending!"

But at that moment he was thinking of the wondrous beauty of the man and of the picture of Maren Le Moyne's brown arms spread wide apart with the laughing child between, and again that little feeling of vexation crept into his wholesome heart.

Without in the soft night the late guest was striding, a graceful figure, hurriedly down toward the gate he had entered so short a time ago, and his slender hand played restlessly at his hip. His heart was seething with swift-roused emotions. So had its quick stirrings brought him into many a scrape in his eventful life. That word of his host, "which speaks almost of foes," sang in his ears.

And yet it had been given only in the spirit of enlightenment.

Behind, John Ivrey gathered up the men idling about the fire and talking with the men of the post, where question and answer had begun to stir uneasiness.

Vingie E. Roe

In a ragged, uneven line they strung out, fading into the darkness, and presently from down the river some forty rods there rose up the columns of their fires.

Fort de Seviere closed its gates and settled into the night with a feeling of something gone awry.

By morning all was early astir, those within to witness the departure of the strangers, and, those without for that same departure.

The canoes were floated, the men embarked, and all in readiness with the first flame of the sun above the eastern forest when Alfred de Courtenay presented himself at the gate and called for McElroy.

Gladly the factor responded, hoping somewhat to soften the awkwardness of the situation by a godspeed, to be met by the Frenchman high-headed and most carefully polite. A servant beside him held a wickered jug.

"With your leave, M'sieu," said De Courtenay, "I wish to leave some earnest of my gratefulness for what we have received at your hands. Therefore accept with my compliments this small gift, which, as you say you have no cantine salope, must come most happily. Once more, farewell."

The man set down the jug at McElroy's feet and strode toward the landing. The master was turning more leisurely away with his uncovered curls shining in the first level beams of morning, when he stopped and looked past the portal within the stockade.

With a small brass kettle in her hand, Maren Le Moyne was coming down the open way toward the well.

With a colossal coolness he forgot the presence of the factor and the ready light began to sparkle in his blue eyes with every step of the approaching girl. Swiftly he glanced to right and left, as if in search of something, and meeting only the green slope of the shore, a growing excitement flushed his face.

Suddenly he snatched from a crevice of the stockade a tiny crimson flower which nodded, frail and fragrant, from its precarious foothold, and sprang forward as she set her vessel on the well's stone wall.

Unsurpassed was the bow he swept her, this daring soldier of fortune, to whose delicate nostrils the taking of chances was the breath of life, and his smile was brilliant as the spring morning itself.

"A chance is a chance, Ma'amselle," he said winningly, "and who would not risk its turning? For me,—I looked upon your face but now, and behold! I must give you something, and this was all the moment offered."

With hand on heart he held forth the little flower.

"In memory of a passing stranger far from all beauty, wear it, I pray you, this day in the dusk of that braid, just there above the temple. Have I permission ?"

He stepped near and lifted the crimson star, smiling down into the astonished eyes of Maren Le Moyne, to whom no man in all her life had ever spoken thus.

For a moment she stared at him, and her face was a field of fleeting sensations. And then, slowly, the sparkle in his eyes lit her own, the smile on his lips curled up the corners of her full red mouth, and the charm of the moment, fresh and

Vingie E. Roe

sweet as the new day, swept over her.

"A venturer,-you!" she said; "some kin we must surely be, M'sieu! 'Tis granted."

She rested her hands on the kettle's rim, and bent forward her head, wrapped round and round with its heavy braids, and with fingers deft as a woman's Alfred de Courtenay placed the flower in a shining fold.

Somewhat lengthy was the process, for the braid was tight and the green stem very fragile, but at last it was accomplished, and Maren lifted her face flushed and laughing.

"Thank you, M'sieu," she said demurely; "God speed your journey."

De Courtenay took the kettle from her, filled it himself, and when he gave it back the smile was gone; from his face, but the light remained.

"Some day, Ma'amselle," he said gravely, "I shall come back to Fort de Seviere."

The tall girl turned away with her morning's kettle of fresh water, and the man stood by the well watching her swinging easily to its weight, forgetful of the canoes, manned and waiting on the river's breast for their leader, forgetful of the factor .of the post, waiting in the shadow of the wall, on whose face there sat a deeper shade.

Then he turned and ran lightly down the bank, leaped into the canoe held ready, once more bowed, and as the little craft swept out to midstream, he shook back his curls and lifted his face toward the country of the Saskatchewan.

CHAPTER VI

SPRING TRADE

So passed out of Fort de Seviere one who was destined to be interwoven with its fortunes.

Anders McElroy watched him go until the shadow of the great trees on the eastern shore, long in the level sun, quenched the light on his silken head and the men of the five canoes had taken up a song of the boats, their voices lifting clear and fresh on the wings of the new day, until the first canoe turned with the curve of the river above and was lost, the second and the third, and even until the last had passed from view and only the song came back.

Then he turned back into the gate and the tender mouth that was all Irish above the square Scottish jaw was set tight together.

His foot touched the wickered jug and he called Jean Saville.

"Take this, Jean," he said, "and give each of the men a cup. 'Tis a shame to waste it."

But for himself he had no taste for the stranger's gift of payment.

He was thinking of the red flower in Maren Le Moyne's black hair and a vexation, past all reason held him.

But the spring was open and there was soon more to occupy his mind than a maid and a posy and a reckless blade from Montreal.

At dusk of a day within that week a trapper brought word of a hundred canoes on the river a day's journey up-country, laden with packs of winter beaver, and bound for the post.

The Indians were coming down to trade.

Picturesque they were, in their fringed buckskin cunningly tanned and beaded, their feathers and their ornaments of elk teeth and claws of the huge, thick-coated bears. At day-dawn they came, having camped for the night a short distance above the fort, to the letter display of their arrival, and they swept down in a flotilla of graceful craft made of the birch bark and light as clouds upon the water.

All was in readiness for them, for the factor had been expecting them for a fortnight back; and, when the crackling shots of the braves announced their coming, McElroy gave orders that the three small cannon mounted on a half-moon of narrow breastwork to the south of the main gate, and just before a small opening in the stockade for use in case of attack, should be fired in salute.

These were the quiet and friendly Assiniboines, and the first of the tribes, being the nearest, to reach the factory that year.

De Seviere was early awake and all was astir within its walls, for this was the great time of the four seasons. Eagerly the maids and the younger matrons flocked down to the great gate to peer out at the gathering craft, afloat like the leaves of autumn upon the breast of the little river,—two braves to a canoe, the gallant front of the young men flanking and preceding that which held the leader of the expedition, chief of the tribe, distinguished by its flag fluttering in the morning wind upon a pole at the stern,—at the bedizened figure of the chief himself, and lastly those canoes which held the women, the few children, and even a dog or two.

Thus they came, those simple children of the forest and the lakes, the open ways and the fastnesses, of the untrammelled summers, and the snow-hindered winters, to the doors of the white man, dependent at last upon him for the implements of life,—the gun, the trap, the knife, the kettle, and the blanket.

Presently Edmonton Ridgar, chief trader of Fort de Seviere, came down the main way between the cabins, passing alone between the rows of the populace, and went forward to the lading to receive the guests.

The canoes had by this time swept swiftly and with utmost skill into two half-moons, their points cutting to the landing; and down the reach of water between them, slightly ruffled into little waves and sparkling ripples by the soft wind and the deftly dipping paddles, there came the larger craft of Quamenoka the leader.

"Welcome, my brothers!" called Ridgar, in their own tongue, for this man had been born on the shores of Hudson Bay and knew the speech of every tribe, from the almost extinct Nepisingues, of the Nepigon, to the far-away Ouinebigonnolinis on the sea coast. His hair was thickly silvered from the years he had spent in the service of the H. B. C., and his heart was full of knowledge gathered from the four winds. Therefore, his worth was above price and he hould have been factor of a post of his own, instead of chief trader for young Anders McElroy.

"We greet our brother," gravely replied Quamenoka as he stepped from his canoe, gathering his blanket around his body with a practised sweep.

Swiftly four headmen disembarked from the first four canoes of the half-moon which closed in with scarce a paddle dip, so deft were the braves with their slender, shining blades of white ash, and stood behind.

Side by side, conversing in a few sentences, the trader and the chief entered the post, followed by the headmen and proceeded to the factory, where McElroy stood to welcome them in the open door.

They entered, to the ceremony of the pipe, the speech, and the bargain, while those without made a great camp two hundred strong all along the bank of the stream, beached the canoes, stacked the beaver packs, set up the tepees of the seventeen sticks, and built the little fires without which no camp is a camp.

In a little space the quiet shore was all a-bustle and activity reigned where the silence of the spring morning had lain, dew-heavy.

Among those most eager who peered at the gate, and who presently ventured forth to the better view the bustling concourse of braves and squaws, was Maren Le Moyne, her dark eyes wide, soft lips apart, and face all a-quiver with keen enjoyment of the scene.

These were the first she had ever seen of those Indians who came from the west. Who knew? Perhaps those moccasined feet had trod the virgin forest of her dreams, those sombre eyes looked upon the Whispering Hills, those grave faces been lifted to the sweet wind that sang from the west and whose caress she felt even now upon her cheeks.

Perhaps,—perhaps, even, some swift forest-runner among them, far on his quest of the home of the caribou or with news of some friendly tribe, had come upon a man, an old man rugged of frame and face, with blue eyes like lakes in his swarthy darkness, and muscles that bespoke the forge and hammer.

Who knew?

Maren's strongly modelled chin twitched a bit while the little flame of tenderness that flickered ever behind the graveness of her eyes leaped up. She longed for their speech that she might go among them and ask.

A little way along the stockade wall to the north there lay a great rock, flat and smooth of surface, and here the girl drew apart from the women and sat herself down thereon, hands clasping her knees and the level sun in her eyes. Her thoughts were soon faraway on the misty trail they had worn for themselves in the many years they had traversed the wilderness in search of what it held, and the eyes between the narrowed lids became blank with introspection. And as she sat thus, a little way withdrawn from the scurrying activity of the scene, there came a, step on the soft green sod and a slim form in buckskins halted beside her.

It was young Marc Dupre, and his devil-may-care face was alert and smiling.

"Is that seat big enough for two, Ma'amselle?" he asked impertinently, though the heart in him was thumping a bit. This was a woman, he recalled having thought, for whom one would fillip the face of Satan, and he was uncertain whether or no he had made a right beginning.

Vingie E. Roe

Maren started and looked swiftly up at him.

"It is, M'sieu," she said quietly, "if those two are in simple, sensible accord. Not if one of the two coquettes."

Over the handsome features of the youth there spread a deep red flush.

"Forgive me, Ma'amselle," he said, "my speech was foolish as my heart. They are both sobered."

"Then," said the girl, drawing aside the folds of her dress, "you may sit beside me."

With a sudden diffidence he sank upon the stone, this handsome boy whose tongue was ever ready and whose heart of a light o' love had taken toll from every maid in the settlement, and for the first time in his life he had no sprightly word, no quip for his careless tongue.

They sat in silence, and presently he saw that her eyes were again half-closed and the dreaming look had settled back in them. She had forgotten his presence.

Never before in his experience had a woman sat thus unmoved beside him when he longed to make her speak, and it stilled him with silent wonder.

He thought of the words of Pierre Garcon that day on the river bank when this maid was new to the post, "if there is, I would not be the one to waken it and not be found its master," and they sent a thrill to his inmost being.

Who would awaken her; he wondered, as he watched the cheek beside him from the tail of his eye, a round womanly cheek, sweet and full and rich as a damask rose with the thick lashes above shining like jet.

Obedient to her silence, he sat still while she dreamed her dream out to its conclusion, and presently she straightened with a little breath like a sigh, unclasped her hands from her knees and turned her glance upon him as if she saw him for the first time.

His head whirled suddenly and he sought for some common word to cover his rare confusion.

"See, Ma'amselle," he said, pointing, "the well-lashed packs of the fat winter beaver. Truly they come well laden, these Assiniboines, and we may well thank le bon Dieu for the wealth of skins. Is it not a heartening sight?"

The eyes of Maren Le Moyne left his face and swept swiftly down the gentle slope to where the Indians had piled their bales of furs. At the sight they darkened like the waters of a lake when a little wind runs over its surface.

"A heartening sight? Nay, M'sieu," she said, shaking her head, "I can find no joy in it."

"What?"

The trapper was aghast.

"No pleasure in the fruits of a fat season?"

"See the packs of marten, the dark streaks showing a bit at the edges where the fur rounds over the dried skin. How were those pelts taken, M'sieu?"

"How? Why, most cunningly, Ma'amselle,—in traps of the H. B. Company, set with utmost skill, perhaps on a stump

Vingie E. Roe

above the line of the heavy snows, or balanced nicely at the far end of a slender pole set leaning in the ground. The delicate hand of a seasoned player must match itself with the forest instinct of these small creatures. The little pole holds little snow and the scent of the bait calls the marten up, when, snap! it is fast and waiting for the trapper and the lodge of the Assiniboines, the women and the drying."

"Yes. And those hundreds of beaver, M'sieu?"

Marc Dupre's eyes were shining and the red in his cheeks flushing with pleasure.

What more to a man's liking than the exploitation of knowledge gained first-hand in the pursuit of his life's work?

"Again the trap," he said, "set this time at the edge of a stream where the beaver huts peek through the ice, or lift their tops above the open water. Neatly they are set, cunning as an Indian himself; hidden in the soft slime at the margin if the water runs, waiting with open jaws in the small runway above the dam where the creatures come out from the swim. A sleek head lifting above the ripples a scrambling foot or two,—snap! again the price of a pound and a half of powder, a tie of tobacco. No footmark must the hunter leave, Ma'amselle, unsplashed with water, no tainting touch of a hand ungloved on chain or stake or trap itself. Ah! one must know the woods and the stream, the cold and the snow and the winds."

"You know them, M'sieu, I have no doubt," said Maren, "for you follow the trapping trail. And those beautiful silver fox, frosty and fine as the sparkle of a winter morning? The heavy hides of the bear, soft and glossy and thick as a folded blanket?"

"All the trap,—unless the latter drops through the flimsy roof of some well-hidden dead-fall, covered with brush."

The girl was not looking at him, her glance being still on the bustling camp below. The fingers on her knee were laced tight together.

Now she began to speak in a low voice, deep and even.

"Aye! All you have said is true. Wealth, indeed, is in those packs, and patience and cunning and utmost skill, defiance of the snows and the crackling cold, long miles on snowshoes and the hardships of the trail, the nights in the bough-tied huts, the pack galling the shoulders. But what is all this beside that which waits the runner of the trail at every 'set' in those many miles? Here he finds his leaning-pole. There have been little tracks up its slim roadway, but those were covered by the fall of three days back and the little creature who made them hangs there at the end, three small feet beating the cold air feebly, a tiny head squirming from side to side, two dull black eyes set at the distorted world. He has caught his marten. It has not frozen, for the snow was light and the forest still and thick, and three days have passed, M'sieu. Three days! Mon Dieu! How much were those three days worth? The trapper taps the squirming head and puts the bit of fur in his pack-bag. On to the next. The beaver? Dead, M'sieu, thanks to the good God, drowned in its own sweet water. The pack is heavy with small bodies ere the Assiniboine reaches the place where he has laid his trap for the silver fox. And what greets him here? Only a foot gnawed off in the silence of the day and the night, and some beauty gone staggering away to lie and suffer with starvation in the cold."

The youth was staring at the averted face beside him, mouth open and utter amazement on his features.

Maren went on.

"And lastly, M'sieu, far at the end of the trail,—at the outer, rim of the circle traced by his traps,—he comes eagerly, to peep and peer for what might have happened at the head of the little dip leading down to the stream where the firs bend heavily under their weight of snow."

"Here he had laid his cunningest instrument, a thing of giant jaws, of sharp ragged points, each inlocking with the other, the whole unholy thing hung to a chain at whose other end there lay a ball of iron, weighing, M'sieu, some eighty pounds. That was for the .great shy bear, rocking along ire his quest of berries or some tree that should ring hollow under his scratching claws, bespeaking the hive of the wild bees. The oiled and fur-wrapped Indian stoops down and looks along the dip. Ah! There he sees that which brings a glint to his small eyes. No bear, M'sieu, nor yet the trap he had left, but a thrashed and broken space where the snow went flying in clouds and the bushes were torn from their roots, where the very tree-trunks bore marks of the conflict and a wide and terrible trail led wildly off to the deeper forest.

"He takes it up."

"All day he follows it. At night he camps and sleeps by his fire in comfort. By daybreak again he is swinging along on that trail. Its word is plain to him. At first it raged, that great shaggy creature, tall as an ox and slow, raged and fought and broke its teeth on the strange thing that bit to the bone with its relentless jaws, and tore along the white silence dragging its hindering ball, that, catching on bush and root, skinned down the flesh from the shining bone. And presently the wild trail narrowed to undisturbed snow, with naught save two great footprints, one after the other. With the cunning of a man, M'sieu, the tortured animal has gathered in its arms that chain and ball, and is walking upright. For another day and night the trapper follows this trail of tragedy and at their end he comes upon it.

"Beside a boulder, where the snow is pushed away there lies a round heap of anguish, curled up, pinched nose flat on the snow and two ears laid lop to a vanquished head. It is still breathing, though the dull eyes open not at sound of the trapper, bold in his safety, who lifts his gun and ends it all.

"A fine pelt,—save that the right foreleg is somewhat spoiled."

"It lies there in that pile, M'sieu, and makes for wealth,—but to me it is no heartening sight. I have followed that trail to the deeper woods."

The eyes of the woman were deep as wells, flickering with light, and the dark brows frowned down the slope. She had drawn her hands tight around her knees, so tight that each knuckle stood out white from the surrounding tan.

The young man shut his open lips and drew in a breath that quivered.

"Ma'amselle," he said huskily, "nowhere in the wide world is there another woman so deep of heart, so strong in tenderness. Never before have I seen that side of the trapping. To a man that is shut. It needs the soul of a woman to see behind those things. And, oh, Ma'amselle!" his voice fell low and trembling, "I have seen more,—the divinity within your spirit. May the good God make me worthy that you may speak so to me again. I would I might serve you,—with my life I would serve you, Ma'amselle, for I have seen no woman like you." He was on his feet, this young Marc

　　　　　Vingie E. Roe

Dupre, and the hot blood was coursing fast in his veins. The awakening was coming, though not for Maren Le Moyne.

"May the time come when I may be a stone for your foot," he said swiftly. "I ask no better fate."

Maren looked up at him and a wonderful tenderness spread on her face.

"I think the time will come, M'sieu,—and, when it does, it will be worth while. I think it would be a lifting sight to see you in some great crisis, before some heavy test."

"You do?" he said slowly; "you do, Ma'amselle? Then, by Heaven, it would!"

"And some day I shall see it."

They little knew, these two in their glowing youth, how true was that word, nor how tragic that sight would be.

"And till then," said this wild youth of the forest, "until then may we be friends?" The head under the crimson cap was whirling.

"Friends?" smiled Maken, and her voice was very gentle; "assuredly, M'sieu—I had destined you for that some time ago."

As she turned away, her glance once more fell upon the long camp of the Assiniboines, and Marc Dupre faded from her mind.

Not so with him, left sitting on the flat stone, the blood hot in his face and a sudden mist before his eyes.

Her last words sang in his ears like the voice of many waters.

He did not look after her,—there was something within that held him silent, staring at the waters of the river, now sparkling like a stream of diamonds in the risen sun, the lightness gone from him and a trembling loosed in his bosom.

Within the big trading-room at the factory, seats had been placed, the chief and his headmen sat in a solemn circle, and McElroy, holding in his two hands the long calumet, stood in the centre of the small conclave.

Very gravely he pointed the stem, clinking with its dangling ornaments, to east and west, to the heavens and to the earth, and then with a deft motion swung it around his head.

"My brothers," he said, glancing around at the solemn visages of these his friends and people, "may the sun smile all day upon us together in peace."

Wherewith he smoked a moment at the carven mouthpiece and handed the pipe to Quamenoka.

With the utmost gravity Ridgar took it from the chief, passed it to the savage on his right, who likewise smoked and passed, it on, and presently the ceremony was done and the visit had begun.

"My brothers are late this year at the trading," said the factor. "For a fortnight has the ox waited in the pen, the bread of the feast been set. So do we love our brothers of the forest. What is the word of the west? What tribes come in to the factory with peltry? We would hear Quamenoka speak."

He fell silent, sat down in his chair, and waited.

In the hush of that moment a shadow falling in the open door of the factory caught his eye and he looked up to see the form of Maren Le Moyne leaning against the lintel, her face filled with eagerness, her eyes, clear as a child's and as far-seeing, fixed on the Indians. He glanced swiftly to that tight braid just above the temple, where he had last seen a small red flower nodding impishly, and was conscious of a feeling of relief to find it gone.

It was irregular, the intrusion of an outsider in the ceremony of the opening of the trade; but for his life the young factor of De Seviere could not have said so to this girl who went fearlessly where she listed and whose eyes held such mystery of strength and wistfulness.

Moreover, Quamenoka was speaking and the council harkened.

CHAPTER VII

FOREST NEWS

He was an old man, this chief of the Assiniboines, and his face was wrinkled like the dried bed of a stream` where the last little ripples have cast up the sand in a thousand ridges. His black eyes were mild, for these Indians were a peaceful people, relying on the trapping and the hunting and the friendship of the white men at the posts which they had held for three generations.

Fear of their more warlike kin had kept them near the factories and driven them into the ways of civilisation.

Now he sat with quiet glance upon the floor looking back into the past year, his feathered head-dress quivering a bit and the blue smoke rising from the pipe.

"The wind in the woods aisles is full of words, my brothers," he said, in his own tongue, "and tales flit down the lakes like the leaves in autumn. From the Saskatchewan come the French, who tell the Assiniboines that at their posts will be given four axes for one beaver, eight pounds of shot and four of powder. Yet thy brothers come down from their lodges to Fort de Seviere because of the love they bear to you, and for the fairness in trade that never varies. Many beavers are in the packs, much marten and fox and ermine. We will do good trade. Guns that are light and neat shaped to the hand, with good locks. Also much tobacco and sweet fruits. Of these things we are sure,—also are we sure of the next year and the next. Therefore do we come down the rivers to the Assiniboine.

"The tales that flit in the forest, my brothers, tell of a new fort of the French far, far to the northwest on the shores of the Slave Lake, whose factor is of the name Living Stone. Also there are whispers that fly like the wintering birds of new people, fair-skinned and red in the cheeks, who come into the upper country from the west where lies the Big Water. These are strange people, like none that trade with the Indians, who are neither friends to the English, nor yet the French, but strive for barter with those tribes that come up from the Blackfeet Hills and down from the frozen regions of the North with bearskins, the one, and seal and sea-otter, the other.

"A runner of the Saulteurs, resting in the lodges of the Assiniboines, has told Quamenoka of their strange customs, their hardness, and their shut forts guarded with suspicion and sentinelled with fear."

He ceased a moment and smoked in silence.

No breath of sound broke the stillness, for this was ceremony and of great dignity.

Only McElroy was acutely conscious of the figure in the doorway and the peering face of the girl, so full of hushed intensity.

"Also do we bring word of a great tribe, the Nakonkirhirinons, living far beyond the River Oujuragatchousibi, who this year journey down to Fort de Seviere with many furs,—more than all that will come from the Assiniboines, the Crees, the Ojibways, and the Migichihilinons put together.

"Past York and Churchill on the Great Bay they come, because of unfair dealings which met them at those places last year and the year before, down to the country of the Assiniboines, in whose lodges they will eat the great feast of the Peace Dance. Not long have the Nakonkirhirinons traded their furs, living to themselves in their hills, and much credit is due Quamenoka by whose word they come this year to his brothers on the Assiniboine."

The chief paused impressively and raised his glance to the factor's face.

McElroy nodded.

"Greatly does the heart of thy brother rejoice at such word, and a present over and above that meant for him shall be given Quamenoka. Let the talk go on. We listen."

But before the chief could speak again, Edmonton Ridgar had broken silence:

"Negansahima is chief of that tribe and my Indian father, he having adopted me with all ceremony once when I sojourned a year among them. The sight of him will gladden my spirit."

Swift surprise spread on the factor's face, but he did not speak. There was much in the checkered life of his friend that had not been set before him, and each revelation was full to the brim of romance, of daring, and of that excitement which attends a life spent in the wilderness.

The Indian nodded and went on:

"And last of the news of forest and lake and river is word of the meeting of canoes, the half of one-ten, laden with goods and going up the river, which passed but few suns back. A sun-man sat in the first, beautiful of face and with hair like light, who strove to barter. But the Assiniboines come to their brothers. They heeded not his words, though they were sweet with promise. I have spoken."

The chief fell silent, for the year had been told, and McElroy spoke presently of his joy at their presence, their words, and their friendship, as was the custom of the H. B. Company's factors on such occasions; and Ridgar rose from the council to bid a young clerk, one Gifford, bring forth the presents for the guests,—a coat with coarse white lace and lining of vermilion, a hat of felt and a sash of many colours for Quamenoka, and lesser glories for his four headmen. These presented with due formality, and actually donned by the recipients without loss of time, the ceremony of the opening council was over, save for the triumphal march of the potentate, accompanied by McElroy and Ridgar, back to the camp on the river bank.

As they passed out the factory door, they brushed by Maren Le Moyne, where she had drawn aside, still wistfully watching the comers from the wilderness.

The young factor's eyes went to her face and for a moment held her glance.

Instantly, with that deep look, the girl's hand shot forth and touched his arm, a light touch with the deftness of strength held in abeyance, and McElroy felt his flesh tingle beneath it.

"M'sieu," she said, "where do they come from, how far in the west?"

"Not far, Ma'amselle,—only from the Lower Saskatchewan. The Assiniboines are our nearest tribe, living along the country from the Hare Hills to the parting of the twin rivers above the Qui Appelle. Hold they interest for you?"

"Nay," she said, shaking her black head, "not if they come not far, other than that excited by their strangeness. I thank you."

She drew back, and McElroy, perforce, followed his way to the encampment, but he thought not this time of the red flower.

Only within him was roused that same desire which had prompted De Courtenay to snatch the bloom from the stockade wall,—a longing to give her something, to offer homage to this tall young woman with the wondrous face of beauty and wistful strength. Since she was but a child had men who looked upon her felt this same longing, this stirring of the worshipper within. But few had dared the wall of quietness about her; therefore, she had remained apart. Only Prix Laroux of all those who had seen her grow into her magnificent womanhood at Grand Portage had come to her with his gift of faith and tied himself to hand for life, and he came not with the love of man but rather as one who follows a goddess. Yet it was that aching desire to serve her which sent him.

And now it gripped the young factor of Fort de Seviere and he looked among the Assiniboines for a gift.

Here a squaw held forth to him a garment that took his eye at once.

Of doeskin it was, soft and white as a lady's hand, and cut after the fashion of the Indian woman's dress, in a single

Vingie E. Roe

piece from throat to ankle, the sleeves straight from the shoulder, and at edge and seam, sewed with thorn and sinew, rippled and fluttered a heavy fringe the length of a man's hand.

Across the breast there gleamed and glittered a solid plastron of the beadwork so justly famed for its beauty of colour and design, which came from the hands of none save the women of this tribe, and at hem and elbow, above the dangling fringe, there ran a heavy band of it. Above the hips there hung a belt made of the brilliant stained quills of the porcupine.

The factor took the beautiful thing in his hands, and the purpose in his mind crystallised.

In a swift moment he had bargained with the silent woman for a price that astonished her and was back within the post, walking hurriedly toward the cabin of the Baptistes.

At the door Marie met him, her bright eyes sparkling with the honour of this visit of him who was the Law, the Head of De Seviere, and at her eager greeting the first abating of the flush within took hold upon him.

He stood like a boy, the gorgeous garment hanging in his hand and the word on his lips forgotten.

"Madame," he stammered, "I would—" and got no further.

Sudden embarrassment took him and he grew angry with himself.

What could he say, how dared he do what he had done?

He could have thrown the white garment into the river in his sudden vexation. Factor of the post, he had made of himself a stammering youth, all for sake of the compelling beauty of a woman's eyes.

But at that moment, while Marie stood blankly on the sill holding to the doorside and the silence grew unbearable, there was a step within the cabin and Maren Le Moyne came from the inner room.

In one moment, so keen was the perception of her, she had seen the red blood in McElroy's face, the wonder on Marie's, and she, too, stood in the open door.

"Ah, M'sieu!" she said quickly, "do some of them, by chance, come from the west?"

The tone of her deep voice broke the spell, so subtly natural was it, and McElroy found his tongue.

"No, Ma'amselle," he smiled, the ease coming back to his blue eyes, "but I have found something very beautiful among them which I wish you to have. It is more beautiful than a red flower."

He held up to her the doeskin garment and his eyes were very anxious.

For a moment Maren stared as she had stared at De Courtenay and a curious expression of perplexity spread on her face.

Truly men were different here in this wilderness from those who lived at the Grand Portage, and for a moment she drew herself up and the straight brows began to frown. But as she had felt the whimsical charm of De Courtenay, so now she felt the eagerness, the taut anxiety of this man, and she noticed that there was no smile on his face as she hesitated.

Moreover, Marie was watching, sharp as a little hawk.

"Why, M'sieu," she said, and there was a baffling note to the voice this time, "why,—you wish me to have this?"

"Yes, Ma'amselle," said McElroy simply.

The girl stooped and took it from him, and for a moment her hand lay against his palm, a smooth warm hand.

"And you wish me to wear it?" she asked.

"If it shall please you."

"Then it shall please me," she said quite easily, "and I thank you."

McElroy turned away and walked back to the factory, and all the way he did not know what he had done. It had been an impulse, and he had rushed to its fulfilling without a thought. Had he bungled in giving her a garment where De Courtenay had played on a wind-harp in giving her a little red flower?

He was hot and cold alternately, and the memory of that momentary frown came turn and turn with that of the gentle manner in which she had reached down for the lifted gift.

And Maren Le Moyne?

Within the cabin she had turned to that portion which was her own, the while Marie's sharp eyes followed her with questions that were ripe on her tongue.

"Maren," she cried, as the girl passed the inner door, unable to longer hold herself, "know you the factor well?"

But Maren only shook her head and closed the slab door between.

Once alone she laid the gift on the bed, covered with a patchwork quilt made from the worn garments that had seen the long trail, and stood bending above, looking closely at each beauty of colour, of softness and design.

She spread the straight sleeves apart, smoothing out the dangling fringe, and her hand lingered with a strange gentleness a-down the glowing plastron of bright beads.

This was the first gift a man had ever given her, other than De Courtenay's red flower, and somehow it pleased her vastly.

She fell to thinking of the factor, of his open face, his light head forever tilted back with the square chin lifted, of the mouth above and of the eyes, clear as the new day and anxious as a child's the while she halted above his offering, and unconsciously she began within her mind to compare him with all other men she had ever known.

There was Prix Laroux. Not like. Also Jean Folliere and Anthon Brisbee of Grand Portage, who came to the wilderness each year. Neither were they like this man, nor Cif and Pierre Bordoux, nor Franz LeClede, nor yet her brother Henri. These she knew and they were of a different pattern.

Also there was that venturer of the great beauty and the silken curls who had spoken so prettily. With all his grace, he was unlike this strong young man whose tongue faltered and whose eyes were anxious.

Verily, for the first time; this maid of the wilderness was thinking of men.

And it was because he had seemed so ill-beset that she had taken the gift so readily.

She would not have him stumble longer under the sharp eyes of Marie.

And then thought of him faded from her mind and she fell to contemplation of the doeskin garment again. Things of its like she had seen at Grand Portage, but nothing of its great beauty, and for the first time she gave thought to self-adornment. She was strong, this woman, and given to serious dreams, and the small things of womanhood had left her wide apart in a land of her own wherein there were only visions of afar country, of travel and of conquest, and perhaps of a man, old and rugged and kindly, who had followed the long trail, and this small new thought lodged wonderingly in her mind.

For the first time she was conscious of the plainness of the garment that folded her form, and she held up her arms and looked at them, brown beneath the up-rolled sleeves.

Yes, some day she would put it on, this gorgeous thing of white fringe and sparkling colour, because she had told that man she would.

Unlike most women, she did not hold it up to her, pointing a foot beneath its pretty edge, gathering it into her waist, trying its effect. She was content to run a hand along its length, to feel the caress of its softness.

Yet even as she touched it she thought of the pretty creature which had worn it first, the slim-legged doe bounding in the forest depth, and a little sigh lifted her breast.

But this had been the quick and merciful death of the bullet, the legitimate death. That she could understand.

More quick and merciful than that which would come in the natural life of the forest. Therefore this pelt held no such repugnance as those stacked on the river bank.

Suddenly, as she bent above the bed, she felt the presence of another, the peculiar power of eyes, upon her, and, turning quickly, she saw a black head, black as her own and running with curls, that dipped from the window.

There was no little head in all the post like that save one, and it belonged to little Francette, the pretty maid who had run by the factor's side that day of the meeting of Bois DesCaut by the river. With the drop of that head from the sill there passed over Maren a strange feeling, a prescience of evil, a thrill of fear in a heart that had never known fear.

She left the tiny room with the gift of the factor still outspread, and joined Marie in the outer space, where yawned a wide fireplace with its dogs on the hearth, its swinging crane made from a rod of iron, its bed and its hand-made table.

Here had come Anon Bordoux and Mora Le-Clede, drawn by the sight of the factor at the Baptistes' door, their tongues flying in eager question.

"—of such gorgeousness," Marie was saying, "such softness of white doeskin, such wealth of the beading—"

"Marie," said Maren sharply, "is there naught to do save gossip?"

Anon and Mora fell into confused silence, the habit of the trail where this girl's word had been the law falling upon them, but Marie, saucy and not to be daunted, was not so easily hushed.

"Is it not true," she cried, "that the factor brought it but now to the door in plain sight of all?"

Whereon Maren passed, out the open door and the tongues began again, more carefully.

In the distance there flashed a crimson skirt at whose beaded edge there hung a great grey dog, his heavy head waist-high to the little maid who wore it.

CHAPTER VIII

FIRST DAWN

Throughout the week that followed Fort de Seviere was gay with the bustle of trading. Packs of furs went up the main way and loads of merchandise went down, carried on the backs of the braves, guns and blankets and many a foot of Spencer's Twist at one beaver a foot, powder and balls in buckskin bags, and all the things of heart's desire that had brought the Assiniboines from the forks of the Saskatchewan.

Kept close to the factory by the bartering, McElroy and Ridgar and the two clerks hardly saw the blue spring sky, nor caught a breath of the scented air of the spring. Within the forest the Saskatoon was blooming and the blueberry bushes were tossing soft heads of foam, while many a tree of the big woods gave forth a breath of spice. It came in at the door and the young factor raised his head many times a day to drink its sweetness in a sort of wistfulness. At dusk he stood on the sill, released from the trade, and looked over his settlement as was his habit, and ever his eyes strayed to that new cabin at the far end, of the northern row.

What was she thinking, that dark-browed girl with the deep eyes that changed as the waters of a lake with each breath of wind, of him and the blundering gift he had carried to her door? What had she done with it, and would he ever see it clinging to those splendid shoulders, falling over the rounded breast?

A feeling of warmth grew at his heart each day with thought of her, and when he saw her swinging down toward the well he felt the blood leap in his veins. The very shine of the sun was different when it struck the tight black braids wrapped round her head.

Verily the little kingdom had brought forth its Princess.

And with her coming there was one heart that burned hot with passion, that fashioned itself after the form of hatred, for little Francette had seen, first a glow in a man's eyes and then a gift in his hand, and she fingered a small, flat blade that hung in her sash with one hand, the while the other strayed on the head of Loup. Dark was the fire that played in her pretty eyes, heavy the anguish that rode her breast.

She hated the memory of that white garment spread out on Maren Le Moyne's bed.

"Tessa," she said one day, sidling up to that Tessa Bibye who had cast a taunt in her teeth, "know you the charm which that doctress of the Crees gave to Marci Varendree when she sickened for love of that half-breed, Tohi Stannard?"

"Oho!" cried Tessa gleefully, "a man again! Who lacks one now, Francette?"

"Nay," said Francette, "but I know of one who sickens inwardly and I would give her the charm."

"Go into the flats of the Beaver House after Marci and her

Indian, whither they went," Tessa laughed. "I know not the charm. But it was good, for she got him, and went to the wilds with him. Follow and learn, Francette."

But Francette, with a gesture of disgust, turned away.

The warm spring days passed in a riot of song from the depths outside the post, the Assiniboine rippled and whispered along its shores and over the illimitable stretches of the wilderness there hung the very spirit of the mating-time.

Within the stockade, mothers sat in the doors crooning to the babes that clutched at the sunbeams, dogs slept in the cool shadows of the cabins, and here and there a youth sang a snatch of a love song.

"Verily, Marie, it is good to be here," sighed Micene Bordoux, sitting on her sill with her capable arms folded on her knees, and her eyes, cool and sane and tolerant, roving over the settlement lolling so quietly in the sun. "After the trail the rest is good, and yet I will be eager long before the year has passed to follow Maren,—may Mary give her grace!—into that wilderness which so draws at her heartstrings."

"Oh, Micene!" cried Marie, a trifle vexed, "if only she might forget her dreams! What is it like, the heart of a maid, that turns from thought of love to that of these wild lands, to the mystery of the Whispering Hills that lie, the good God knows where, in that dim and untracked West! I would that Maren might love! Then would we have peace and stop forever at this pleasant place."

Good Micene, with her brave heart and her whole-souled sense, smiled at Marie.

Vingie E. Roe

"Love," she said,—"and think you THAT could turn that exalted spirit from its quest? Still the stir of conquest within her bosom, hush the call of that glorious country which we know from rumor, and. plain hearsay lies at the heart of the Athabasca?"

"Little do you know Maren, Marie, though the same mother gave you birth. There is naught that could turn the maid, and I love her for it. It is that undaunted faith, that steadfast purpose, that white fire in her face which holds at her heels the whole of us, that turns to her the faces of our men, as those legions of France turned to the Holy Maid. Love? She would turn not for it if she could not take it with her."

Micene looked off across the cabins, and there was a warm light in her eyes.

"Nay, Marie," she said, "make ready for the trail the coming spring, for we will surely go."

It was this day, golden and sweet with little winds that wafted from the blossom-laden woods, that Maren Le Moyne, drawn by the dusky depths, passed, out the stockade gate, traversed slowly the length of the Indian camp, stopping here and there to hold out a hand to a frightened pappoose peeking from behind its mother's fringed leggings, to watch a moment at the cooking fires, to smile at a slim young boy brave in a checkered shirt, and entered the forest.

From the door of the factory McElroy saw her go and the call of the spring suddenly became unbearable.

With a word to Ridgar he stepped off the long log step and deliberately followed.

The Irish blood within him lifted his head and sent his heart a-bounding, while the half-holy mysticism that came from the Scottish hills drew his glance upward to the blue sky arching above.

A tumult surged in his breast and every pulse in his body leaped at thought of speech with her, and yet again a diffidence fell upon him that set him trembling.

As the conqueror he went, pushing toward victory, yet humble in his ambition.

He felt a mist in his eyes as he entered the high arched aisles, cool beneath their canopy of young green, and he looked eagerly here and there for sight of a tall form, upright, easy, plain in its dark garb.

Along the river bank he went where he saw a footprint in the soft loam, and presently it turned deeper into the great woods and he swung forward into those depths whose sweetness had called him subtly for these many days.

She was a strong traveller, that straight young creature of the open ways, and a full hour went swiftly before he caught the sight he wanted.

At sight of her he halted and stood a moment in hushed joy, looking with eyes that knew their glory, for with every passing second Anders McElroy was learning that nowhere in all the world, as had said that flaming youth Marc Dupre, was there another woman like this Maren Le Moyne.

She stood in a little glade, cool, high-canopied, where the sunlight came in little spots to play over the soft carpet of the pale forest grass thick-starred with frail white flowers, and her back was to a tree that towered to heaven in its height. At her sides her brown arms hung, palms out in an utter abandon of pleasure, while her lifted face, with its closed eyes, communed with the very Spirit of the Wild. Like some priestess she was, and McElroy felt an odd sensation of unworthiness sweep over him as he stood silent, his sober blue eyes on the beauty of her face. He cast swiftly back across his life. Was there anything there which might forbid him now, when he would go forward to so pure a thing as this maid, dreaming her dreams of prowess in the wilderness?

Nay, he saw no unworthy deed, nothing to spoil the page of a commonplace life spent at his old father's side across the sea, nothing of the so common evils of the settlement. Within him there was that which thanked its Maker unashamed that he had kept himself from one or two temptations which had beset him in these stirring years of service on the fringes of the great country spreading from the bay.

With that thought he went forward, and Maren did not hear his step on the soft grass, so far was she on her well-worn trail of dreams, until he stood near and the feeling of a presence finally brought back the wandering soul.

Then she opened her eyes and they fell full upon the factor, his light head bared to the dancing sun-spots, his blue eyes sober and touched again with that anxiety which had compelled her to take his gift.

There was no sudden start of fear, no little startled breath, for this woman was calm as the dreaming woods and as serene.

"Bon jour, M'sieu," she said, and at sound of her voice, so deep and full of those sliding minors, McElroy felt her power sweep over him in a tumultuous flood.

"Ma'amselle," he said, "Ma'amselle!"

And in the next moment stopped, for the words of love were on his tongue and the wide dark eyes were looking at him wonderingly.

"No longer could I withstand the call of the springtime and the woods," he finished falteringly; "the trading-room and the bargain were grown hateful to me in these warm days with the scent of flower and leaf and heated mould coming in at the door and bidding me come. I left my post, a traitor, Ma'amselle, betrayed by the forest. Too weak am I for courage when the big woods call."

Maren looked at him and the light grew up in her eyes, that little flame that flickered and leaped and gave so baffling a charm to her beauty.

"Ah!" she said softly; "you love it too, the great wilderness?"

"Aye, most truly."

"And you can hear the whisper of the far countries, the ripple of distant streams, the wind in the pines that have never sheltered a white man? You know these things, M'sieu?"

She leaned forward from the great smooth-barked tree and looked at him eagerly.

"They are what brought me over seas," he said quietly, "what sent me to De Seviere, what hold me to the tribes that come each year to my doors."

Maren's lips were parted, the fire of her passion in her flaming face. "Then you know why I come to the woods, why I grieve that the spring is passing, why I can scarcely hold my soul in patience through this delay!"

Vingie E. Roe

With the suddenness of her words her breath had leaped to a heaving tumult, the wide eyes, so calm, so cool, had filled first with fire and then with a mist. That clouded them like tears.

"Oh, M'sieu!" she cried tensely; "know you of that country which lies far to the west and which the Indians call the Land of the Whispering Hills?"

"Aye. It lies circling a great lake, blue as the summer skies, its waters forever rippled by the winds of the west which sing in the grassy vales and over the rounded knolls that stud the region,—a land of waving trees, of high coolness, or rich valleys thick with rank grasses and abounding with the pelt animals. It is the country of the Athabasca and from it came last year a band of the Chippewas heavily laden with furs. They told fine tales of its beauty. It is for that land you are bound?"

"For that land, M'sieu," said Maren Le Moyne, and her lips trembled; "for that virgin goddess of the dreams of years! I have seen its hills, its waving grass, wind-blown, its leaping streams,—I have breathed the sweet air of its forests and gazed on its beauties since my early childhood, in dreams, always in dreams, M'sieu, until I could bear the strain no longer. And now, when it beckons almost within my reach, when its very breath seems in my nostrils, I must stop for a year's space! You know, M'sieu,—you comprehend?"

She leaned forward looking earnestly into McElroy's eyes, and a surge of painful ecstasy shot to the man's heart, so near she seemed in the suddenly created sympathy of the moment, so near and gracious, so strong in her pure passion, so infinitely sweet.

"I know," he said, and his voice sounded strange in his ears;

"I know every pulse of your heart, Ma'amselle, every longing of your spirit, every pure thought of your mind,—for these many days I have trembled to every vibration that has touched or thrilled you. Oh, Ma'amselle!"

With the surge of that overwhelming thing within him the young man had forgot all things,—that this girl was near a stranger, that he had quaked at his temerity of the gift, forgot all but that she leaned toward him with the mist in her wide eyes, and he strode forward the step between them, his arms reaching out instinctively to enfold her.

With the swiftness of the impulse he swept her into them until the eager face lay on his breast, the smooth black braids pressing his lips with their satiny folds.

For one intoxicating moment he held her, as the primal man takes and holds his woman, tightly against his beating heart as though he would defy the world, lost in a sea of strange new emotions that rolled in golden billows high above his head.

Then from the depths there came a cry that cleared his whirling brain, a very embodiment of startled amaze, of indefinable horror, of mixed intonations.

"M'sieu!"

Maren Le Moyne wrenched herself free and lifted her face to look at him.

It was a warring field.

Upon it lay a great astonishment, a wonder, and a newness. Behind these there came, creeping swiftly with each moment of her startled gaze, an odd excitement that mounted with

Vingie E. Roe

each panting breath that left his lips, for it was from him that it took its life. Her red mouth dropped apart, showing the gleam of the white teeth between. She looked like a child rudely shaken from its sleep, startled, perhaps vaguely frightened at the strange shapes of familiar things distorted by the vision not yet adjusted.

"M'sieu!" she stammered; "M'sieu!"

And with her voice McElroy felt the arrested blood rush back to his heart again, for it held no anger. Instead it was full of that startled wonder, and it was as gold to him.

"Maren," he said, the emotion choking him; "Maren—" and with that new courage he put both hands on her shoulders and drew her near, looking down into the eyes so near on a level with his own.

Deliberately, slowly, that she might fully catch the meaning of what he was about to do, he drooped his lips until they rested square on the red mouth.

This was the thing he had left the factory for, this was what had drawn him, unconsciously perhaps, to the path along the river's bank, that had made him follow deliberately the light trail of the girl into the woods.

"Maren," he said, so thrilled that his words shook, "from this day forth you are mine. Mine only and against the whole world. I have taken you and you are mine."

He was full of his glory, dominating the dark eyes that had never left his own, and his soul was big within him. He was still very much a boy, this young factor, and the crowning moment of life had him in his grip.

He knew no fear, no thought of her next word or action touched him until she, as deliberately as he had acted, reached up and took both his hands from her shoulders.

"Adieu, M'sieu," said Maren Le Moyne quietly, the excitement of that breathed "M'sieu! M'sieu!" quite lost in the calmness that was her usual characteristic, and turning she walked away down the glen toward the river bank, the little spots of sun dancing on her black head like a leopard's gold as she passed in the checkered shade, and not once did she turn her head to see the factor of De Seviere standing where she had left him beside the forest giant.

CHAPTER IX

GOLD FIRE

If that time in the tuneful spring was crowded full to the brim of emotions scarce bearable to McElroy, how much more wonderful was it to Maren Le Moyne, for the first time in her life trembling in all her being from the touch of a man's lips?

To the outward world there was no sign of the tumult within her as she came and went about the business of the new cabin by the stockade wall, but in her virgin heart there stirred strange new things that filled her calm eyes with wonder.

In the seclusion of the little room to the east she spread out on the patchwork quilt the Indian garment and looked at it with a new meaning.

Never before in her life had she thought of a man's eyes as she thought of McElroy's, thrilling to the very tips of her fingers at memory of the blue fire in them, and never before had she been conscious of anything as she was conscious of the flesh on her shoulders where his hands had rested, her lips sealed under the warm caress of his. Verily, there was nowhere another such man as this one who knew the longing of the wild as did she, whose heart responded to the same call of the great wilderness.

Night and day she thought of him, and the memory of that day in the forest glade haunted her like a golden melody newly heard.

Yet something within her held her back from his sight, kept her eyes from that part of the small settlement where stood the factory with its wide doorway. She could not bear to look upon him yet in the newness of this awakening.

And McElroy, deep in the work of the trading, was eaten by a thousand qualms and torments. All those doubts that beset lovers tore at his heart and made of his days a nightmare.

With the cooling of his exalted intoxication what time the touch of the girl's young body had fired him with all confidence, came a thousand condemnations for his blundering haste, his stupid boasting of conquest.

To what depths of scorn might he not now be fallen in the mind of such a girl as Maren Le Moyne with her calm judgment; how far might he not be from the object of his longing!

And the fact that he could catch no sight of her, no matter how often he stepped near the door nor how diligently he sought for a glimpse of the shining braids and plain garment among the women at the well, but added fuel to the fire that scorched him.

But the times were getting very busy at Fort de Seviere. Before the Assiniboines were ready to depart back up the waterways down which they had come, their canoes laden with the wealth of the coming season, other flotillas were on the little waves of the river, other chiefs made their entrance up the main way of the post, and the goods of the Hudson's Bay Company went out in a stream as the priceless pelts came in.

"Lad," said Edmonton Ridgar with that easy probing of the well-known friend, "there is something eating at your mind these days. The trade goes differently from that of last year. It is not so all-absorbing. I fear me that the Nor'westers, with their plundering and their tales of deportation, have entered a wedge of worry."

"'Tis not of the Nor'westers I give a thought, Ridgar," he smiled, accepting the veiled raillery, "for you well know that we of the Company are above them, though it was but yesterday that an Indian brought word of a trapper at Isle a La Crosse being maltreated in the woods by a couple of their sneaking cutthroats and two packs of beaver taken from him for which they laughingly offered him in payment a bundle of mangy skins cast out from the summer's pickings. 'Twas Peter Brins and I'll wager that those two are marked for a long reckoning when the tables turn. And by the same Indian I hear that the young blade from Montreal with his light-haired brigade who stumbled upon us a while back, has reached his post on the Saskatchewan and has taken hold with a high hand, doing his utmost to intercept our Indians and turn the tide of the Company's furs into the trading-rooms of the Nor'westers. I think it will be a bootless process, for we hold our people with the hand of surety."

"Aye, but what of the Nakonkirhirinons, making their initial trip by way of Rapid River and Deer Lake, coming through the country of the Saskatchewan and held by no bond of loyalty? I see trouble ahead if this young De Courtenay gets wind of their coming, for they will be rich in peltry and they are a warlike tribe."

"But they are to celebrate the Peace Dance in the lodges of the Assiniboines. Surely they will come straight to their friends before trusting their trade to any."

Edmonton Ridgar shook his head.

"Hey fear nothing, these Nakonkirhirinons, and would as soon enter trade with one as another, having come for trade, if the values were above those at York and Churchill. I hope they swing eastward to Winipigoos and thus miss that young hot-brain on the Saskatchewan."

"By the way, Ridgar, Pierre Garcon says that Bois DesCaut is at Seven Isles on the Qui Appelle with Henderson. Since telling that wanton lie to the Nor'wester he has not had enough to show his face here. A bad lot Bois, and one to be watched for tricks."

"Aye, a bad lot, but salted with a prudence that savours of cowardice. His tricks are all turncoats that slip danger like an old garment."

But for all Ridgar's hope, at that very moment the great tribe from the far north country, even twelve leagues beyond the Oujuragatchousibi, was swinging down through the wilderness bound for the lodges of the Assiniboines, burdened with a wealth of peltry to make a trader's eyes stand out and clad in all the glory of the visiting tribes, and it was heading straight for the country of the Saskatchewan.

Towering head-dresses swept above their moving columns, pomp and ceremony showed in the panoply of carved spearheads, feathered shafts, and slung bows of the white ash which decked them on their peaceful mission, while underneath fringed garments of buckskin, stained and beaded with porcupine quills, were bands and stripes of war-paint.

Vingie E. Roe

They were ready for anything that might happen in this unknown country into which they journeyed at the word of their friends the Assiniboines, given at the buffalo hunt the fall before, above the Great Slave Lake.

Never before had the Nakonkirhirinons been so far in the south.

And long before they reached Deer Lake word had been brought to that new venturer in his post on the Saskatchewan, Alfred de Courtenay, and he was keenly alert.

About the same time a half-breed trapper came into Fort de Seviere, loud in his lamentations, and sought McElroy.

From the flats south of the Capot River, where he had wintered amid a band of Blackfoot Indians, a rare thing for a white man, he had come laden with rich furs from that unopened country, bound for De Seviere, and on the banks of the Qui Appelle three men had come upon him who had shared his lonely campfire. Rollicking fellows they were, brawny of form and light of head, and they had carried much liquor in flasks in their leg-straps, which liquor flowed freely amid songs and fireglow.

In the morning when he awoke late with, Mon Dieu! such a head! there were no three men, who had vanished like dreams of the liquor, likewise there was no well-strapped pack of fat winter beaver!

The man, a French half-breed, whimpered and cursed in impotent wrath, and showed McElroy one of the flasks that had been in the leg-straps of his visitors. It was covered with a fine light wicker weave, of the same pattern as that jug which De Courtenay had left at the post gate that morning in early spring.

"Ridgar," said the factor, showing the thing to him, "our friend from Montreal is taking a high hand with the country. The freedom of the wild has gone to his head."

Indeed it seemed as though that were true, for the tales of the reckless doings of that post of the Nor'westers on the Saskatchewan over which De Courtenay presided became more frequent and always they were characterised by a wildness and folly that were only exceeded by their daring.

The young adventurer had already made a headlong sally into the fringes of that country which came too near his Tom-Thumb garrison, and along which roving bands of the sullen Blackfeet trailed with a watching eye on the white men at the forts, and returned without two of those long curls of which he was so proud, a spear-head pinning them in the trunk of a tree which happened to form a convenient background.

To add to the small resentment against him which began to rankle in McElroy's heart, and which had never really left it since that evening in De Seviere when Maren Le Moyne had passed behind the cabin of the Savilles with some voyageur's tot on her shoulder and the handsome gallant from Montreal had lost his manners staring, one day in this same week a Bois-Brules came to the post gates and asked for one Maren Le Moyne.

He stood without and stubbornly refused to give his message, and at last McElroy himself went to the cabin of the Baptistes.

He had not seen the girl since that day in the forest, and his heart beat to suffocation as he neared the open door and caught the sound of her voice singing a French love song. He stopped on the step, and for a moment his glance took in the interior: By a window to the north she stood at a table, its wooden surface soft and white as doeskin from water and stone, and prepared the meal for ash-cakes, her sleeves, as usual, rolled to her shoulder and the collar of her dress open at the throat.

To the young factor's eyes she was a sight that weakened the knees beneath him and set him quaking with a new fear. He dared not speak and bring her gaze upon him, the memory of his boastful words in the forest was too poignant.

But it needed not speech. Had he but known the wonder that had lived within her all these days he would have understood the force that presently stopped the song on her lips, as if her soul listened unconsciously for tangible knowledge of the presence it already felt near, that slowed her nimble brown fingers in the pan, that presently lifted her head and turned her face to him.

Instantly a warm flush leaped up to the dark cheeks, and McElroy felt its answer in his own.

"Ma'amselle," he stammered, far from that glib "Maren" of the glade, "there is one at the gate who demands speech of you."

The words were commonplace enough and the girl did not get their import for the intensity of her gaze into the eyes whose blue fire had set her first wondering and then a-thrill with these strange emotions.

"Eh, M'sieu?" she smiled, and McElroy, revived through all his being with that smile, repeated his message.

She took her hands from the yellow meal and dusted them on a hempen towel, and was ready to go forth beside him.

That short walk to the stockade gate was silent with the silence of shy new joy, and once the factor glanced sidewise at the drooped lashes above the dusky cheeks.

"Had you expected any messenger, Ma'amselle?" he asked indifferently as they neared the portal with its fringe of peeping women and saw beyond them the tall figure of the Bois-Brule, his lank hair banded back by a red kerchief.

"Nay, M'sieu," replied the girl, and went forward to stand in the gate.

The messenger from the woods asked in good French if she were Maren Le Moyne, and being answered in the affirmative, he took from his hunting shirt a package wrapped in broad green leaves and placed it in her hands.

The leaves were wilted with the heat of the man's body and came easily off in her fingers, disclosing a small square box cunningly made from birchbark and stained after the Indian fashion in brilliant colours. A tiny lid was fastened with a thong of braided grass.

Wonderingly she slipped the little catch and lifted the cover.

Inside upon a bed of dampened moss there lay a wee red flower, the exact counterpart of that one which Alfred de Courtenay had fastened in her hair that morning by the well.

McElroy, at her shoulder, looked down upon it, and instantly the warmth in his heart cooled.

When Maren looked up it was to find his eyes fixed on the messenger whose tall figure swung away up the river's bank toward the north forest, and they were coolly impersonal.

She was unversed in the ways of men where a maid is concerned, this woman of the trail and portage, and she only knew vaguely that something had gone wrong with sight of the little flower.

She stood, holding the box in her hand, among the women craning their necks for a glimpse of the contents, and looked in open perplexity at McElroy until a light laugh from the fringe behind her broke the silence.

"A gift!" cried the little Francette, her childish voice full of a concealed delight; "a gift from the forest; and where do such trinkets come from save the lower branch of the Saskatchewan! It savours of our pretty man of the long gold curls! Mon Dieu! The cavalier has made good time!"

Whereat there was a stirring at the gate, and the peeping fringe drew back while the factor turned on his heel and strode away toward the factory, leaving the tall girl alone at the portal, holding her gift.

There was a devilish light in the dancing eyes of Francette as she flirted away.

But Maren Le Moyne walked slowly back to the cabin, wondering.

CHAPTER X

THE SASKATOON

It was at dusk of that same day that McElroy, as near sullen anger as one of his temperament could be, sat alone on the log step of the factory, his pipe unlighted in his lips and his moody eyes on the beaten ground worn hard by the passing feet of moccasined Indians from the four winds.

Edmonton Ridgar, with that keenness which gave him such tact, had shut himself in the living-room, and the two clerks were off among the maids at the cabins.

Once again McElroy had made himself ridiculous by that abrupt turning away because of a small red flower sent a maid by a man he now knew to be his foe and rival in all things of a man's life.

Down by the southern wall an old fiddle squeaked dolefully, and from beyond the stockade came the drowsy call of a bird deep in the forest depths.

On the river bank young Marc Dupre sang as he fumbled at a canoe awaiting the morn when he was to set off up-stream for any word that he might pick up of the coming of the Nakonkirhirinons. There was no moon and the twilight had

Vingie E. Roe

deepened softly, covering the post with a soft mantle of dreams, when there was a step on the hard earth and the factor turned sharply to behold a little figure in a red kirtle, its curly head hanging a bit as if in shame, and at its side the shadowy form of the great dog Loup.

"M'sieu," said Francette timidly, and the tone was new to that audacious slip of impudence; "M'sieu."

"What is it, little one?" said McElroy gently, his own disgust of his morning's quickness softening his voice that he might not again play the hasty fool, and Francette crept nearer until she stood close to the log step.

The small hands were twisting nervously and the little breast lifting swiftly with an agitation entirely new to her.

Presently she seemed to find the voice that eluded her.

"Oh, M'sieu!" she cried at last, breaking out as if the words were thick crowded in her throat; "a heavy burden has fallen upon me! Is it right, M'sieu, for a maid to die for love of a man, waiting, waiting, waiting for the look, the word that shall crown her bondage? Love lives all round in the post save in the heart that is all the world to Francette! Why should there be happiness everywhere but here?"

With a gesture pathetically dramatic the little maid threw her hands across her heaving breast and gazed at McElroy with big eyes, starry in the dusk.

Her emotion was genuine he could not help but see, even through his astonishment, and he stared at her with awaking sympathy.

"Is there some one who is so much to you, little one?" he

asked. "I thought there wasn't a youth in the post—no, nor in any other this side the Red River-who did not pay homage to France Moline's little daughter. Who is of such poor taste? Tell me, and what I can do I will do to remedy the evil."

He was smiling at the little maid's pretty daring in coming straight to the very head of De Seviere with her trouble, and he reached out a hand to draw her down on the step beside him. There was never a woman in distress who did not pull at the strings of his heart, and he longed to soothe her, even while he smiled to himself at her childishness.

But Francette was not so childish, and he was one day to marvel at her artless skill.

At the touch of his hand she came down, not upon the step beside him as he meant, but upon her knees before him, with her two little hands upon his knees and her face of elfin beauty upheld to him in the starlight.

"Oh, M'sieu, there is one who is so much,—oui, even more than all the world, more than life itself,—more than heaven or hell, for whose sake I would die a thousand deaths! One at whose feet I worship, scorning all those youths of the settlement and the posts. See, M'sieu," she leaned forward so close that the fragrance of her curls blew into the man's nostrils and he could see that the little face was pale with a passion that caused him wonder; "see! Today came one from the forest bringing love's message to that tall woman of Grand Portage,—the little red flower in the birchbark case. It spoke its tale and she knew,"—subtle Francette!—"she knew its meaning by the eye of love itself. So would I, who have no words and am a woman, send my message by a flower."

The hands on the factor's knees were trembling with a rigour that shook the whole small form before him.

"See, M'sieu!" she cried, with the sudden sound of tears in the low voice; "read the heart of the little Francette!"

She took from her bosom a fragile object and laid it in his palm, then clasped her hands over her face and bowed until the little head with its running curls was low to the log step.

McElroy strained his eyes to see what he held.

It was a dried spray of the blossoms of the saskatoon.

For a moment he sat in stupid wonder. Then swiftly, more by intuition and that strange sense which recalls a previous happening by a touch, or a smell, than by actual memory, he saw that golden morning when he had stopped by the Molines' cabin and watched the great husky balance on his shaky legs. He had twirled in his fingers the first little spray of the saskatoon, brought in by Henri Corlier to show how the woods were answering the call of the spring.

"Why," he said, astounded beyond measure, "why, Francette,— little one, what does this mean?"

But Francette had lost her tongue and there was no answer from the bowed figure at his knees.

He put out a hand and laid it on her shoulder and it was shaken with sobs,—the sobs of a woman who has cast her all on the throw of the die and in a panic would have it back.

Off in the forest a night bird called to its mate and the squeaky fiddle whined dolorously and a profound pity began to well in the factor's heart. She was such a little maid, such a childish thing, a veritable creature of the sunlight, like those great golden butterflies that danced in the flowered glades of the woods, and she had brought her one great gift to him unasked.

Some thought of Maren Le Moyne and of that reckless cavalier with his curls and his red flowers crept into his voice and made it wondrously tender with sympathy.

"Sh, little one," he comforted, as he had comforted that day on the river bank when she had wept over Loup; "come up and let us talk of this." He lifted her as one would lift a child and strove to raise the weeping eyes from the shelter of her hands, but the small head drooped toward him so near that it was but a step until it lay in the shelter of his shoulder, and he was rocking a bit, unconsciously, as the sobbing grew less pitiful.

"Sh—sh-little one," he said gently; "sh—sh."

Meanwhile Maren Le Moyne sat in the doorway of her sister's cabin with her chin on her hands and stared into the night. Marie and Henri were at the cabin of the Bordoux, laughing and chattering in the gay abandon of youth. She could hear their snatches of songs, their quips and laughter rising now and again in shrill gusts. Also the wailing fiddle seemed a part of the warm night, and the bird that called in the forest.

All the little homely things of the post and the woods crept into her heart, that seemed to her to be opening to a vague knowledge, to be looking down sweet vistas of which she had never dreamed among her other dreams of forest and lake and plain, and, at each distant focus where appeared a new glory of light, there was always the figure of the young factor with his anxious eyes. Strange new thrills raced hotly through her heart and dyed her cheeks in the darkness. She tingled from head to foot at the memory of that day in the glade, and for the first time in her life she read the love-signs in a man. That change in his eyes when he had looked upon De Courtenay's red flower was jealousy. With the thought came a greater fulness of the unexplainable joy that had flooded her all these days. Aye, verily, that red flower had caused him pain,—him,—with his laughing blue eyes and his fair head tilted back ever ready for mirth, with his tender mouth and his strong hands. The very thought of that killed the joy of the other. If love was jealousy, and jealousy was pain, the one must be healed for sake of the other. With this girl to think was to do, and with that last discovery she was upon her feet, straight and lithe as a young animal beside the door. She would go to this man and tell him that the red flower was less than nothing to her, its giver less than it.

At that moment a figure came out of the dusk and stopped before her.

It was her leader, Prix Laroux, silent, a shadow of the shadows.

"Maren," he said, in that deep confidence of trusted friends, "Maren, is all well with you?"

"All is well, Prix," said the girl, her voice tremulous with pleasure, "most assuredly. Thought you aught was wrong?"

"Nay,—only I felt the desire to know."

"Friend," said Maren, reaching out a hand which the man took strongly in both his own; "good, good friend! Ever you are at my back."

"Where you may easily reach me when you will."

"I know. 'Tis you alone have made possible the long trail. Ah! how long until another spring?"

But, when Prix had lounged away into the dusk and the girl

had stepped into the soft dust of the roadway, she fell to wondering how it was that mention of the year's wait brought no longer its impatience, its old dissatisfaction.

She was thinking of this as she neared the factory, her light tread muffled in the dust.

"Foolish Francette! What should I do with a gay little girl like you? Play in the sunshine years yet, little one, and think not of the bonds and cares of marriage. How could these little hands lift the heavy kettles, wash the blankets, and do the thousand tasks of a household? You are mistaken, child. It is not love you feel, but the changing fancies of maidenhood. Play in the sun with Loup and wait for the real prince. He will come some day with great beauty and you will give no more thought to me. He must be young, little one, a youth of twenty; not one like me, nearer the mark of another decade. It would not be fitting. Youth to youth, and those of a riper age to each other." He was thinking of a tall form, full and round with womanhood, whose eyes held knowledge of the earth, and yet, had he been able to define their charm, were younger even than Francette's.

The little maid had ceased her weeping long since and the face on McElroy's shoulder, turned out toward the night, was drawn and hard. The black eyes were no longer starry with passion, but glittering with failure. And the man, stupid and good of heart as are all men of his type, congratulated himself that he had talked the nonsense out of her little head.

Suddenly he felt the slender figure shiver in his arms and the curly head brushed his cheek as she raised her face.

"Aye, M'sieu," she whispered, "it is as you say, but only one thing remains. Kiss me, M'sieu, and I go to—forget."

The factor hesitated.

He felt again his one passionate avowal on the lips of his one woman.

This was against the grain.

"Please, M'sieu," begged the childish voice, with a world of coaxing; and, thinking to finish his gentle cure, he bent his head and kissed her lightly on the cheek.

"And now—" he started to admonish, when she threw her arms about his neck, stiffling the words in her garments.

At the corner of the factory Maren Le Moyne stood looking through the twilight at the scene.

When Francette released him there were only they two and he had heard no step nor seen the silent beholder.

When the little French maid slipped away with the husky she fingered the carved toy of a knife in her sash and tossed her short curls in triumph.

Her failure had taken on a hue of victory.

CHAPTER XI

LEAVEN AT WORK

"M'sieu," said Marc Dupre, coming up the slope from the river, his buckskins much tattered, showing a swift cross-country run, "I have news of the great tribe. Like the forest leaves in fall in point of numbers they are, and they wear a wealth of wampum and elk teeth, so much that they are rich beyond any other tribe. Their young men are tall and heavy of stature and wonderful in the casting of their great carven spears. Also do they excel in the use of the bow. Warlike and suspicious, scouting every inch of country before them, they come down by way of Dear Lake,—and the young Nor'wester at Fort Brisac has already sent forth his messengers to meet them."

McElroy frowned.

Double anger swelled suddenly within him. In two ways had De Courtenay crossed his plane at opposing angles. It was evidently war that the adventurer wanted, the hot war of the two fur companies coupled to that of man and man for a maid. He stood a while and thought. Then he turned to Dupre.

"You have done well, Dupre," he said shortly. "Get you to

your cabin and rest, for I may want your wit again. Only, on the way, send Pierre Garçon to me."

The young man touched his red toque, symbol of safety to all trappers in a land where the universal law is "kill," for no wild animal of the woods bears a crimson head save that animal man who is the greatest killer of all, and turned away. He was draggled and stained from a forced march through forest and up-stream, over portage and rapid, carrying his tiny birchbark craft on his head, snatching a short sleep on a bed of moss, hurrying on that he might learn of the Nakonkirhirinons travelling slowly down from that unknown land to the far north, even many leagues beyond York factory on the shores of the great bay.

As he went toward his own cabin he glanced swiftly at the open door of the Baptistes. Always these days he glanced that way with a sick feeling in the region of his heart. Who was he, Marc Dupre, trapper of the big woods, that he should dare think so often of that woman from Grand Portage, with her wondrous beauty and her tongue that could be like a cold knife-blade or the petal of a lily for softness? And yet he was conscious of a mighty change that had come over him with that day on the flat rock by the stockade when she had talked to him of the trapping,—a change like that which comes to one when he is so fortunate as to be in distant Montreal and sits in the dusk of the great church there among the saints and the incense.

There was no longer pleasure in flipping jests and love words with the red-cheeked maids, and something had happened to the dashing spirit of the youth. All through those long days in the forest, those short blue nights under the velvet sky, one image had stood before him, calm, smiling, quivering with that illusive light which held men's hearts. Never a day that he could win forgetfulness of the face of

Maren Le Moyne, and now he glanced toward her doorway. It lay in the sunlight without a foot upon its sill, and Marc sighed unconsciously. He was not to see her, perhaps, to-day.

But suddenly, as he rounded a corner among the cabins, he came full upon her, and his flippant tongue clove to the roof of his mouth without speech.

She came toward him with a bread-pan in her hands and her eyes were cast down. The heart in him ran to water at sight of her, and he stopped.

Once more thought of his unworthiness abased him.

Then she felt his presence and raised her eyes, and the young trapper looked deep into them with that helplessness which draws the look of a child. Deep he looked and long, and the woman looked back, and in that moment there sprang into life the first thrill of that thing which was to lead to the great crisis which she had predicted that day by the stockade.

With it Marc Dupre found his tongue.

"Ma'amselle!" he cried sharply, "what is it? Mon Dieu! What is it?" For the dark eyes, with their light-behind-black-marble splendour, were quenched and dazed and all knowledge seemed stricken from them. The look of them cut to his very soul, quick and sensitive from the working of the great change, made ready as a wind-harp by the silent days of dreams, the nights of visions. To him alone was the devastation within them apparent. He stretched out a timid hand and touched her sleeve.

"What is it, Ma'amselle?" he begged abjectly. "I would heal it with my blood!"

Extravagant, impulsive, the boy was in deadly earnest, and Maren Le Moyne was conscious of it as simply as that she lived.

Just as simply she acknowledged to him what she would have to none other in De Seviere, that something had fallen from a clear sky.

"Nay," she said, and the deep voice was lifeless, "I am beyond help."

Dupre's fingers slipped, trembling, around her arm.

"But I am a stone to your foot, Ma'amselle,—always remember that. When the way becomes too hard there shall be a stone to your foot. I ask no better fate and you have said."

The miserable eyes were not dead to everything. At his swift words they glowed a moment.

"Aye,—I have said, and I thank God, M'sieu, for such friendship. I am rich, indeed."

"Oho! Marc Dupre does better at the lovemaking than at the trapping! His account at the factory suffers from les amours!"

A childish voice broke in upon them, and Francette's mpish face peeped round the corner of the nearest cabin.

"Let it be, Marc Dupre," as the youth dropped his and from Maren's arm. "Ma'amselle does not object,—a trapper or a cavalier, all are fish to Ma'amselle's net. Mon Dieu! If all were so attractive as Ma'amselle!"

The little maid sighed in exaggerated dolour.

Dupre flashed round on his moccasined heel and reached her in a stride.

"Aha! It is you, by all the saints!" he said beneath his breath, as he took her none too gently by the shoulder. "I know your tricks."

Aloud he said, "Francette, children should keep from where they are not wanted. Get you back to your mother."

"Children, you say, M'sieu Dupre? Is eighteen so far behind twenty-two? Grow a beard on your cheek before you give yourself the airs of a man. And, anyway, grown men of twice eighteen have been known to love children of that age."

It was a dagger thrust, and it found its mark even as the girl glanced slily at her victim. Maren's full mouth twitched and she looked dully away to the fort gate. Dupre gave Francette an ungallant push. "Begone!" he cried angrily; "you little cat!"

With a ringing laugh the maid danced away in the sunshine, and Dupre faced Maren.

"It is that imp of le diable, Francette?" he asked. "What has she done to you, Ma'amselle?"

But Maren shook her head.

"The maid is not to blame. She is but a child in spirit and what le bon Dieu has seen fit to give her has gone to her head. That is all, save as your quick eye has detected, M'sieu, I have received a heavy hurt."

Suddenly, with that whimsical youthfulness of soul which glimmered at times through her apparent strength, she looked at Dupre with a sort of fright.

"Merci, M'sieu! For what reason does the good God let some things befall? ... But I have still a stone. Throughout I will remember that."

In a moment she was gone, walking toward the cabin of Micene Bordoux, and Marc Dupre went on his quest of Pierre, wondering and all a-tremble with pity and thought of that promise.

Where Marc, with the revelation of adoration, had seen sharply, Micene with her good sense felt vaguely that something was wrong with the intrepid leader of the long trail.

"Maren," she said this day, as she took the bread pan which had been borrowed, "I fear there is something troubling you. Is there bad news from Athabasca?"

Always there lay behind Maren's eagerness a fear, sleeping like a hidden fawn but ever ready to quiver into life, a fear of news from the Whispering Hills, news that should make the promise of the trail a sudden void.

"Nay, Micene," smiled Maren, "these latest Indians come from the south."

"And all is well with the plans?"

The vague uneasiness was not stilled in Micene.

"All is well with the plans. There is not a year now."

The girl looked straight in her friend's eyes without a trace of the dazed misery which Marc Dupre had surprised in her own.

Micene smiled back, but that night she lay far into the dark hours thinking of the subtle change in the maid of the trail. With a woman's intuition she knew that the girl had lied, that all was not well with her.

And one other there was of that small party of venturers housed in the new cabins of De Seviere who knew vaguely that something had gone wrong-Prix Laroux, the sturdy prow of that little vessel of progress of which the girl was the beating heart, the unresting engine.

He had felt its coming even before it fell, that mighty shadow which blotted out the heavens and the earth, for to Maren, once given, there was no recalling the gift, and with that day in the glade she had lost possession of her soul and body forever.

Dazed in all the regions of her being, enshadowed in every vista of hope and scarce-tasted joy, she went quietly about the cabin, her mind a dark space in which there flashed sudden, reiterated visions,—now McElroy's blue eyes, anxious and eager as he held up the doeskin dress at the door-sill, burning with fire and truth and passion in the glade in the forest, again tender and diffident what time they walked together to the gate to meet De Courtenay's messenger, and again it was that scene at the factory steps that haunted her,—McElroy with his arms about Francette Moline, the grey husky crouching in the twilight. Throughout the whole sick tangle there went a twisting thread of wonder, of striving for understanding. What was this thing which had come clutching sweetly at her heart, which had stilled the very life in her with holy mystery, and whose swift passing had left her benumbed within as some old woman numbling in the sun on a door-sill? Where was the glory of the spring? What had come upon the face of the waters, that the light had gone from them? What was this thing that the good God wished her to learn, where was the lesson?

Given to reason and plain judgment of all things, the girl tried to think out her problem, to fathom the meaning of this which had befallen her, and to find if there was any good in it. But everywhere she looked there was the laughing face of the factor with his sunburnt hair and his blue eyes. The spring days were heavy as those steel-grey stretches that pass for the days in winter.

Too dull for sharp pain, she went about in a sort of apathy.

For several days McElroy watched uneasily for her, hoping for a chance meeting. He was anxious to speak about his boyish jealousy, to beg forgiveness for that abrupt leaving at the gate. So close did she stay at the cabin, however, that at last he was forced to go to her. It was twilight again, soft, filled with the breath of the forest, vibrant with the call of birds off in some marshy land to the south, and he found her alone, sitting upon the step, staring into the gathering dusk, listening to the laughter of the young married folk from the cabin next where Marie and Henri were loudest.

A lump rose in his throat as he caught the outline of the braided head bowed lower than he had ever seen it, saw the whole attitude of the strong figure, every line relaxed as if in a great weariness.

"Maren," he said, with the wonder of love in his voice, "Maren—my maid!"

And he strode forward swiftly, stooped, and laid his hand on her shoulder.

With a jerk the drooped head came up. She drew from his touch as if it burned her.

"If you please, M'sieu," she said coldly, "go away."

McElroy sprang back.

"What? Go away! You wish that,—Ma'amselle?"

The tone more than the words drove out of him all daring of her sweet name, took away in a flash all the personal.

"Of a surety,—go away."

The factor stood a moment in amazed silence. Did the red flower mean so much to her, then? Had she accepted its message? And yet he knew in his heart that the look in her eyes, the smile on her lips had told their own tale of awakening to his touch. What but the red flower in its birchbark case had wrought the change?

He thought swiftly of De Courtenay's beauty, of his sparkling grace, his braided blue coat, his wide hat, and the long golden curls sweeping his shoulder. Truly a figure to turn a woman's head. But within him there rose a tide of rage, blind vent of the hurt of love, that boded ill for the dashing Nor'wester on the Saskatchewan.

Sick to the very bottom of his heart, he bowed ever so slightly to the tense figure on the step and strode away in the shadows.

So! Thus ended his one love.

For this he had kept himself from the common lot of the factors in their lonely posts; for this he had never looked with aught save friendly compassion upon the maids of the settlements, the half breed girls of the wilderness, the wild daughters of the forest.

Waiting for this one princess in his small kingdom, he had thrown himself on the out-bearing tide of love only to be stranded on some barren beach, to see her taken from him by some reckless courtier not fit to touch a woman's hand!

Thus they turned apart, these two meant for each other from the beginning, and in each love worked its will of pain.

Maren on the step stared dry-eyed into the night, uncomprehending, unrebelling, and McElroy strode ahead, blind with sudden anguish, scarce knowing which way his steps tended.

And, like a ghoul behind a stone, a small dark face peeped keenly from a corner.

Francette was watching her leaven work.

CHAPTER XII

THE NAKONKIRHIRINONS

In the week that followed the waters of the Assiniboine grew black with myriads of canoes. Like the leaves in fall, truly, they came drifting out of the forest, long slim craft, made with a wondrous cunning of birchbark peeled from the tree in one piece, fitted to frames of ash fragile as cockleshell and strong as steel under the practised hand, and smeared in every crinkle and crease and crevasse with the resinous gum of the pine tree. By scores and hundreds and battalions, it seemed to the traders at De Seviere, they poured out of the wilderness, choking the river with their numbers, spilling their contents on the slope under the bastioned walls until a camp was made so vast that it stretched into the forest on each side the clearing of the post and even extended to the marsh at the south.

Half-naked braves stalked in countless numbers among the tepees that went rapidly up, tall fellows, mighty of build and fearless of carriage and of eagle eye, aloof, suspicious, watching the fort, guarding the rich piles of peltry and exchanging a word with none.

These were the great Nakonkirhirinons from that limitless region of the Pays Ten d'en Haut.

　　　　　　　　Vingie E. Roe

If McElroy's heart had not been so full of his own trouble he would have exulted mightily in their coming, for did it not prove one failure for that reckless Nor'wester on the Saskatchewan? They had come, past all his blandishments of trade, to Fort de Seviere, and their coming spelled a number of furs this season far in advance of any other for that small post. If he wondered at first how they had held out against De Courtenay it was all made plain when among the strangers he espied many Assiniboines and saw in the great canoe of the chief Negansahima, old Quamenoka, who had boasted of the coming of this tribe to De Seviere as his work.

He had spoken truly and had evidently made his word good by meeting the approaching columns and returning with them.

To him alone was due the failure of De Courtenay, McElroy felt at once, and determined in his mind on that present which he had promised for this zeal.

With the coming of the strangers Fort de Seviere was put under military rule. The half-moon to the right of thegate, with its small cannon, received a quota of menwho strayed carelessly all day within reach of the low rampart; a guard lounged in the great gate, ready at a moment's notice to clang it shut, and seemingly matter-of-course precautions were taken throughout, for these Indians were as uncertain as the flickering north lights crackling in a frosty sky.

There was a scene not to be likened to any other outside the region of the Hudson Bay country, where strange relations existed between white trader and savage, when Edmonton Ridgar met the canoe of the chief at the landing.

Savage delight overspread the eagle features of Negansahima as he beheld the white man.

Towering mightily in the prow of his canoe, the sweeping head-dress of feathers crowning him with a certain majesty, he fixed his keen glance on Ridgar and came gliding toward him across the rippled water.

As the canoe cut cleanly up and stopped just short of scraping on the stones at the edge, obeying the paddles like a thoroughbred the bit, the chief trader of De Seviere stepped forward and held out his arms.

"Who art thou?" he called.

Deep and guttural as thunder from the broad chest, naked under the lines of elk teeth, came the reply,

"Thy father"

"And master of my goods. The heart of thy son melts as the snow in spring. Wiskendjac has sent thee."

McElroy, standing near, saw the face of his friend illumined with a real affection as the savage landed and, contrary to the custom of the Indians in the lower country, embraced with every sign of joy the lean white man whose skin was nearly as dark as his own and whose greying temples bespoke almost a as many years as the chief's black locks could boast.

In the eyes of both, as they regarded each other, were memories known to no one else. McElroy wondered what they were and what that year, of which Ridgar had spoken only once, had held.

The trader spoke their tongue as easily as he spoke any other that came to the post, naturally and with quiet fluency.

So deep was the apparent pleasure of the meeting that, when

the interpreting was done and the ceremonies over, Ridgar went with the Indian among the tepees and no more did McElroy see him until he came to the factory at dusk.

"Mother of Heaven!" he ejaculated, flinging himself down at the table in the living-room where Rette's strong coffee tempted the nostril; "such furs! Beaver in countless packs, all the fat winter skins, no Bordeaux, no Mittain. Fox, also of the best only,—black fox, fine and shining, fox of those far-north regions where they hunt beyond the sun, white as the snow it runs on, and Mon Dieu, McElroy! Seven silvers as I hope for salvation! Verily are they a prize beyond price, these Indians that have come in to us, and I fancy that young Nor'wester is swearing at his luck in losing them. Old Quamenoka struts as if their wealth belonged to his meek Assiniboines.... But the furs! Ermine and nekik and sakwasew and wapistan, all the little fellows that, taken from those virgin north lands, are worth their weight in gold! Nowhere have I seen a common pelt. They are connoisseurs, these wild Nakonkirhirinons, and they carry a king's ransom in their long canoes. White bear and brown arctic wolf and everywhere the best of its kind! To-morrow's trade will be worth while—but keep the guns in evidence and quiet above all things."

"Ah!" said McElroy, "what is there to fear, think you? Is not the chief bound to you by all ties of ceremony and regard?"

"Most assuredly," returned Ridgar quietly, "but those young braves are strung like a singing wire and swift as a girl to take suspicious fright; and there are somewhere near five hundred of them, as near as I can make out from the numbers seething among the lodges. They are in a strange country and watching every leaf and shadow."

Thus the sun went down on De Seviere, with the eager maids

and women passing and repassing near the gate to peep out at the rustling throng, at the tepees with their fine skin coverings painted with all the wonders of battle and the chase, at the comely squaws and maidens, the chubby brown children, the dogs snarling arid savage, for they had full complement of the grey northern huskies.

To a woman they peeped at the gate from all the cabins of the post, save only that one who had been most eager before when the Indians came, Maren Le Moyne, sitting in idle apathy on her sister's doorstep.

"Ma'amselle," said Marc Dupre, stopping hesitant before her, "have you seen the Nakonkirhirinons?"

"Nay," she said listlessly, "I care not, M'sieu."

And the youth went gloomily away.

"Something there is which preys on her like the blood-sucker on the rabbit's throat. But what? Holy Mother, what?"

His handsome eyes were troubled.

By dawn on the following day the trading had begun. Up the main way passed a line of braves, each laden with his winter's catch of furs, to barter at the trading-room, haggle with the clerks by sign and pantomime, and pass down again with gun and hatchet and axe, kettle and bright blanket, beads, and, most eagerly sought of all, yards of crimson cloth.

There was babble of chatter among the squaws, shrill laughter, and comparison of purchases.

In the trading-room sat the chief with his headmen and old

Quamenoka of the Assiniboines, smoking gravely many pipes and listening to the trading. Like some wild eagle of the peaks brought down to earth he seemed, ever alert and watchful behind his stately silence.

For two days the trading progressed finely, and McElroy had so far laid aside his doubts as to take delight in the quality of the rare furs.

Never before had such pelts stacked themselves in the sorting-room.

It was a sight for eyes tired by many springs of common trade.

Then, like a bomb in a peaceful city, came a running word of excitement.

The Nor'wester from the Saskatchewan was among the Nakonkirhirinons! Was at the very gates of De Seviere! When Pierre Garcon brought the news, McElroy flushed darkly to his fair hair and went on with his work.

This was unbearable insolence.

"An', M'sieu," pursued Pierre, "not only the man from Montreal, but, like the treacherous dog he is, among the Nor'westers is that vagabond Bois DesCaut."

"Turncoat?" said the factor.

"Aye."

True enough. When McElroy, after trading hours, strolled down to the gate between the bastions, whom should he behold but the hulking figure of his erstwhile trapper, sulky of appearance, shifty eyes flitting everywhere but toward his old factor. And farther down the bank, among a group of warriors, a brown baby on his shoulder and his long curls shining in the sunset, was that incomparable adventurer, Alfred de Courtenay.

Apparently he had not come for barter, nor for anything save the love of the unusual, the thirst for adventure that had brought him primarily to the wilderness.

"A fine fit of apoplexy would he have, that peppery old uncle at Montreal, Elsworth McTavish, could he see his precious nephew following his whims up and down the land, leaving his post in the hands of his chief trader," thought McElroy, as he looked at the scene before him.

While he stood so, there was a rustle of women behind him and voices that bespoke more eager eyes for the Indians, and he glanced over his shoulder.

Micene Bordoux and Mora LeClede approached, and between them walked Maren Le Moyne. McElroy's heart pounded hard with a quick excitement as he saw the listless droop of the face under the black braids and stopped with a prescience of disaster. His glance went swiftly to the long-haired gallant in the braided coat. Surely were the elements brought together.

It seemed as if Fate was weaving these little threads of destiny, for no sooner did Maren Le Moyne step through the gate among the lodges than her very nearness drew round upon his heel De Courtenay.

His eyes lighted upon her and the sparkling smile lit up his features. With inimitable grace he swung the child from his shoulder, tossed it to a timid squaw watching like a hawk, and, shaking back his curls, came forward.

"Ah, Ma'amselle!" he said, bending before her with his courtly manner, "you see, as I said in the early spring,—I have come back to Fort de Seviere."

"So I see, M'sieu," smiled Maren, with a touch of whimsical amusement at the memory of that morning, and his venturesome spirit. "Have you by chance brought me a red flower?"

"Why else should I come?" he returned, and, with a flourish, brought from his bosom a second birchbark box which he held out to the girl.

Over her face there spread a crimson flood at this swift, literal proving of a secret pact and she stood hesitating, at loss.

The stretch of beach was alive with spectators. Near the wall a group of girls hugged together, with Francette Moline in the centre; down by the canoes Pierre Garcon and Marc Dupre stood, the dark eyes of the latter watching every move, while at the door of the chief's lodge, directly before the fort and between it and the river, Edmonton Ridgar talked in low tones with Negansahima. Indeed, like father and son seemed this strangely assorted pair. Maren remembered afterward how near together they had stood, the wild savage in his elk teeth and scant buckskin garments, an indiscreet band of yellow paint showing a corner above his blanket, and the dark, wiry trader with the grey eyes. Scattered, here and there among the braves were many Bois-Brules, lean Runners of the Burnt Woods, belonging she knew to the North-west Company. Also in that moment she saw the frowning face and ugly eyes of Bois DesCaut beneath the white lock on his temple. Long afterward was the girl to recall that evening scene.

For another moment she hesitated, and then, from sheer loss of poise, reached out her hand. The dancing eyes of the cavalier lit with all the daring of conquest.

"My heart, Ma'amselle," he said gallantly, as he pressed the fragile thing in her palm; and in another second he had stooped and kissed her, as he had kissed many another woman, lightly, delicately, in the face of the populace, joying to the depths of his careless nature in the dare of the thing.

With a cry the girl sprang back, crushing the birchbark case with its red flower into shapeless ruin. There was a muffled word, the flash of a figure, and McElroy the factor had flung himself before her. She caught the thud of a blow upon flesh and in a moment there were two men locked in deadly combat before the post gate. In less time than the telling, a circle of faces drew round, dark faces of Indians and Bois-Brules, light faces of De Courtenay's men, and in all there leaped swift excitement as they saw the combatants. White with passion, his brilliant eyes flaming and dancing with fury, De Courtenay fought like a madman to avenge that blow in the face, while McElroy, flushed and calmer, took with his hands payment for all things,—slighted kindliness, Company thefts, and, above all else, the stolen heart of his one woman.

How it would have ended there is no telling, for these two were evenly matched—what De Courtenay lacked in weight he made up in swiftness and agility,—had it not been for the side arm that hung at his hip, one of those small pistols in use across the water where gentlemen fight at given paces and not across a frozen river or through a mile of brush.

Once, twice, he tried to reach it, and twice did McElroy

Vingie E. Roe

snatch the groping hand away. Three times he passed swiftly for the inlaid handle and, as if there lay luck in the number, the weapon flashed in the red light.

Swift as was the draw, McElroy was swifter.

With an upward stroke he flung up the hand that held it. There was a shot, ringing down the Assiniboine and echoing in the woods, and little Francette by the stockade wall screamed. With the first flash of metal Maren Le Moyne had gripped her hands until the nails cut raw, standing where she had sprung at the stranger's kiss.

She could no more move than the bastioned wall behind her.

For a moment there was deathly silence after that shot. Then pandemonium broke loose as Negansahima, chief of the Nakonkirhirinons, flung up his arms, the dull metal bands with their inset stones catching the crimson light, and fell into the outstretched arms of Edmonton Ridgar.

A long cry broke from his lips, the death-cry of a warrior.

CHAPTER XIII

"A SKIN FOR A SKIN"

For a moment the whole evening scene, red with the late light, was set in the mould of immobility. The two fighting men at sound of that cry following hard upon the shot stopped rigidly, still clasped in the grip of rage, the women staring wide-eyed from the wall, the Bois-Brules, the leaning eager faces of the wild Nakonkirhirinons, the figure of the girl in the foreground, all, all were stricken into stillness by that dirge-like cry. For only the fraction of a second it held, that tense waiting.

Then from nine hundred throats there shot up to the sky, turquoise and pink and calm, such a sound as all the northland knew,—the wild blood-cry of the savage.

It filled the arching aisles of the shouldering forest, rolled down the breast of the river, and echoed in the cabins of the post, and with it there broke loose the leashed wildness of the Indians. There was one vast surging around the lodge where Ridgar knelt with the figure of the chief in his arms, another where a tumbling horde fought to get to the factor and De Courtenay.

At the stockade gate Prix Laroux, swift of foot and strong as twenty men in the exigency of the moment, swept the women into his arms and rushed them within the post. Above the hideous turmoil his voice rose in carrying command,

"Into the post! Into the post,—every man inside! Man the rampart!"

It fell on ears startled into apathy by the suddenness of the tragic happening, and there was a wild confusion of white people pulling out of the mass like threads, all headed for the open gate. Swift as light those guards of the guns on the rampart sprang to place, the watcher of the portal swung the great studded gate ready for the clanging close, and, in a twinkling, so alert to peril do they become who pierce the wilderness, there were without only that howling mass of savages, De Courtenay, McElroy, and Edmonton Ridgar gazing with dimmed vision into the fast glazing eyes of the dying chief.

Only they? Standing where she had leaped at the cavalier's kiss, her eyes wide, her lips apart, was Maren Le Moyne. In the hurrying rush of frantic people she had been forgotten and she was utterly helpless.

As in a dream she saw the leaping forms close in upon the two men who fought for her, knew that those of De Seviere were pouring past her to safety, heard the boom of the great gate as it swung into place, and for her life she could move. neither hand nor foot. Her body stood frozen as in those horrid dreams of night when one is conscious, yet held, in a clutch of steel.

Over the heaving heads with their waving eagle feathers she saw the head and shoulders of De Courtenay rise, tipped sidewise so that his long curls swung clear, shining in the light, and already he was bound with thongs of hide.

She saw his handsome face again sparkling with that smile that was so brilliant and that bore such infinite shades of meaning.

Now it was full of devil-may-care, as if he shrugged his shoulders at a loss at cards, and in that second it fell upon her standing in horror.

"Ah, Ma'amselle!" he called, across the surging feathers; "the tune changes! But you have my heart, and I,—I have one kiss! Adieu, my Maid of the Long Trail! The chance was worth its turning."

Then the shining head sank into the mass and she heard no more.

She was conscious only of a giant form lurching, red-eyed and yelling, out of the turmoil, of brown hands that clutched her arms, and of another form which shot past her. For the second time in a few moments one man had reached for her and another flung himself to her rescue. She saw the Indian reel back with a red line spurting across his eyes, felt herself lifted and flung across a shoulder, and knew that the gate behind was swinging open. The next instant she slid down to her feet with her face in the buckskin shirt of Marc Dupre, who leaned shaking against the stockade wall and held her in a grip like steel, while Henri Corlier shot the bolts into place.

Huddled in white groups were the women, some of them already raising their voices in weeping, others silent with the training of the women of the wilderness. The men faced each other with lips drawn tight and breath that came swiftly. Prix Laroux, his dark eyes cool and sharp, looked swiftly over the populace as they stood, for with that first shot every man in Fort de Seviere had rushed to the gate, and in that first moment of getting breath he calculated their strength and their ability.

A leader born himself, he was looking for a leader among McElroy's men; but, with that intrepid factor himself gone and Edmonton Ridgar also, there was nowhere a man with the signs of leadership upon him.

Through Prix's mind this went while they stood listening to the death-wail that was beginning to rise from the tepees without.

Then he quietly took command, knowing himself to be best fitted.

"Corlier," he said quietly, "leave the gate to Cif Bordoux. Take one man and get to the southwest bastion. You, Gifford," turning to that young clerk who worked in the sorting-room, "man the northwest. Garcon and Dupre will take the forward two. The rest will stand ready with guns and ammunition along the four walls and at the gates. We know not what will transpire."

As if their factor spoke, the men of De Seviere turned to obey, feeling that strange compelling which causes men to follow one man to death on the field of battle, and which is surely the gift of God.

Out of his shaking arms Marc Dupre loosed Maren, the trembling lessening as the danger passed. That sight of the defenceless girl among the Indians had shaken him like a leaf in the wind, had nerved his arms with iron, had worked in him both with strength and weakness.

Now he looked into her eyes and said never a word, for once again he saw that they were dazed and void of knowledge.

As he set her upon her own strength, she swayed. Her eyes went round the hushed groups of faces with wild searching. At last they found the face of her leader, and clung there, dark and dull.

"Prix!" she cried. "Prix! Open the gate!"

"I cannot, Maren," he said quietly; "'twould be but madness."

"But they are without!"

All horror was in the cry.

"They are among the Indians!"

"Aye,—and may the good God have mercy on them!"

Laroux hastily made the sign of the cross.

"We must guard the post, Maren."

"But—" She turned her eyes slowly around from face to face and not a woman there but read her secret plain, the open script of love,—but for which man?

"But-they-will—be—" She did not finish the sentence, staring at Laroux. Once she moistened her lips.

"They will—Prix,—as I am your leader, open that gate!"

With sudden reviving the daze went out of her features and the old light came back to her eyes, the far-seeing, undaunted light that had beaconed the long way from Grand Portage. She was every inch the leader again, tall, straight against the logs, her brown arm pointing imperiously to the closed gate.

"Open, I say!"

For a moment Laroux faced her squarely, the man who had tied himself to her hand, pledged himself to forge the way to the Whispering Hills, who followed her compelling leadership as these lesser men had turned to follow his but now. Then he set his will to hers.

"I will not," he said quietly.

With no more words she flung herself upon the gate and tore at the chains, her strong hands able as a man's. As the sight of her in peril had worked for both weakness and strength in Dupre, so had McElroy's plight affected her. That helpless moment was the one defection of her dauntless life.

Now again she was herself, reaching for the thing of the moment, and the roar outside the palisade, constantly rising in volume, in menace and savagery, brushed out of her brain every cloud of shock. Laroux caught her from behind, pinioning her arms.

"Maren," he said quietly, "hear me. Out there are five hundred warriors wild as the heart of the Pays d'en Haut, howling over the body of their dying chief. What would be the opening of the gate but the massacre of all within? Could forty men take the factor from them? There would be but as many more scalps on their belts as there are heads within the post. See you not, Maren?"

In his iron grip the girl stood still, breathing heavily. As he ceased speaking a great sigh came from her lips, a sigh like a sob.

"Aye," she said brokenly, "I see,—I see! Mary Mother! Let me go, Prix. I see."

Laroux loosed her, knowing that the moment was past, and went at once about his duties of throwing the post into a state of defence.

Once more strong and quiet, Maren went to the cabin by the gate. Here Marie knelt at her bed with a crucifix grasped in her shaking hands, her face white as milk and prayers on her trembling lips.

"Maren!" she gasped, with the child's appeal to the stronger nature. "Oh, Maren, what will befall? For love of God, what will befall?"

"Hush, Marie," answered Maren; "'tis but a tragedy of the wild. Naught will befall us of the post."

"But those without? What is that roaring of many throats? Little Jean Bleaureau but now ran past crying that the Nakonkirhirinons were killing the factor"

"No!" Marie jumped at the word like one shot, so wild and sudden it was. "No! No! Not yet!"

Even in the stress of the moment Marie stared open-mouthed at her sister.

"Holy Mother! It is love,—that cry! You love the factor!"

"Hush!" whispered Maren, dry-lipped.

The roar from the river bank had sharpened itself into one point of utterance which pierced the calm heavens in a mingling of native speech, French and broken English from

Nakonkirhirinon and halfbreed, and, worse than both, dissolute "white Indian," and its burden was,

"A skin for a skin!"

CHAPTER XIV

FELLOW CAPTIVES

After that tense moment of hush following the shot, McElroy had no distinct recollection of what occurred. He was conscious of a sickening knowledge of Negansahima with his banded brown arms stretching into the evening light, of the tepees, of the river beyond, of the face of Edmonton Ridgar, and of all these etched distinctly in that effect of sun and shade which picks out each smallest detail sometimes of a rare evening in early summer. Then the whole scene went out in a smother as an avalanche of bodies descended upon him. He could smell the heavy odour of flesh half-naked, the scent of the hidden paint, he felt arms that fought to grip him and fingers that clutched like talons. Under it all he went down in the grass of the slope, fighting with all his strength, but powerless as a gnat in a pond. Above the turmoil of cries and guttural yells, even while he felt himself crushed at the bottom of that boiling mass, he heard the light voice of De Courtenay ringing clear in his whimsical farewell to Maren Le Moyne. Then he was wrenched up through the mass, something struck him on the head with a sharp blow, a shower of stars fell like a cataract, and the sickening scents in his nostrils faded away.

When he again opened his eyes it was to behold real stars

shining down from a velvet sky, to hear the river lapping gently at the landing, and the night birds calling in the forest. From the prairie beyond the fringe of woods to the east there came the yapping of the coyotes, and far to the north a wolf howled.

At first a sense of bewilderment held him. Then in a rush came back the memory of what had happened. He listened intently. Back and forth, back and forth somewhere near went a soft footstep, the swish and glide of a moccasin. He strained his eyes, which smarted terribly, into the darkness, and presently descried a tall form pacing slowly up against the skyline of his vision and back again into the shadows. A single feather slanted against the stars. A guard pacing the place of captives.

With a slight movement McElroy tried to lift a hand.

It was immovable. He tried the other. It likewise refused his will.

So with both feet when he attempted, ever so cautiously, to move them.

He was bound hand and foot, and with cruel tightness, for with that tiny slipping of his muscles there set up all through him such a tingling and aching as was almost unbearable.

His head seemed a lump of lead, glued to whatever it lay upon, and big as a buttertub.

Turning his eyes far as he could to the right, he looked long in that direction. Faintly, after a while, he picked out the straight line of the stockade top, the rising tower at the corner. The line of the wall faded out in darkness the other way, strain as he might. To the left were the ragged tops of the tepees, their two longer sticks pointing above the others.

From the sound of the river, he must be between it and the stockade gate.

Presently his numbed hearing became conscious of a sound somewhere near, a sound that had rung so ceaselessly since his waking that it had seemed the background for the lesser noise of the sentry's slipping moccasin. It was the weird, unending, unbeginning wail of the women, the death-song of the tribe mourning the passing of a chief, the voices of some four hundred squaws blending indescribably.

McElroy listened.

With consciousness of that his mind grew clearer and he began to think.

What a fool he had been!

Once more had he played like an unbalanced boy at the game of love.

What right had he to strike De Courtenay for kissing the woman whom he had won with his red flowers and his curls before the populace? That he himself had fancied for a brief space that she was his was no excuse for plunging like a boy at his rival's throat. If he had held his peace, all would be well now and the old chief would not be lying stiff and stark somewhere in the shadowed camp, the women wailing without fires.

It was no balm to his sore heart that he in his blundering wrath had wrought this fresh disaster. And his post, De Seviere, which he had won by daring service and loyalty to the H. B. C., what would become of it?

Who after him would rule on the Assiniboine?

For well he knew that death, and death thrice,—aye, a million times refined,—awaited so luckless a victim as he whose hand had killed the great chief. But he had not killed Negansahima. It was the gun in De Courtenay's hand. Ah, De Courtenay! Where was De Courtenay? A captive assuredly, if he was one. They had both gone down together under the foam of that angry human sea. And, if he was here, his antagonist must be somewhere near. With exquisite torture, McElroy slowly turned his head to right and left. At the second motion his face brushed something close against his shoulder. It was cloth, a rough surface corrugated and encrusted with ridges,—what but the braid on the blue coat of the Montreal gallant!

There was no start, no answering movement at his touch. The rough surface seemed strangely set and still.

He lay silent and thought a moment with strange feelings of new horror surging through him.

Was De Courtenay dead?

Or was it by chance a stone under the braided coat, a hillock where it had been thrown? That strange feeling of starkness never belonged to a human body soft with the pulse of life.

For hours McElroy lay staring into the night sky with its frosting of great northern stars, and passed again over every week, every day,—nay, almost every hour,—since that morning in early spring when she had stepped off the factory-sill to accompany little Francette to the river bank where Bois DesCaut stood facing a tall young woman against the stockade wall.

The Maid of the Whispering Hills   137

With dreary insistence his sore heart brought up each sweet memory, each thrill of joy of those warm days. He saw every flush on her open face, every droop of her eyes. Again he saw the white fire in her features that day in the forest glade when she spoke of the Land of the Whispering Hills. He pondered for the first time, lying bound and helpless among savages, of that unbending thing within her which drove her into the wilderness with such resistless force. Granted that she had loved him as he thought during that delirious short space of time, would love have been stronger than that force, or would it have been sacrificed? She was so strong, this strange girl of the long trail, so strong for all things gentle, so unmoving from the way of tenderness. Proving that came the picture of the tot on her shoulder. "dipping as the ships at sea, ma cherie," and the look of her face transfigured. And yet home for her was "the blue sky above, the wind in the pine-tops, the sound of water lapping at the prow of a canoe." So she had said on that last day they spoke together in happiness, passing in diffident joy to the gate to meet De Courtenay's fateful messenger.

Of all women in the vast world she was the one woman. There was never another face with that strange allurement, that baffling light of strength and tenderness.

Sore, sore, indeed, was the heart of the young factor of Fort de Seviere as he lay under the stars and listened to the death-wail in the darkened camp.

Nowhere was there a fire.

Desolation sat upon the Nakonkirhirinons.

Along toward dawn, presaged by the westward wheeling of the big stars, tom-toms began to beat throughout the maze of lodges. They beat oddly into the air, cold with the chill of the coming day,

McElroy's thoughts had left the great country of the Hudson Bay and travelled back along the winding waterways, across the lakes, and at last out on that heaving sea which bore away from his homeland. Once more he had been in the smoke of London town, had looked into the loving eyes of his mother and gripped the hand of his tradesman father. Once more he had wondered what the future held.

The sudden striking up of the tom-toms answered him.

This.

This was to be the end of his eager advance in the Company's favour, the end of that good glass of life whose red draught he had drunk with wholesome joy, the end of love that had but dawned for him to sink into aching darkness.

He sighed wearily. So poignant was his sense of loss and the pain of it that the end was a weariness rather than a new pain.

The thing that hurt was the fact that he himself had juggled the cards of fate to this sorry dealing.

The sudden rage concerning De Courtenay had spent itself. There remained only the deep anger of the man who has lost in the game of love. And yet, what right had he to cherish even this wholesome anger against his rival when the maid had chosen of her own free will? As well hold grudge to the great Power whose wisdom had given the man such marvellous beauty. As he lay in the darkness listening to the unearthly noises he worked it all out with justice.

He alone was to blame for the sorry state of things.

De Courtenay was but a man, and what man, looking upon Maren Le Moyne, could fail to love her?

Therefore, he freed his rival of all blame.

And Maren,—oh, blameless as the winds of heaven was Maren!

What had she given him that he could construe as love?

Only a look, a blush to her cheek, the touch of a warm hand.

In his folly he had hailed himself king of her affections when perchance it was but the kindliness of her womanly heart.

And what maid could be blind to De Courtenay's sparkling grace,—compared to which he was himself a blundering yokel?

Thus in bound darkness he reasoned it all out and strove to wash away the anger from his heart.

And presently there came dawn. First a cold air blowing out of the forest, and then a deeper darkness that presently gave way to faint, shadowy light.

Here and there tall figures came looming, ghostly-fashion, out of chaos, to take slow shape and form, to resolve themselves into tapering lodges, into hunched and huddled groups.

And with light came action.

McElroy saw that around the central lodge before the gate

there was a solid pack of prostrate Indians covering the ground like a cloth, and from this centre came the tom-toms and the wailing.

It was the lodge of the chief and within lay the stark body of the murdered Negansahima.

As the faint light grew, one by one the warriors rose out of the mass like smoke spirals, drawing away to disappear among the tepees. Soon there came the sound of falling poles and McElroy knew that they were striking the camp.

For what?

Why, surely, for one thing.

A chief must go to the great Hunting Ground from his own country; in his own country must his bones seek rest.

They would journey back up the long and difficult trail down which they had just come to that vague region from which they hailed.

But what of him, and of De Courtenay, if he was yet alive?

He wondered why they had been reserved.

The light came quickly and he looked eagerly around on the moving camp.

With quickness and precision the whole long village was reduced in a few minutes to rolled coverings, gathered and tied utensils, stacked packs of furs, and ranged canoes already in the water lining the shore.

He could not help a feeling of regret for this wild people,

coming but few suns back with their rich peltry, their pomp, and their hopes of gain, as they prepared for the back trail, the whole tribe in deepest mourning.

Of all the tents, that one before the post gate alone stood, silent reproach to the white man's ways.

Around it still knelt a solid pack, wailing and beating the drums.

As the grey light turned whiter, he turned his stiffened neck for a glance at the thing against his shoulder.

He looked into the smiling eyes of Alfred de Courtenay.

"Bonjour, M'sieu," whispered that ardent venturer; "you nuzzled my arm all night. Apparently we are fellows in captivity, as we have been opposed in war,—and love."

"Aye, M'sieu," whispered back McElroy, not relishing the turn of the sentence but passing it by; "and a sorry man am I for this state of events. I owe you my regrets,—not for what I did, mark you,—but for the way and the time and place. Had I waited and proceeded as a gentleman, we should not be in this devilish plight, nor that fine old chief a victim to our blunder."

"Tish!" said De Courtenay lightly; "'tis all in a day's march. And, besides, I have,—memories,—to shorten the way."

The pacing guard came back and the two men fell silent.

At that moment a stentorian call pealed above the dismantled camp, and there began a vast surge of the mass of Nakonkirhirinons toward the waiting canoes, a dragging of goods and chattels, a hurry of crying children, a scurrying of squaws. In the midst of it the flaps of the big lodge were opened and, amid redoubled wailing, a stark wedge of the length of a tall man came headforemost out, carried on the shoulders of six gigantic warriors; and walking beside it, bareheaded in the new day, was Edmonton Ridgar, his face pale and downcast. He paid no heed to the two men on the ground, though one was his factor and his friend.

CHAPTER XV

LONG TRAIL

The women changed their wail as the procession started for the waiting canoes, and from all the long camp there drew in a horde of savages, their eagle feathers slanting in the light, bare shoulders shining under unhidden paint, skin garments and gaudy shirts alike cast to the winds.

They surged along chanting their unearthly song, and the mass of them swept by where lay the two men.

Not a glance was given them, no taunts, no jeers with which the tribes of the North-west were wont to torment their captives.

The swish of the moccasined feet was as the sound of many waters.

"No time for play," thought McElroy; "that will come later,—when we have reached the Pays d'en Haut."

For he knew now that he and De Courtenay were to be taken along.

The body of Negansahima was placed in the first canoe,

Vingie E. Roe

covered with a priceless robe of six silver foxskins laced together; the six big warriors, their halfnaked bodies painted black, manned the paddles, and at the prow there stood the sad figure of Edmonton Ridgar.

At one side had drawn out old Quamenoka and his Assiniboines, their way lying to the west. They raised a chant as the first canoe circled out and headed down the stream. Behind it fell in five canoe-loads of Bois-Brules, their attachment a mystery, and the river became alive with the great flotilla.

Not until the death-boat had passed the far bend did the pacing Indian give way to a dozen naked giants, who lifted the captives with ceremony and carried them down the slope.

As he swung between his captors McElroy looked back at the closed gates of De Seviere and a sharp pain struck at his heart, a childish hurt that the post he had loved should watch his exit from the light of life with unmoved front. It seemed almost that the bastioned wall was sensate, as if the small portholes here and there were living eyes, cold and hard with indifference, nay, even a-glitter with selfishness.

But quick on the sense of hurt came the knowledge which is part of every man in the wilderness; and he knew well that every face in the little fort was drawn with the tragedy, that from those blank portholes looked human eyes, sick with the thing they could not avert, that whoever had taken charge within was only working for the safety of the greatest number, and with the thought his weakness passed.

Only one more pang assailed him.

He gave one swift thought to Maren Le Moyne. Where in Fort de Seviere was she, and what was in her heart?

Then he was swung, still bound, into the bottom of a canoe, saw De Courtenay tossed into another, felt the careless feet of Nakonkirhirinons as the paddlemen stepped in, and existence became a thing of gliding motion, the lapping of water on birchbark, and the passing of a long strip of cloud-flecked sky, pink and blue and gold with the new day.

Lulled by the rocking of the fragile craft that shot forward like a thing of life beneath the paddles dipping in perfect unison, McElroy lay its a sort of apathy for hours, watching the sliding strip of sky and the bending bodies of the Indians. He knew that the end awaited him somewhere ahead, but it was far ahead, very far, even many leagues beyond York factory, and his mind, again dropping into the dulness of his early awakening, refused to concern itself with aught save the blue sky and the sound of water lapping on birchbark. That sound was sweet to his befuddled brain, suggesting something vaguely pleasant.

Ah, yes, it was the deep voice of the maid of the long trail speaking of the streams and the waving grass of that visionary Land of the Whispering Hills.

He fell to wondering at broken intervals if she would ever reach it, to see drowsy visions of the tall form leading its band of venturers into the wilderness beyond Lac a la Croix, penetrating that country which tried the hearts of men, and with the visions came a sadness.

She would go without love, mourning her cavalier of the curls, and who would be responsible for the desolation of the heart he would fain have made happy but himself?

McElroy sighed, and the visions faded.

When he again awakened it was evening and camp had been

made. Fires danced and crackled all up and down the reach of shore set like a half-moon of pearl in a sea of emerald, where the forest shouldered down to the stream, and the smell of cooking meat was poignantly sweet. Women were busy at the work of the camp, carrying wood, mending the fires, tending the kettles swung from forked sticks, and scolding the scrambling children.

Here and there a half-naked Indian stalked silently, his long feather slanting in the light, but for the most part the warriors were gathered in a silent mass a little way apart where the big tepee had been set up.

The clouds were gone from his brain, and he was keenly conscious of hunger.

He was still bound, though not so tightly, some of the thongs having been taken off entirely, and he found that he could sit up with comparative ease, though his hands were still fast behind him and his ankles tied.

There was no pacing guard this time, distance and possession making such precaution needless, for well the Nakonkirhirinons knew that none from the little post on the Assiniboine would attempt rescue in face of so great a horde as an entire tribe.

McElroy sat up and looked around.

One of the first things he encountered was the face of the cavalier, still smiling and looking very much as it had looked in the dawn.

Like that encounter, too, De Courtenay was the first to speak in this.

"Aha, my fighter of the H. B. C.," he laughed from his seat

against a towering maple, "have your laggard wits come in from wool-gathering?"

He, too, was more comfortably bound, and McElroy noticed that there were little rubbed creases in the sleeves of the gay blue coat where the numbing bonds had cut. The sparkling spirit was as high in his handsome face as it had been that long past morning morning by the well. The factor wondered if there was in heaven or earth anything with power to dim it.

He was to see, and marvel at, the test.

"Aye," he answered the cheerful query; "it has been a weary day, M'sieu, it would seem, with my senses drifting out and in at ragged intervals of which I have only vague impressions. How has it fared with you?"

"Much as another day. There has been plenty to see and enjoy, even from under the feet of our hasty friends of the paddles."

"Enjoy! Holy Mother! Have you not been thinking over your sins, M'sieu?"

"Sins? I have none. Who thinks of sins while the red blood runs? Rather have I dreamed dreams of,—memories. Ah, no, M'sieu, it has not been a weary day to me, but one of swift emotions, of riots of colour in a strip of racing sky when the sun turned his palette for a gorgeous spread. The sunset was stupendous at its beginning. Now the darker greys come with so much forest."

McElroy fell silent, biting his lip.

Sorry as he felt for the plight of his rival, the old anger was close to his heart, and it seemed that the rascal knew it and probed for a weak spot with his smiling allusions to his memories. Memories of what but of the red lips of a girl?

The young factor, too, had memories of those red lips, though they gave him only a pain so bitter as not to be borne.

Almost it forced from his heart the gentle justice he had striven so hard to keep in sight.

As he sat thinking and staring at the twilight river rippling below, a man came from the forest at the back of the camp and passed near on his way to the fires.

It was Bois DesCaut, and he did not lift his evil eyes.

The white lack on his temple gleamed with a sinister distinctness amid his black hair.

"Double foe," thought McElroy; "I am to pay for my own words and Maren's blow."

As the trapper passed he sidled swiftly near the Nor'wester and something dropped from a legstrap. It was a small knife, and it tumbled with seeming carelessness close to De Courtenay's knee.

"So," thought McElroy again; "by all rights that should have been for me."

DesCaut went on into the heart of the camp among the women, and De Courtenay began moving ever so cautiously toward the priceless bit of steel.

With that hidden in one's garments what not of hope might rise within a daring heart?

What not, indeed! Life and liberty and escape and a home-coming to a rival's very hearthstone, and more,—soft lips and arms of a woman.

The cavalier was smiling still as he edged inch by inch along the little way, his back against the maple.

"See you, M'sieu," he whispered; "how loyal are the servants of the North-west Company?"

McElroy did not answer. Bitterness was rife within him. Even his one friend in the wilderness, Edmonton Ridgar, on whose sound heart he would have risked his soul, had passed him by without a look.

Verily, life had suddenly been stripped, as the hapless birch, of all its possessions.

He was thinking grimly of these things when a young squaw came lightly up from somewhere and stopped for a second beside De Courtenay. She looked keenly at him, and stooping, picked up the knife.

"Another turn to the wheel, M'sieu," said that intrepid venturer; "what next?"

As if his thought had reached out among the shadows of the wood where stood the death tepee and touched its object, Edmonton Ridgar appeared among the lodges. He was bare-headed, and McElroy saw that his face was deep-lined and anxious, filled with a sadness at which he could but marvel and he passed within a stone's throw without so much as a glance at his superior.

No captive was this man, passing where he listed, but McElroy noticed the keen eyes watching his every move.

What was he among this silent tribe with their war-paint and their distrust of white men?

It was a hopeless puzzle, and the factor laid it grimly aside. Next to the closed and impregnable front of his own post what time he passed from its sight, this cold aloofness of his chief trader cut to inmost soul.

But these things were that life of the great North-west whose unspeakable lure thralled men's souls to the death, and he was content.

It was chance and daring and danger which drew him in the beginning to the country, love of the wild and breath of the vast reaches, something within which pushed him forward among these savage peoples, even as the same thing pushed Maren Le Moyne toward the Whispering Hills, sent De Courtenay to the Saskatchewan.

At any rate he was very hungry, and when a bent and withered crone of a squaw brought food and loosed his right hand, the young factor tossed up his head to get the falling hair out of his eyes and fell to with a relish.

"Faugh!" said De Courtenay with the first mouthful; "I wonder, M'sieu, is there nothing we can do to hasten the end? Many meals of this would equal the stake."

Whereat the gallant smilingly tossed the meat and its birchbark platter at the woman's feet.

"If you would not prefer starvation, I would suggest that you crawl for that, M'sieu," said McElroy gravely; but the wrinkled hag gathered it up, and left them to the night that was fast settling over the forest.

Thus began the long trail up to the waters of Churchill and beyond into that unknown region where few white men had yet penetrated, and fewer still. returned.

CHAPTER XVI

TRAVEL

Day followed day. Summer was upon the land, early summer, with the sweet winds stirring upon the waters, with gauze-winged creatures flitting above the, shallows where willow and vine-maple fringed the edges and silver fish leaped to their undoing, with fleecy clouds floating in a sapphire sky, and birds straining their little throats in the forest.

McElroy and De Courtenay were loosed of their bonds and given paddles in the canoes, a change which was welcomed gladly.

At night a guard paced their sleeping-place and the strictest surveillance was kept over them.

Down the Assiniboine, into Red River, and across Portage la Prairie went the great flotilla, green shores winding past in an endless pageant of foliage, all hands falling to at the portages and trailing silently for many pipes, one behind the other, all laden with provisions and packs of furs, the canoes upturned and carried on heads and shoulders.

Of unfailing spirits was Alfred de Courteray.

"'Od's blood, M'sieu," he would laugh, oddly mixing his dialect, "but this is seeing the wilderness with a vengeance! Though there is no lack of variety to speed the days, yet I would I were back in my post of Brisac on the Saskatchewan, with a keg of good-liquor on the table and my hearty voyaguers shouting their chansons outside, my clerks and traders making merry within. Eh, M'sieu, is it not a better picture?"

"For you, no doubt. For me, I had rather contemplate a prayer-book and recall my mother's teaching in these days," answered McElroy simply.

"What it is to have sins upon one's conscience!" sighed the venturer. "Verily, it must preclude all pleasant thoughts." And he fell to humming a gay French air.

Presently the foaming river, growing swifter as it neared the great lake, leaped and plunged into the wide surface of Winnipeg, shooting its burdens out upon the glassy breast of the lake like a spreading fan.

Here the blue sky was mirrored faithfully below with its lazy clouds, the green shores rimmed away to right and left, and the swarming canoes, with their gleaming paddles, made a picture well worth looking at.

The Nakonkirhirinons were going back to the Pays d'en Haut by another way than that by which they had come.

Hugging the western shore, the flotilla strung out into the formation of a wedge, with the canoe of the dead chief at the apex, and went on, day after day, in comparative silence.

With the passing of the sleeping green shores, the ceaseless slide of the quiet waters, a tender peace began to come into

McElroy's soul.

With the gliding days he could think of Maren without the poignant pain which had been unbearable at the beginning, could linger in thought over each .detail of her wondrous beauty, the clear dark eyes, sane and earnest and full of the hope of the dreamer, the full red mouth with its sweetness of curled corners, the black hair banded above the smooth brow, the rounded figure under the faded garment, the shoulders swinging with the free walk after the fashion of a man.

Verily, the wilderness held healing as well as hurt.

So followed each other the dawns and the summer noons and the marvellous twilights, with pageantry of light and colour and soft winds attuned to the songs of birds, and the two men neared the mystery of Fate.

CHAPTER XVII

THE COMPELLING POWER

Back in De Seviere the gloom of the forest in bleak winter sat heavily on every cabin.

Women went about with misty eyes and men were oddly silent.

Not one of all his people who did not love the whole-hearted factor with his ready laugh, his sympathy in all the little life of the post, his unfailing justice; not one who did not strive to keep away the haunting visions of leaping flames above fagots, and all the ugly scenes that imagination, abetted by grim reality, could conjure up.

On that fateful morning when the rising sun saw the slim canoes of the Nakonkirhirinons trailing around the lower bend, Maren Le Moyne stood by the little window in the small room to the east of the Baptiste cabin and covered her face with her hands.

Great breaths lifted her breast, breaths that fluttered her open lips and could not fill the gasping lungs beneath, that sounded in the little room like tearless tearing sobs.

"Heavenly Mother!" she gasped between them; "Thou who art woman... Mary..."

But the prayer hung aborted between the shuddering sighs.... Who shall say that it is not such a cry, torn from the depths of the spirit by instinct groping for its god, which reaches swiftest the Eternal Infinite?

Until the last sound had faded into the morning, until the last little ripple had widened to the shores and died among the willows, until the screaming birds, startled from the edges of the river, had settled into quiet, she stood so, fainting in her Gethsemane. She alone of all the post had remained away from the great gate where was gathered the populace at the nearest vantage point.

Silence of the young day hung in the palisade, a silence that cut the soul with its tragic portent.

Even little Francette Moline, weeping openly, pressed close in the mass and jerked with unconscious savagery of spirit the short ears of the husky at her heels,—that Loup whom no man dared to touch save only the master his fierce spirit must needs acknowledge. It had been DesCaut by brutality. Now it was the little maid by love.

Strange cat of the woods, Francette could be as riotous in her tenderness as in her enmity.

In the bastions Dupre and Garcon and Gifford watched the scene with the grim quiet of men born in the wilderness, while at the portholes trapper and voyageur and the venturers from Grand Portage handled their guns and waited.

None knew what might happen, for these Indians were not to be judged by any standard they knew.

Henri Baptiste held the trembling Marie in his arm, while Mora and Anon and Ninette clung together in a white-faced group. A little way aside Micene Bordoux comforted a frightened woman and held a child by the hand.

Big Bard McLellan stood by a porthole, his eyes always pensive with his own sadness, gazing with grave sorrow to where McElroy swung down the slope between his captors.

Thus they watched his going, and he had been spared that sick pain had he known.

When it was over, Prix Laroux turned back to the deserted factory and stood hesitating on its step.

This was one of the crises which so commonly confronted the fur industry in the North-west.

What had he a right to do?

The simple man considered carefully. What right but the right of humanity to do the best for the many could send a servant into the seat of power?

And yet who among them all was fitted?

Not the clerks, youths from the Bay, not the traders nor the trappers.

With a daring heart the venturer from Grand Portage went in across the sill.

To a man the men of De Seviere rallied to him and council was held.

Everywhere in the trading-room, the living-room behind,

were evidences of the factor and Ridgar. It seemed as if the two men had but just stepped out-were not in hostile hands drifting down the river toward an unspeakable fate.

In the midst of the grave-faced council another step sounded on the sill and once again Maren Le Moyne stood looking in at the factory door, though this time there was no eager interest on her face, only a drawn tenseness which cut to the heart of her leader like a knife.

"Come in, Maren," he said in aching sympathy.

"Men," she said straightly, "is there none among you who will turn a hand to save his factor?"

Over every face her eyes travelled slowly, hot and burning.

In every face she read the same thing,—a pitying wonder at the folly of her words.

"Aye," spoke up Henri Corlier, grizzled and weathered by his years of loyal service to the Great Company, "not a man among us, Ma'amselle, but would give his life if it would serve. It would not serve."

"And you?" her gaze shifted feverishly to Laroux; "you, Prix?"

"'Tis useless, Maren. What would you have us do?"

"Do?"

She straightened by the door, and the hand on the lintel gripped until the nails went white.

"Do? Anything save sit with closed gates in safety while

savages burn your factor at the stake! The Hudson's Bay brigade comes from York this very month. What easier than to meet it and get help of men and guns?"

"Nay," said Laroux gently; "you do but dream, Maren."

Whereat the girl turned abruptly from the doorway and went down among the cabins.

Here and there in the doorways groups of women stood together, their voices hushed and trouble in their eyes.

As Maren passed, seeing nothing to right or left, they looked in pity upon her.

The heart of this woman was drifting with the canoes,—but with which man?

"'Tis the gay Nor'wester with his golden curls," whispered Tessa Bibye sympathetically.

"The Nor'wester? 'Tis little you know, truly, Tessa," said the young wife of old Corlier. "What maid in her senses would look twice at yonder be-laced dandy when a man like Anders McElroy stood near?"

"Aye, an' may the Good God have mercy on our factor!" whimpered a withered old woman, wife of a trapper, making the sign of the cross; "nor hold back His mercy from the other!"

Night seemed to fall early on Fort de Seviere, waiting sadly for its healing touch on fevered hearts.

Throughout the long day a waiting hush had lain upon the post, an expectancy of ill.

　　　　　　Vingie E. Roe

Over the dark forest the stars came out on a velvet sky, and a little wind came out of the south, nightbirds called from the depths, and peace spread over the Northland like a blanket.

While the twilight lasted with its gorgeous phantasmagoria there were none of the accustomed sounds of pleasure in the post,—no fiddle squeaked by the stockade wall, no happy laughter wafted from the cabins. Even the sleepy children seemed to feel the strangeness and hushed their peevish crying.

Night and darkness and loneliness held sway, and in one heart the shadows of the world were gathered.

What was the meaning of this Life whose gift was Pain, where was the glory of existence?

By the window to the east Maren Le Moyne stood in the darkness, with her hands upon her breast and her face set after the manner of the dreamer who follows his visions in simpleness of soul.

Once again a great call was sounding from the wilderness, as that which lured her to the Whispering Hills had sounded since she could remember, once more the Long Trail beckoned, and once more she answered, simply and without fear.

She waited for the depth of night.

Long she stood at the little window, facing the east like some worshipper, even until the wheeling stars spelled the mid hour.

To Marie she gave one thought,—child-like Marie with her dependence and her loving heart. But Marie, to whom she had been all things, was safe in the care of Henri. There remained only the dream of the Whispering Hills and the illusive figure of a man,—an old man, sturdy of form and with blue eyes set in swarthy darkness.

Poignant was the pain that assailed her at that memory. Would she ever reach that shadowy country, ever fulfil the quest that was hers from the beginning? Did she not wrong that ghostly figure which seemed to gaze with reproach across the years? Her own blood called, and she turned aside to follow the way of a stranger, an alien whose kiss had brought her all sorrow.

And yet she was helpless as the water flowing to the sea. The primal quest must wait. Her being turned to this younger man as the needle to the pole, even though his words were false, his kiss a betrayal.

When the mid hour hung in silence over the wilderness a figure came out of the darkness and stood at the gate beside that watcher, Cif Bordoux, who paced its length with noiseless tread.

A strange figure it was, clad in garments that shone misty white in the shadow, whose fringes .fluttered in the warm wind and whose glowing plastron glittered in the starlight.

"Cif Bordoux," said the figure, "I would go without."

Wondering and startled, Bordoux would have refused if he dared; but this was the leader of the Long Trail and her word had been his law for many moons, nor had he ever questioned her wisdom.

Therefore he drew the bolts and opened the gate the width of a man's body, and Maren Le Moyne slipped outside the palisade into the night.

A rifle hung in her arm and a pouch of bullets dangled at her knee.

Swiftly and silently she pushed a canoe into the water at the landing, stepped in, and with one deep dip of a paddle sent the frail craft out to midstream. She did not turn her head for a farewell glance toward the post, but set her face toward the way that led to the Pays d'en Haut and the man who journeyed thither.

Deep and even her paddle took the sweet waters and the current shot her forward like a racer. The dark shores flowed by in a long black ribbon of soft shadow, their leaning grasses and foliage playing with the ripples in endless dip and lift. No fear was in her, scarce any thought of what she did, only an obeying of the call which simplified all things.

McElroy was in danger, and she followed him.

That was all she knew, save the mighty sorrow of his falseness which never left her day or night.

He had taught her love in that one passionate embrace in the forest, and it was for all time.

What mattered it that he had turned from her for another? That was the sorry tangle of the threads of Fate,—she had naught to do with it.

Love was born in her and it set a new law unto her being, the law of service.

Every fibre in her revolted at thought of his death. If it was to be done beneath the pitying Heaven, he should be saved.

He must be helped to escape. The other was insupportable. Nothing mattered in all the world save that. Therefore she set herself, alone and fearless, to follow the tribe of the Nakonkirhirinons to the far North if need be, to hang on their flank like a wolverine, to take every chance the good God might send. Chief of these was her hope of the Hudson's Bay brigade which should be coming into the wilderness at this time of year. Somewhere she must meet them and demand their help.

There was no rebellion in her, no hope of gain in what she did. Love was of her own soul alone, since that evening by the factory when she had seen the factor bend his head and kiss the little Francette.

No more did she think of his words in the forest, no more did she dream of the wondrous glory of that first kiss.

Far apart and impersonal was McElroy now,—only she loved him with that vast idolatry which seeks naught but the good of its idol.

Even if he loved Francette he must be saved for that happiness.

Therefore she knelt in a cockleshell alone on a rushing river and sped through, a wilderness into appalling danger.

Such was the compelling power of that love which had come tardily to her.

CHAPTER XVIII

"I AM A STONE TO YOUR FOOT, MA'AMSELLE"

At dawn Maren shot her craft into a little cove, opal and pearl in the pageantry of breaking light, and drawing it high on shore, went gathering little sticks for a micmac fire.

The bullet pouch held small allowance of food. She would eat and sleep for a few hours.

Deep and ghostly with white mist-wraiths was the forest, shouldering close to the living water, pierced with pine, shadowy with trembling maple, waist-high with ferns. She looked about with the old love of the wild stirring dumbly under the greater feeling that weighted her soul with iron and wondered vaguely what had come over the woods and the waters that their familiar faces were changed.

With her arms full of dead sticks she came back to the canoe,—and face to face with Marc Dupre. His canoe lay at the cove's edge and his eyes were anguished in a white face.

"Ma'amselle," he said simply, "I came."

No word was ready on the maid's lips. She stood and looked at him, with the little sticks in her arms, and suddenly she saw what was in his eyes, what made his lips ashen under the weathered tan.

It was the same thing that had changed for her the face of the waters and the wood. She had learned in that moment to read a man better than she had read aught in her life beside the sign of leaf and wind.

"Oh, M'sieu!" she cried out sharply; "God forbid!"

The youth came forward and took the sticks from her, dropping them on the ground and holding both her hands in a trembling clasp.

"Forbid?" he said and his voice quivered; "Ma'amselle, I love you. Though my heart is full of dread, I am at your feet. By the voice of my own soul I hear the cry of yours. We are both past help, it seems, Ma'amselle,-yet am I that stone to your foot which we pledged yonder by the stockade wall. You will let me go the long trail with you? You will give me to be your stay in this? You will let me do all a man can do to help you take the factor from the Nakonkirhirinons?"

The infinite sadness in Dupre's voice was as a wind across a harp of gold, and it struck to Maren's heart with unbearable pain.

Her eyes, looking straight into his, filled slowly with tears, and his white face danced grotesquely before her vision.

"M'sieu," she said quite simply, "I would to God it had been given me to love you. We have ever seen eye to eye save in that wherein we should have. And I know of nothing dearer than this love you have given me. If you would risk your life and more, M'sieu, I shall count your going one of the gifts of God."

"I cannot ask you to return, Ma'amselle,—too well do I know you,—nor to consider all you must risk for, this,—life and death and the certain slander of the settlement,—though by all the standards of manhood I should do so. The heart in me is faithful echo of your own. This trail must be travelled,—therefore we travel it together. And, oh, Ma'amselle! Think not of my love as that of a man! Rather do I adore the ground beneath your foot, worship at the shrine of your pure and gentle spirit! See!"

With all the prodigal fire of his wild French blood, the youth dropped on his knee and, catching the fringe on the buckskin garment, pressed it to his lips.

For once Maren, unused to tears, could speak no word.

She only drew him up, her grip like a man's upon his wrists, and turned to the making of the fire.

Dupre drew up his canoe and took a snared wild hen from the bow.

*　*　*　*　*　*　*　*　*

"I think, Ma'amselle," said the youth when Maren awaked some hours later from a heavy sleep, during which Dupre had killed the little smoke of the fire and kept silent watch from the shore, "that we had best leave your canoe here and take mine. It is much the better craft."

"So I see. Mine was but the first I could put my hands upon in the darkness."

"'Tis that of old Corlier, and sadly lacking in repair. If you will steer, Ma'amselle?"

Thus set forth as forlorn a hope as ever lost itself in that vast region of hard living and daily tragedy, with the strength of the man set behind the woman's wisdom in as delicate a compliment as ever breathed itself in silken halls, and the blind courage of the dreamer urged it on. .

At the forks of Red River they passed the signs of a landing.

Here had the Indians summarily sent ashore all of the Nor'westers who had been with De Courtenay and who had followed in the uncertainty of fear, not daring to desert lest they be overtaken and massacred.

All, that is, save Bois DesCaut and the lean, hawk-faced Runners of the Burnt Woods.

Thanking their gods, the North-west servants had lost no time in taking advantage of the fact that they were not wanted, leaving their Montreal master to whatever fate might befall him.

Dupre went ashore and examined the reach of land, the trampled grass, a broken bush or two.

"Ten men, I think," he said, returning, "and all in tremendous haste. The Nor'westers escaping, I have no doubt. Would our captives were among them."

"No such fortune, M'sieu," said Maren calmly, "Heard you not the cry before the gate in that unhallowed scramble what time they took the factor and the venturer? 'Twas 'a skin for a skin.' There are many guards."

The summer day dreamed by in drowsy beauty, like a woman or a rose full-blown, and Maren, who would at another time have seen each smallest detail of its perfection through the eye of love, saw only the rushing water ahead and counted time and distance.

Dupre, kneeling in the bow, his lithe brown arms bare to the shoulder, where the muscles lifted and fell like waves, was silent. Sadness sat upon him like a garment, yet lightened by a holy joy.

Odd servers of Love, these two, who knew only its pain without its pleasure, yet who were standing on the threshold of its Holy of Holies.

Of nights they sat together at the tiny fire of a few laid sticks and talked at intervals in a strange companionship.

Never again did they speak of love, nor even so much as skirt its fringes, though the young trapper read with wistful eyes its working in the woman's face. Out of her eyes had gone a certain light to be replaced by another, as if a star had passed near a smouldering world and gone on, changed by the contact, its radiance darkened by a deeper glow.

The firm cheeks, dusky as sunset, had lost something of their contour.

Like comrades, too, they shared the work and the watches, the girl standing guard with rifle and ball while Dupre snatched heavy sleep, herself dropping down like the veriest old wolf of the North on mossy bank or green grass for the rest they sternly shortened.

"'Tis near the time of the Hudson's Bay brigade, is it not, M'sieu?" she would ask sometimes. "Think you we shall meet them surely if we skirt the eastern shore of Winnipeg?"

And Dupre would always answer, "Assuredly. By the third

week in July they will be at the upper bend where the river comes down from York. The Nakonkirhirinons will hold to the west, going up Nelson River and west through the chain of little lakes that lie to the south of Winnipeg, thence gaining Deer River and that Reindeer Lake which sends them forth into their unknown region beyond the Oujuragatchousibi. We, then, will make straight for the eastern shore, skirting upward to the interception of the ways, and we will surely meet the brigade."

"And they will surely lend help, think you, to a factor of the Company in such grave plight?"

"Surely, Ma'amselle."

So the hours of day and darkness slipped by with dip of paddle and with portage, with snatched rest and fare of the wild.

In a plentiful forest and on an abundant stream Dupre was at no loss for food. Trout, sparkling and fresh from the icy water, roasted on forked sticks stuck in the ground beside a bed of coals, made fare for an epicure, and the young trapper, watching Maren as she knelt to tend them, shielding her face with her hand, thought wistfully of a cabin where the fire leaped on the hearth and where this woman passed back and forth at the tasks of home.

"'Tis too great a thing to ask of le bon Dieu," he said in his heart; "'tis not permitted even that one dream of such joy,— 'twould be heaven robbed of its glory."

So he fished and hunted for her, as the primal man has hunted and fished for his woman since time began, tended her fires and guarded her sleep, and the wistful sadness within him grew with the passing days.

Vingie E. Roe

Down that northbound river the lone canoe with its two people hurried after the great flotilla, silent and determined, like a starved wolf on the flanks of a caribou herd.

Out on the breast of the great blue lake it, too, was shot by the rushing waters, lone little cockleshell, to head its prow to the eastward, where the green shore curved away, to take its infinitesimal chance of victory against all odds.

When the sun came out of the eastern forest, a golden ball in a cloud of fire, it saw the light craft already cutting the cool waters of Winnipeg. When it sank into the western woods the bobbing dot was still shooting forward.

Child of the wilderness by birth was Dupre, child of the wilderness by dream and desire was Maren, and its simple courage was inborn in both.

The Indians were a day and night ahead, hurrying by dawn and dusk to the north, that the body of the dead chief, cured like a mummy by the smoke curling from the big tepee at every stop, might have burial, the earth-bound spirit begin its journey to the shadowy hunting-grounds.

When McElroy took his last look backward at the blue lake from the northern end, Maren and Dupre were making their last camp before the Big Bend on the eastern shore.

"How soon, think you, M'sieu?" she asked that night, standing beside the little fire; "how soon will they come,— the H. B. C.'s from York?"

"To-morrow, most like, or in a few days at most."

This evening luck had deserted his fishing, so the trapper took a rifle and went into the woods after a fool-hen.

Thoughts kept him company; thoughts of love and its strangeness, of the odd decrees of Fate and the helplessness of man. How all the world had changed with its coming, this love which hail been born in an hour what time he had listened to a woman's voice beside the stockade wall, and how the very soul within him had changed also.

Where had been lightness and the recklessness of youth there was now a wistful tenderness so vast that it covered his life as the pearly mist covered the world at dawn.

Where he had taken all of joy that post and settlement, friend and foe could give, lived for naught but his sparkling pleasures, he was now possessed of a great yearning to give to this woman, this goddess of the black braids; to give, only to give to her; to give of his strength, of his overwhelming love; aye, of even his heart's blood itself as he had told her in the beginning.

He was long in finding a fat grouse this evening, and when he returned night was thick on forest and shore.

Light of tread in his moccasins, Dupre came quietly out not far from the blaze of the small fire, and stopped among the shoulder-high brush that fringed the forest.

In the glow of the fire Maren knelt before a green stake set upright in the earth, from a fork of which there hung a black iron crucifix, its ivory Christ gleaming in the light. On either side of this pitiful altar there flamed, in lieu of candles, a fagot taken from the pine.

On her knees, her hanging hands clasped and her face, raised to the Symbol, she spoke, and the deep voice was sweet with its sliding minors.

"Jesu mia," she said softly, "forgive Thou our sins—Ours. Teach me Thy lesson,—me with pain that will not cease. For him,—Oh, Thou Lord of Heaven, comfort him living,—shrive him Thyself in dying! Let not the unspeakable happen! Send, send Thou that help without which I am helpless, and failing that, send me the strength of him who wrestled with the Angel, the wisdom of Solomon! Not for my love, O Christ, but for him, grant that I may find help to save him from death! And more,—deliver also that venturer who, but for my thoughtless words of the red flower, would be now safe on the Saskatchewan. These I implore, in mercy. And for this last I beg in humbleness of spirit complete,—Grant Thou peace to the friend whose eyes eat into my heart with pity! Peace, peace, Jesu of the Seven Scars, have mercy on him, for he is good to his foundations! I beg for him peace and forgetting of unhappy me! Reward him in some better fate, this youth of the tender heart, of the great regard! Save us, Thou Lamb Jesus—"

In the dark eyes there was a shine of tears, the lips, with their curled corners, were trembling. The face upturned in the fitful light was all tenderness. The calm brown hands clasped before her were all strength.

Marc Dupre, in the forest's edge, felt his breast heave with an emotion beyond control as he stood so, looking upon the scene, listening to the sliding voice. Darkness hid the wilderness, out on the face of the lake a fish leaped with a slap, and a nightbird called shrilly off to the south. With aching throat the trapper turned softly back into the woods. When he came later along the shore, with heavier step than was his wont, the fagot and the forked stake were gone, there was no black crucifix, and Maren waited by the fire, water brought from the lake in Dupre's small pail, the little sticks ready for the roasting.

"Let me have the grouse, M'sieu," she said; "the hunt was long?"

But Dupre did not answer.

CHAPTER XIX

THE HUDSON'S BAY BRIGADE

The two days that followed were heavy ones to Maren.

No farther did they dare venture lest they pass to the west and miss the brigade coming down from the north and entering the lake at the northeast extremity.

So they waited on the shore in anxiety of spirit, watching the bright waters with eyes that ached with the intensity of the vigil, and Dupre hunted in the forest and over the sand dunes, among the high meadows that broke the heavy woods in this region, and down along the reaches of the water.

"Farther with each day!" thought Maren to herself. "Holy Mother, send the brigade!"

And Dupre echoed the thought in sadness of soul.

"More pain for her heart in each hour's delay. Would the trial were done!"

About three of the clock on the first day of waiting there came sounds of singing and a string of canoes rounded a bend of the shore at the south.

"M'sieu!" cried Maren swiftly; "who comes?"

Dupre, tinkering at the canoe overturned on the pebbly beach, straightened and looked in the direction she indicated.

He looked long with hand to eye, and presently turned quietly.

"Nor'westers, I think, Ma'amselle. They come from Fort William to the Wilderness."

Fort William!

Back along the trail went memory with mention of the post on the distant shore of Lake Superior. How oft had she peeped with fascinated eyes from behind her father's forge at sturdy men in buckskins who spoke with the blacksmith about the wonders of the country of the Red River, and they had come from Fort William. She saw again the bustle and activity of Grand Portage, the comfortable house of the Baptistes. Once more she felt the old yearning for the unknown.

And this was it,—this gleaming stretch of inland sea, one man who stood by her and another who betrayed her with a kiss, yet who drew her after him as the helpless leaf, fallen to the stream, is whirled into the white destruction of the rapids.

Aye, verily, this was the unknown.

She was looking down the lake with the sun on her uncovered head, on the soft whiteness of the doeskin garment, and to young Dupre she had never seemed so near the divine, so far and unattainable.

"Ma'amselle," he said presently, "if these newcomers speak

us, heed you not what I may say. There are times in the open ways when a man must lie for the good of himself—or others."

The girl turned her eyes from the canoes, some twenty of them, to his face. It was grave and quiet.

"Assuredly," she said after a moment's scrutiny. "Had I best hide in the bushes, M'sieu?"

"No, they have seen us."

Sweeping forward, the brigade of the Nor'westers, for such it proved to be, headed near in a circle and the head canoe turned in to shore.

"Friend?" called a man in the prow; whom Dupre knew for a wintering partner by the name of McIntosh of none too savoury report.

"Hudson's Bay trapper, M'sieu," he said politely, going a step nearer the water. "I wait, with Madame my wife, the coming of our brigade from York, now one day overdue."

"Ah,—my mistake. I had thought the H. B. C.'s this fortnight gone down. As ever, they are a trifle behind."

While he addressed Dupre his bold eyes were fastened on Maren, where she hung a dressed fish on a split prong.

"Not behind, M'sieu," said the young man gently. "They but take the time of certainty. A Saulteur passing this way at daylight reported them as at McMillan's Landing."

"Then your waiting is short. I am glad,—for Madame. So lone a camp must be hard for a woman."

With the words the Nor'wester scanned the girl's face with a glance that pierced her consciousness, though her eyes were fixed on her task. Not a tinge of deeper colour came to her cheeks. There was no betrayal of the part Dupre had assigned her, and with a word of parting the canoe swung out to its place, though McIntosh's eyes clung boldly to her beauty so long as he could see her.

"Ah-h,—a close shave!" thought the trapper as he picked up a splinter and once more fell to upon the boat.

Twenty-four hours later there came out of the north the thrice blessed brigade of the H. B. C., bound down the lake to Grand Rapids, where the canoes would separate into two parties, one going up the Saskatchewan to Cumberland House, the other down to the country of the Assiniboine.

Eager as a hound for the quarry Maren stood forth beside Dupre to hail them.

Head of the brigade was Mr. Thomas Mowbray, a gentleman of fine presence and of gentle manners.

In answer to the hail from shore he came to, and presently he stood in the prow of his boat listening to an appeal that lightened his grave eyes.

"Men we must have, M'sieu," Maren was saying passionately; "men of the Hudson's Bay. Against all odds we go of a truth, but strategy and wit accomplish much, and the Nakonkirhirinons have no thought of rescue. Besides, the farther north they get the less keen will be their vigilance. With men, M'sieu, we may retake, by strategy alone of course, the factor of Fort de Seviere. Therefore have we come across your way, In the Name of Mary, M'sieu, I beg that you refuse me not!"

She was like some young priestess as she stood in the westering light on the green-fringed shore, one hand caught in the buckskin fringe at her throat and her eyes on Mr. Mowbray's upright face.

"Upon my word, Madame—?" he said when she had finished.

"Ma'amselle, M'sieu," she corrected simply.

"Ma'amselle,—your pardon,—upon my word, have I never seen such appalling courage! Do you not know that you go upon a quest as hopeless as death? This tribe,—I have heard a deal too much about them, and once they came to York two seasons back,—are unlike any others of the Indians of the country. Ruled by a peculiar justice which takes 'a skin for a skin'—not ten or an hundred as do the Blackfeet or the Sioux,—they yet surpass all others in the cruelty of that taking. Have you not heard tales of this surpassing cruelty, Ma'amselle?"

"Aye, we have heard. It hastens our going. M'sieu the factor awaits that cruelty in its extremest manner with the reaching of the Pays d'en Haut."

"Mother of God!" said Mr. Mowbray wonderingly. "And yet,—I see!"

"And he is Hudson's Bay, M'sieu," said the girl sharply; "a good factor. Would the Company not make an effort to save such, think you?"

Mr. Mowbray stood a moment, many moments, thinking with a line drawn deep between his eyes. Out on the burnished water the canoes lay idly, the red kerchiefs of the trappers making bright points of colour against the blue background.

Presently he said slowly

"What yon ask is against all precedent, Ma'amselle, and I may lose my head for tampering with my orders,—but I will see what can be done."

The brigade drew in, and when dusk fell upon the wilderness a dozen fires kept company with the lone little spiral from Dupre's camp.

Sitting upon the shingle with her hands clasped hard on her knees, Maren shook her head when the young trapper brought her the breast of a grouse, roasted brown, along with tea and pemmican from the packs of the H. B. men.

"I thank you, my friend," she said uncertainly; "but I cannot —not now. Not until I know, M'sieu. Without many hands at the paddles how can we overtake the Nakonkirhirinons?"

Thus she sat, alone among men, staring into the fire, and it seemed as if the heart in her breast would burst with its anxiety. A woman was at all times a thing of overwhelming interest in the wilderness, and such a woman as this drew every eye in the brigade to feast upon her beauty, each according to the nature of the man, either furtively, with tentative admiration, or openly, with boldness of daring.

And presently, after the meal was over, she saw Mr. Mowbray gather his men in a group. For a few moments he spoke to them, and a ripple of words, of ejaculations and exclamations, went across the assemblage like a wave.

"Nom de Dieu! Not alone?"

"To the Pay d'en Haut,—those two?"

"A woman? Mother of God!"

Wondering eyes turned to the figure in the glow of the fire, to the brown hands hard clasped, the face with its flame-lit eyes.

"Five men and a good canoe I send with them," said Mowbray quietly; "who goes? Know you it is a quest of death."

"Who goes, M'sieu?" cried a French trader. "I! 'Tis worth a year of the fur trade!"

"And I!"

"And I!"

"And I!"

Once more she had made her appeal to man, man in the abstract, and once more he had come to her, this maid of dreams.

Mr. Mowbray had lost half his brigade had he not fixed on those who were the strongest among the volunteers, the best canoe-men, the best shots.

Such were these men of the wilderness, excitable, ready for any hazard, drawn by the longest odds, and to serve a woman gave the last zest to danger.

Seldom enough did a woman appeal to them in such romantic wise.

"Brilliers,—Alloybeau,—Wilson," picked out Mr Mowbray, with a finger pointing his words; "McDonald,—Frith,—

make ready the fourth canoe, Take store of pemmican and all things necessary for light travel and quick. From to-morrow you will answer to Ma'amselle. When she is through with you report to me, either at Cumberland or York, according to the time."

And he left his men to walk over and seat himself beside Maren Le Moyne on the shingle.

It was dark of the moon and the night was thick with stars and forest sounds. Out on the lake beyond the ranged canoes at the water's edge, the fish were slapping.

"Ma'amselle," said Mr. Mowbray gravely, "I have detailed you five men, a canoe, and stores. May God grant that they may serve your purpose"

A long sigh escaped the girl's lips.

"And may He forever hold you in His grace, M'sieu!" she said tremulously; "and bless you at the hour of death!"

"And now, Ma'amselle," he said gently, "tell me more of this strange adventure. How comes it that a young maid, alone but for a youthful trapper, goes to the Pays d'en Haut after a factor, of the Company? Why did this duty not fall to the men of the post?"

"They said, as you, M'sieu, but an hour back, that it was a quest of death. They love life. I love the factor."

She made her explanation simply, in all innocence, looking gravely into the fire, and Mr. Mowbray gasped inwardly.

"I see. So Anders McElroy is your lover. A fine man, worthy of the love of such a woman, and blessed above men in its

Vingie E. Roe

possessing if I may make so bold, Ma'amselle."

"Nay,—you mistake."

Maren shook her head.

"Not my lover. I but said that I love the factor He does not love me, M'sieu."

"What? Heaven above us! What was that? Does not love you! And yet you go into the Pays d'en Haut after the North Indians? You speak in riddles."

"Why, what plainer? Life would die in me, M'sieu, did I leave him to death by torture. I can do no less."

Mr. Mowbray sat in silence, amazed beyond speech.

When he rose an hour later to go to his camp he laid a hand on the beaded shoulder wet with the night dew.

"Ma'amselle," he said, "I have seen a glimpse of God through the blind eyes of a woman. May Destiny reward you."

Thus it came that before the dawn reddened the east the camp of the brigade broke up for the start to the south and west, and one big canoe with six men waited at the shore for one woman, who held both the hands of Mr. Mowbray in her own and thanked him without words.

As the lone craft shot forth upon the steel-blue waters the leader of the Hudson's Bay brigade looked after the figure in the bow, glimmering whitely in the mists, and an unaccustomed tightness gripped his throat.

He had two daughters of his own, sheltered safe in London,—two maids as far from this woman of the wild as darkness from the light, soft, gentle creatures, and yet he wondered if either were half so gentle, so truly tender.

Ere the paddles dipped, the men in the canoes with one accord, touched off by some quick-blooded French adventurer, set up a chanson,—a beating rhythmic song of Love going into Battle,—and every throat took it up.

It flowed across the lightening face of the waters, circled around the lone canoe and the woman therein, and seemed to waft her forward with the God-speed of the wilderness.

She lifted her hand above her without turning her head, and it shone pale in the mist, an eerie beacon, and thus the boat passed from view in the greyness, though as the paddles dipped for the start the song still rung forth, beating along the shore.

* * * * * * * * * * *

"Men," said Maren Le Moyne at the first stop, "this is a trail of great hazard. There is in it neither gift nor gain, only a mighty risk. Yet I have asked you forth upon it as men of the H. B. C. because the man I would save is a factor of the Great Company."

"Ma'amselle," said Bitte Alloybeau, a splendid black-browed fellow, "it is enough."

"Aye,—and more." So was bound their simple allegiance.

CHAPTER XX

THE WOLF AND THE CARIBOU

Northward along Nelson River went the concourse of the Nakonkirhirinons, turning westward into the chain of little lakes above Winnipeg of which Dupre had spoken, sweeping forward over portage and dalle, and after them came the lone canoe, leaping the leagues like a loup-garou, for it never rested.

Day and night it shot forward, pulled by sturdy arms, half its people sleeping curled between thwarts, the other half manning the paddles, stopping for snatched rations, reading the signs of passing. So it crept forward upon the thing it sought, untiring, eager, absurd in its daring and its hope.

Like an embodiment of that very absurdity of courage so dear to the hearts of these men, the girl sat in the prow, taking a hand in the work with the best of them, beaconing the way as she had done before her venturers of Grand Portage, firing them with her calm certainty, binding them to her more firmly with each day.

To each bit of courtesy done eagerly to her there was her grave "I thank you,"—at each portage and line her hand to the rope, her shoulder to the pack, and all in the simple unconsciousness of her womanhood that made her what she was,—a leader.

Before forty-eight hours had passed they would have followed her to the brink of death,—to the Pays d'en Haut, to the heart of an hostile camp.

They fixed their eyes on her shining braids, bare to the sun, and anticipated her commands, obeyed her few words implicitly, and who shall say that many a dream did not weave itself around her in the summer days, for every man in the boat was young.

Who knew?

Perhaps the Nakonkirhirinons had already yielded to the savage wrath that takes a "skin for a skin,"—perhaps they had passed somewhere in the forest, hidden from view from the water, the too well-known blackened stake, the trodden circle. Perhaps there was no factor of Fort de Seviere.

Only Marc Dupre, nearest Maren in every change and arrangement, had no such thoughts. Dreams enough he wove in all surety, but they had to do with the blinding heights of sacrifice, the wistful valleys of renunciation.

His heart was full to overflowing with idolatry. From shadow and fireglow his dark eyes looked upon her with a love that had passed far beyond the need of word or touch, that buoyed her up and supported her in strength and purity, like the silver cloud beneath the feet of the Madonna.

And Maren, too, dreamed her dreams, for she had dreamed since the days of the forge in Grand Portage, and they were sad as death. No more did she list the sound of a western wind in the bending grass of a far country, the rush of virgin rivers, the whisper of pine-clad hills. The joy of the great quest was dead within her, the love of forest and stream, the lure of trail and trace. Sadness sat upon her like a garment. She only knew the pain that had birth that night in De Seviere when she sought McElroy to disclaim the giver of the red flower and found him kissing the red-rose cheek of the little Francette.

So went forth this little barque o' dreams.

Meanwhile what of the two men who journeyed ahead?

With each day they lost a little of the love of life, for with the cunning which gave them their hazy fame the Nakonkirhirinons were tightening the screws of cruelty.

Work beyond a man's strength was meted out to them. Alone in a long canoe heavily laden, McElroy and De Courtenay were forced to keep the pace set by the boats, each of which carried five men. Blisters came in their hands, broke and rose again, sweat poured from their straining bodies, and if they fell slow a spear-prod from the boat behind sent them forward.

How much more exquisite could be made the torture of a victim already worn to the ragged edge, how much sooner the scream be wrung from his throat. With each passing league that brought them nearer the end of the journey could be seen the fiendish eagerness rearing in the glittering eyes.

Turn and turn they took, these two, of the hindmost seat in the canoe, for the back of each was unspeakable from the spear-prods. Without a word McElroy took his punishment as the lagging became more pronounced from arms over-taxed at the paddles, but the long-haired adventurer from the Saskatchewan taunted them to their faces.

Taunt and fling were unavailing. Of an unearthly poise were these savages from the distant north. With grinning good humour they withheld their anger, knowing full well that time would doubly repay.

Here and there among them appeared those worst monsters of the wilds, INDIANS WITH BLUE EYES AND SQUARED-OUT TOES.

Far up ahead went forward the canoe of the dead chief, with Edmonton Ridgar sitting in silence among the blackened warriors.

Never once did he glance backward, never once at the night camps did he come near his factor.

Throughout the long days McElroy pondered this in his heart and turned it over and over without satisfaction. Unable to form any conclusion he fell to thinking of their friendship and of the gentle nature of the man, the unbending faith of him.

It was all a sorry riddle.

"Brace up, M'sieu," De Courtenay would laugh, even in the midst of exhaustion; "sing,—smile,—perhaps it will be only the stake, not something worse. Console yourself, as do I, with—memories."

And McElroy would say nothing, trying in his heart to hold back his wrath against this man for whose death he was to be responsible.

So went the uneven chase. Day's march of the savages and night's rest on the green shores, mummying fires in the big tepee and the captives lying in the sleep of exhaustion with

Vingie E. Roe

one guard pacing the lodge opening,—day's pursuit of the lone canoe, brief landings for tea made at a micmac fire, scanning of lake and river and forest, night's unceasing forging .ahead with Maren asleep in the prow, her head on Dupre's blanket.

When the last hard portage was made which carried them into Deer River, the girl looked to the west with a sudden fire of the old passion in her eyes.

"So, M'sieu?" she said to Dupre, "it lies yonder, the Land of the Whispering Hills? Would God our course lay there!"

And Dupre, wondering, answered, "Aye, at the Athabasca," for it was to McElroy alone that she had uncovered her soul concerning the great quest.

In Deer River the signs began to be plainer and fresher, showing the passing of the Indians,—here a camp but two days deserted, there scraps of refuse not yet cleared away by forest scavengers, and the pursuers knew they drew close to danger and excitement.

All day the men of Mowbray's brigade bent to the paddles in growing eagerness, and at the evening's stop Maren spoke to them, gathered around with cold rations in their hands, for no fire was lighted now.

"To-morrow we will overtake the Nakonkirhirinons," she said simply, as if that meant no more than speaking a brother brigade of Hudson's Bays, "and then will come the time of action. At night-camp we will make our effort of deliverance. You, Alloybeau, and you, McDonald, will keep within my call whatever happens, while Frith and Brilliers and Wilson will stay with the canoe, ready for instant flight. M'sieu," she laid a hand on Dupre's arm and her voice deepened softly, "is scout and captain and he goes at my side. More I cannot say until we know the lie of land to-morrow."

So they again took boat, this little band of venturers than whom there were no more daring threaders of the wilderness in all the vast unknown country; and Maren sat in the prow, her hands idle in her lap, for she had paddled since four by the sun.

Beside her, huddled half under the feet of Wilson on the foremost thwart, Dupre watched the stars as they came out in a turquoise sky, for the sleep that was due him would not come. He thought of the morrow and what it would bring, and the sadness in his heart grew with the deepening shades.

The fringed garment of white doeskin lay under his elbow and a fold of it brushed his cheek, and, boy that he was, its touch brought the quick tears to his eyes.

"Ma'amselle," he said presently, when the turquoise had faded to purple and the purple to velvet black, with the stars like a dowager's diamonds thickset upon it, "Ma'amselle, what think you is behind the stars?"

Maren turned her face to him like a sweet young moon, pale in the night.

"Behind the stars? Why, Heaven, M'sieu, where all is glory; Heaven assuredly."

"Aye. Where all is glory. Yes, for those who keep the holy mandates, whose hearts are pure as that heaven itself. For such as you. Oh, Holy Mother!—" his voice fell to a whisper; "there is no heaven, Ma'amselle, so pure as the white heart of you! But for him whose days have gone like the butterfly's flight from one prodigal joy to the next, whose heart has known neither love of God nor love of a good woman, save for a little space, whose tongue has boasted and blasphemed, and whose life has been worth no jot of good,— what, think you, awaits so lost a man as this?"

The light "whoosh,—sst—whoosh" of the dipping paddles, the occasional rattle of a handle on a gunwale, formed a blending background against which his low words were distinguishable only to the girl beside him.

She looked long into his upturned face. The wistfulness sat heavy upon it. The youthfulness of this dashing trapper of the posts and settlements came out plain in the starlight. She saw again the pliant strength beneath the slender grace, caught the suggestion of contradicting forces that she had felt one day in Marie's doorway when young Dupre swung up the main way of Fort de Seviere, and beneath it all she saw that which had caused her to say on that first morning of the long trail when he faced her in the hidden cove, "Would it had been given me to love you, M'sieu!"

All this passed through her aching heart, and presently she said with a little catch in her deep voice,

"What awaits a man like this? A man who has done all these things and who speaks of their folly, who thinks of God in the nighttimes, whose heart turns with longing to that land behind the stars, and who gives,"—she paused a moment,— "I cannot say the rest,—But—but—Oh, there awaits this man the smile of that Christ of the Seven Scars, the loving tears of Our Lady of Sorrows, the very grace of the Good God!"

"Truly,—Ma'amselle?" asked Marc Dupre wistfully, "in your heart—not out of its goodness?"

"In my heart of hearts I think this, M'sieu."

They fell silent for a long time, while the stars travelled with them in the broken water and the ripples lapped and sucked at the shores and the swift stream hurried to the bay.

At length the trapper tentatively raised his hand and touched the bare arm of Maren where it shone brown beneath the white of the fringed sleeve.

"I thank you for those words, Ma'amselle," he said simply; "they are healing as the Confessional to my ragged soul."

CHAPTER XXI

TIGHTENED SCREWS

"M'sieu," said De Courtenay, "what think you? It would seem that something stirs in this camp of squaws and old men. Gaiety and festive garb appear. Behold yonder brave with a double allowance of painted feathers and more animation than seems warrantable. What's to do?"

The man was worn to the bone with the day's work, yet the old brilliance played whimsically in his eyes. This day a wearing burden of skin packs had been added to the canoe, ladening it to the water's lip, and the vicious prodding from behind had been in consequence of redoubled vigour.

McElroy, reclining beside him on his face,—to lie on his back was unbearable,—to one side of the camp, looked at the scene before them.

Surely it seemed as if something was toward.

Here and there among the Indians appeared strangers. More Bois-Brules, lean half-breeds more to be feared than any Indian from the Mandane country to the polar regions, decked half after the manner of white man and savage, all more animated than was the wont of these sullen Runners of the Burnt Woods, they passed back and forth among the fires, and presently McElroy caught the gleam of liquid that shone like rubies or topaz in the evening light.

"Aha!" he said, "these Bois-Brules that have joined our captors appear to have had dealings with the whites. Yonder is the source of your discovered animation. Whiskey, as I live, and circling fast among the braves. It bodes ill for us, my friend."

"So? Why so?"

"Because never was redskin yet who could hold fire-water and himself at the same time. No matter how determined they are to reach their stamping-ground before the ceremonies of our despatch, their determination will evaporate like morning mists before the sun in the warmth of the spirit, or I know not Indian nature. Prepare for something, M'sieu."

As the evening fell and the fires leaped against the darkness, sounds increased in the camp. Groups of warriors gathered and broke, voices rose; and shrill yells began to cut above the melee of the noise.

From time to time a brave would come running out of the bustle and, stopping near, glare ferociously at the captives. Twice a hatchet came flittering through the firelight, its bright blade flashing as it circled, to fall perilously close, and several times a squaw or two prodded one or the other with a moccasined toe.

Once a young brave, his black eyes alight with devilishncss, sprang out from the bushes behind and caught McElroy's face in a pinching clasp of fingers. With one bound the factor was on his feet and had dealt the stripling a blow which sent him sprawling with his oiled head in a squaw's fire. Instantly

Vingie E. Roe

his long feather was ablaze and his yelp of dismay brought forth a storm of derisive yells of laughter.

McElroy sat quietly down again.

"It has begun, M'sieu," he said grimly.

All night the liquor circled among the savages, as the spirit fired the brains in their narrow skulls the aproar became worse. A huge fire was built in the centre of the camp, tom-toms placed beside it in the hands of old men, and, forming in a giant circle, the braves began a dance.

At first it was the stamp-dance*, harmless enough, with bending forms and palms extended to the central fire and the ceaseless "Ah-a, ah-a-a, ah-a," capable of a thousand intonations and the whole gamut of suggestion and portent, blood-chilling in its slow excitement.

*I have witnessed this.—V. R.

Without the circle the squaws fought and quarrelled over the portion of liquor doled out to them by their lords, and their clamour was worse than the rest.

No sleep came to the two white men lying at the foot of a tree to the west of the camp, with a guard pacing slowly between them and liberty.

Instead, thoughts were seething like dalle's foam in the mind of each.

If only this giant guard might drink deep enough of the libations of the others,—who knew?—there might be the faint chance of escape for which they had watched cease-lessly since leaving Red River.

But, with the irony of fate, this one Indian became the model warrior of the tribe. As the confusion and uproar grew in intensity, one after another joined the dancing circle, until it seemed that every brave in the camp was leaping around the fire. Blue-eyed Indians, Bois-Brules, Nakonkirhirinons, they circled and uttered the monotonous "Ah-a, ah-a," and in the light could be seen the white lock on the temple of Bois DesCaut.

"I should have killed him long ago," thought McElroy simply, "as one kills a wolf,—for the good of the settlement."

As they lay watching the unearthly orgy at the fire a plan slowly took shape in McElroy's mind. They were unbound as they had been for many days, the silent guard proving sufficient surety for their retention, and they were two to one in the wild confusion of the growing excitement. What easier than a swift grapple in the dusk, one man locked in combat with the sentinel and one lost in the forest and the night? It was a desperate chance, but they were desperate men with the post, the hatchet, and the matete before them. As the thought grew it took on proportions of possibility and the factor threw up his head with the old motion, shaking out of his eyes the falling sun-burnt hair.

"M'sieu," he said, in a low voice, carefully modulated to the careless tone of weary speech which was their habit of nights; "M'sieu, I have a plan."

The cavalier looked up quickly.

"Ah!" he said; "a plan? Of what,—conduct at the stake? The etiquette of the ceremony of the Feast of Flame?"

"Peace!" replied McElroy sternly; "you jest, M'sieu. We are

in sore straits and a drowning man snatches at straws. It is this. The fire of liquor is rising out there. Hear it in the rising note of the blended voices. How long, think you, will they be content with the dance and the chanting, the tom-toms and the empty fire? How long before we are dragged in, to be the centre of affairs? In this plan of mine there is room for one of us, a bare chance of escape. This guard behind,—he is a powerful man, but, with every warrior wild in the circling mass yonder, he might be engaged for the moment needed for one to dart into the darkness and take to the river. Once there, the mercy of night and bending bushes might aid him. What think you?"

"Truly 'tis worth the try. My blood answers the risk. At the most it would but hasten things. But give the word and we'll at it."

"Nay,—we must understand each other, lest we bungle. As the plan was mine, I take the choice of parts. There is a stain upon my conscience, M'sieu." McElroy spoke simply from his heart, as was his wont. "Throughout this long journey it has lain heavy. Though I hold against you one grave offence, yet I grieve deeply that it was through my hasty anger you were brought to such sorry plight. As I am at fault, so would I heal that fault. This the way I find given me. When I spring for our friend of the painted feather, do you, M'sieu, waiting for nothing, take to the bush with all the speed there is in you. And before we part know that, were we free, I would punish you as man to man for that moment before the gate of De Seviere with all pleasure."

"Ah! You refer to Ma'amselle Le Moyne? By what right?"

"By the right of love, whose advances were more than half-reciprocated before the advent of your accursed red flowers,—the right of man to fight for his woman."

"Nom de Dieu!" De Courtenay threw back his head and laughed, the flecks of light from the fire flittering across his handsome features. "You speak a lost cause, my friend! She was mine since that first morning by your well when the high head bent to my hand. What a woman she is,—Maid of the Long Trail, Spirit of the Woods and Lakes! A lioness with a dove's heart! I have seen the Queen of the World in this God-forsaken wilderness; therefore is it worth while."

"Stop!" cried McElroy sharply; "let the old wound be. Only make ready to act at once."

"Aye,—I am ready now."

"Then rise with me,—swiftly as possible,—when I count to three. One—"

The two men strained their bodies, leaning forward, for both had risen to sit facing the fire when the dance began.

"Two,—" breathed McElroy, "ready, M'sieu,—three!"

With one accord they leaped to their feet, and the factor in a flash was upon the Indian just passing behind him. He had leaped high, for the Nakonkirhirinon was taller than a common man, and he clutched the muscled neck in a grasp of steel, pressing his shoulder against his adversary's face, to still the outcry he knew would come.

The orgy at the fire was lifting its tone of riot into one of savagery and menace, the tom-toms beat more swiftly with gaining excitement, and the yapping yells were growing more frequent.

It was an auspicious moment and the heart of McElroy throbbed with a savage pleasure, but suddenly he felt other hands disputing his grip on the astonished Indian, who was raining blows upon him having dropped his gun in the first shock. Over the bare shoulder of the warrior, shining like bronze in a gleam of light, he saw the face of De Courtenay, its blue eyes alight.

In a flash his grip was torn from behind, and, as the Indian reared his head and threw back his great shoulders, lifting him clear of the earth, he heard the joyous voice of the cavalier.

"Run!" it cried, as he fell clear; "run! And tell Maren Le Moyne that her name is last upon my lips,—her face last before—"

Out above the words there rang the shrill cry of the guard, his mouth uncovered by McElroy's shaking off.

The Indian had whirled and grappled with De Courtenay, and, before McElroy could tear him loose, fighting like a madman, out from the yelling circle there poured an avalanche of lunatics, jerked from Gehenna by that ringing cry.

Foremost was Bois DesCaut, his evil eyes glinting like a witch's omen.

Yelling, jumping, flaming with the liquor of the Bois-Brules, they fell upon the two men and dragged them, half-falling, half-running, toward the circle, into it, and up to the fire.

"Ho-ho! ho-ho-o! Ha-ha! ha-ha-a! ha-ha!"

Faces wild as the devil's dreams pushed close, hands plucked at them, and suddenly a dozen painted braves caught up handfuls of live coals and flung them upon them.

In the midst of it McElroy looked stupidly at De Courtenay.

"For the love of God!" he said, "why did you not run?"

"Why didn't you?"

The cavalier was laughing.

"I could not, M'sieu," he added; "the charm of the hazard was too great."

And that was the last word he offered the man who would have delivered him, turning to face the savages.

"Dogs!" he cried in French; "dogs and sons of dogs!"

Stooping suddenly, he snatched a horned headdress from the crown of an aged medicine man, scooped it full of glowing brands, and tossed its contents straight into the wild faces before him.

Then he straightened, crossed his arms, and smiled upon them in contempt.

Pandemonium was loose.

In breathless swiftness the captives were stripped to the skin, tied hand and foot, and fastened to stakes set hastily up on either side the fire.

"It begins to look, M'sieu," called De Courtenay, across the space and the roaring flames, "as if the Nor'westers and the Hudson's Bays must scratch up a new wintering partner and a fresh factor,—though, 'ods blood! this one is fresh enough! Will they cure us as as they have Negansahima?"

At mention of the dead chief a dozen missiles cut the night air and struck the speaker. One, a lighted torch, landed full in his face, and McElroy groaned aloud.

If De Courtenay hoped by his taunts and his jeers to reach a swifter end, he was mistaken in that hope. No fire was kindled at their stakes, no sudden stroke of death maul or tomahawk followed his words. The Nakonkirhirinons had keener tortures, torments of a finer fibre than mere physical suffering, and the Bois-Brules' liquor had stirred the hidden resources.

Again the dancing commenced, but this time it was not the harmless measure of the stamp-dance. Instead of the bending bodies, the rhythmic stamping of soft-shod feet, the extended palms, there were unspeakable leapings, writhings, and grimaces revolting in their horror, brandishing of knives, and yelling that was incessant.

McElroy closed his eyes and forced his mind to the Petition for Mercy.

Through the tenor of the beautiful words there cut from time to time De Courtenay's voice, cool, contemptuous, a running fire of invective, now in French, now in English, and again in the Assiniboine tongue, which was familiar to the Nakonkirhirinons, they being friends with that tribe.

As the hubbub rose with the liquor two slabs were brought, rough sections of trees hastily smoothed with axe and hatchet, of the height of a man and the thickness thereof, with a slight margin at top and sides. These were set up behind the stakes that held them, thus forming a background, and the two naked forms stood out in the firelight like pictures in white frames.

A wise old sachem, hideously painted, drew a line on the ground at thirty feet, facing the central fire, and with a bony finger picked out a certain number of warriors.

Full fifty there seemed to McElroy when he opened his eyes to see them ranged before the line, all armed with knives that shone in the glow, and (grim irony of fate!) in the blades of some there was a familiar stamp—H. B. C.!

"Ah! Yuagh!" called the sachem, and two young men stepped forward, toe on the line, glanced each at a framed picture, drew up an arm, and, "Whut-t-t t-e-e-p," whined two knives that flittered through the light and struck quivering, one with its cool kiss on McElroy's cheek, the other just in the edge of the slab at De Courtenay's shoulder.

A shout of derision greeted this throw, and two more took the place of the retiring braves, this time a Runner of the Burnt Woods, wearing the garments of the white man, but smeared with bars of red and yellow paint across the cheeks, and a white renegade.

"A Nor'wester's man once," thought McElroy; "another DesCaut."

Again the "whut-t" of the whimpering blades, again the little impact in the wood behind, this time with more indifferent aim; for never was white man yet who sank or rose to Indian level in the matter of spear or tomahawk.

They were brave men, these two, and they faced the singing knives without a quiver of muscle, a droop of eye, while the joy of the savages, at last turned loose, rose and rose in its wildness.

For an hour the mob at the line threw and shifted, the vast

circle sitting or standing in every attitude of keenest enjoyment. The slabs bristled with steel, to be cleaned and decorated anew, while the fire in the centre leaped and crackled with an hundred voices.

A stone's-throw away the grim tepee of the dead chief glimmered now out of the shadow, now in, and to the east behind a rocky bluff, through which led a narrow gorge, the river hurried to the north.

Blood-painted brilliant splotches here and there against the white pictures, but neither man was limp in his bonds, neither fair head drooped, neither pair of blue eyes flinched. De Courtenay's long curls hung like cords of gold against his bare shoulder, enhancing the great beauty of him, while his brilliant smile flashed with uncanny steadiness. McElroy's face was grave, lips tight, eyes narrow, and forehead furrowed with the thought he strove in vain to make connected.

Suddenly every shade of colour drained out of his countenance, leaving it white as the virgin slab behind.

On the outskirts of the concourse, just at the edge of shadow and light, Edmonton Ridgar stood apart and the look on his face was of mortal agony. As his eyes met those of his factor all doubt was swept away. This was his friend, McElroy knew in that one swift moment, even as he watched his torture, his friend on whose faith and goodness he would stake his soul anew. It was strange what a keen joy surged through him with that subtle knowledge, what smart of tear-mist stung his eyes.

Long their gaze clung, filled with unspeakable things, things that were high as Heaven itself, that pass only between men clean of heart on the Calvaries of earth.

Then, as gleaming eyes began to follow the fixed look of McElroy, heads to turn with waving of feathers on scalp-locks, the factor with an effort took his eyes from Ridgar's.

"Dog-eaters!" De Courtenay was laughing. "Birds of carrion! Old men! Squaws of the North!"

And above the hubbub the ritual chanting in his brain turned into an Act of Thanksgiving.

CHAPTER XXII

"CHOOSE, WHITE WOMAN!"

Another day had gone into the great back country of time, from which the hand of God alone can pluck them and their secrets. Soft haze of blue and gold hung over forest and stream, sweet breath of summer fondled the high carpet of interlaced tree-tops, blew down the waters and wimpled the bending grasses, and the wolf had sighted the caribou herd.

In a shelter of spruce within sight of the Indian smoke the lone canoe and its people lay hidden, awaiting the coming of night.

"Now, Ma'amselle," said Dupre earnestly, "do you remain close here with Frith and Wilson and Alloybeau while Brilliers and McDonald go with me to reconnoitre."

Maren knelt beside a fallen log binding up the heavy ropes of her hair. Before her were spread the meagre adjuncts of her toilet, in all conscience slim enough for any masculine runner of the forest,—a dozen little pegs hand-whittled from hard wood and polished to finest gloss by contact with the shining braids.

She looked up at him with eyes that were unreadable to his

simple understanding.

"Remain?" she said; "and send you into my danger alone? You know me not, M'sieu."

Purple dusk was thick upon the underworld of lesser growth beneath the towering woods. In its half-light the trapper saw that her face, usually of so sad a calm, was glowing with excitement.

"Brilliers," she said, rising and fastening the last strand, "bring me the brown no-wak-wa berries from the pail yonder."

She stood crushing the ripe fruit in her hands and looked into the faces of her little band. In every countenance she read what she had read in men's faces all of her life, the dumb longing to serve, and it lifted her heart with tenderness.

"My men," she said presently, "remember we are Hudson's Bays, and that we have behind us the Great Company which punishes guilt and upholds loyalty, and that we go to rescue a factor of the Company. Alloybeau and McDonald go with me, flanking either side. You, Frith, take up position a hundred yards inland to cover what retreat may happen. Wilson and Brilliers stand at the canoe, and, M'sieus, keep hand at prow ready for instant action. We know not what may happen. I, who am most concerned, go first. You, Marc Dupre, go with me."

Her voice dropped as it ever did of late when she spoke to this good friend.

"And now we wait only for full darkness."

"You must go, Ma'amselle?" said Alloybeau miserably.

"Cannot another make the first scouting? Send me."

"And me!" Frith pushed softly forward. "At the last, Ma'amselle, we are old women. We cannot let you go."

"Cannot?" said Maren sharply. "Do Mr. Mowbray's men so soon forget his orders? I am good as a man, M'sieus. See!"

She held up her right arm, with the fringed sleeve falling loose. The muscle sprang up magnificently.

"Fear not for me,—and yet,—I thank you! Now we wait."

One hour,—two,—passed and the last light crept, afraid, out of the forest to linger a trembling moment on the waters and be drawn up to the darkening sky.

At last the maid arose, tall and quiet, save for the excitement in her eyes, and one by one her chosen followers stepped noiselessly after.

Silent as the wood around, the forlorn hope crept forward.

"Here, Frith," commanded Maren, when they had reached a vantage point of higher ground, "and here you, Alloybeau and McDonald, separate. If during this night the good God shall deliver into our hands Mr. McElroy and the venturer from Montreal, you will hear a panther's far-off call. Make for the canoe, for that will mean swift flight. If, on the other hand, aught should befall us ahead, a night-hawk will cry once. Hide and wait. Wait one day, two, three. There is always hope. So. We go now."

Thus they separated, that small band, as hopeless together as apart in case of discovery, and at last Dupre followed alone, his heart heavy within him and a grip in his throat of tears.

On through the leafy forest, parting the lacing vines, holding each branch that it might not swish to place, they went, far from safety and the commonplace of life, and a prescience of disaster weighed on the trapper's soul like lead.

At last it grew more than he could bear, and he reached a hand to Maren's shoulder, a tentative hand, hesitating, as if it felt its touch blasphemy.

"Ma'amselle," he faltered, "forgive me! But, oh! without confession this night I am sick to my heart's core! I lied to you back at the cove, though with a clean conscience, for it is love,—love of a man warm and wild that tears my soul to tatters! I love you with all love, of saint and sinner, of Heaven and earth, and I would have you know it!"

His low voice was shaking, as was his whole slim body, and Maren felt it in the hand on her shoulder.

"As a man, Ma'amselle, I would give my life for one touch of your lips! As a lost monk I would kiss your garment's hem! See!"

He dropped to his knee and, catching her beaded skirt, pressed it to his lips again and again, passionately, swept away by his French blood.

"As I live I love you as the dog loves his master! I am naught save the dust under your feet, the thorn you brush in the forest, yet like them I catch and cling! Forgive, Ma'amselle, and if the future is fair for you, think sometimes in the dusk of Marc Dupre!"

"Hush!" said Maren, catching the hand at her knee, a shaking hand more slender than her own; "hush, my friend! You break my heart anew. I know the inmost grace of you, the glory of the love you tell, and be it of heaven or earth, of angel or man, I would to the Good God there was yet life enough within me to buy it with my own! I have seen naught so holy, so worth all price, in the years of my life. It is dear to my heart as that life itself. Dear as yourself, my more than friend."

In all tenderness she stooped from her fair height and laid her arm around the shoulders of the youth, drew his head against the beadwork of McElroy's gift, and kissed him upon the lips,—once, twice, yearningly, as a mother kisses a weakling child.

At that moment there came, borne on a waking breeze of the night, the sound of the tom-toms, the yapping of many throats.

"The gods beckon," she said sadly; "this life and love is all awry and we who are bound against our will must but abide the end."

"Aye," whispered young Dupre, from the warm depths of her shoulder, and his voice was like gold for joy; "aye,—the end."

He rose swiftly.

"Forgive the passion that could forget the great business of the night," he said, and they went forward, though Maren's fingers still rested in his clasp.

Through the thinning wood which neared the stream presently there came a glow and then the shine of a great fire ahead, with massed figures that leaped and sprang, fantastic as a witch's carnival, and a roar of frightful voices.

"Stay now, Ma'amselle!" begged Dupre, at last, for he had caught a sight that shook him through and through; "stay you here in the wood while I go forward!"

But his protest was lost on the maid. Eagerly she was pushing on, hid by the shadows,—nearer and nearer, until suddenly she stopped and stared upon the scene, the fingers in his clasp gripping Dupre's hand like steel.

"God! God! God!" breathed Maren Le Moyne at the forest's edge as she looked once more upon the face of the factor of Fort de Seviere.

Unspeakable was that scene. All reason had fled from the North savages.

What small veneer of docility had been spread over them by their three years' dealing with the Hudson's Bays and their intercourse with the quiet and tractable Assiniboines, had vanished. They were themselves as nature made them, cruel to the point of art.

The work of the day was visible upon the captives tied to their stakes on either side the fire. Half-clothed, for they had been thrown into a lodge to recuperate for the night's festivities, they stood in weariness, that from time to time drooped one head or the other, only to lift again with taunt and jeer.

De Courtenay, his thin face between the curls thinner, was still facing the mob with the smile that would not down. McElroy was as Maren had ever known him, patient and strong, and from time to time he tossed up the light hair falling in his eyes.

"We are none too soon," she said tensely; "tonight it must

end. Go you around to the east, M'sieu, between the camp and the river. Look for the lodge of the dead chief, for there will be the trader, Ridgar. Look for him and read his face,—whether or no he will help us. I will skirt to the north."

"I—Ma'amselle! Stay far from their sight, for love of Heaven!"

"Sh! Go, my friend;" and Maren turned into the darkness.

"Mary Mother, now do thou befriend!" she whispered, as she felt her way forward. With touch of tree trunk and slipping moccasin, lithe bend and sway and turning, as sure in the forest as any savage, this Maid of the Trail took into her hands the saving of a man. It was simple. Wit must play the greater part, wit that invades a sleeping camp, risks its life, and laughs at its victory. So would she work in the late hours when revelry had worked its own undoing. Now she would learn the camp and the safest side of it, the place of the captives and a way of escape. With thought and eager plan she pushed from her mind the look of McElroy's body.

She would—

In the darkness she stopped with inheld breath. Her groping foot had touched an object, a soft object that stirred and rolled over on its side and presently sat up. So near it was that she could feel the movements of its garments, which fact told her it was human.

Then, without warning, a hand shot out and caught her knee in a grip of steel. With all her strength the girl tore away, leaping backward. But a tangle of vines snatched at her foot and she fell crashing forward with a figure prone upon her, and in the darkness she fought silently for life.

As in the camp of the Nakonkirhirinons the thin veneer had slipped away, so now in the forest its heavier counterpart fell from this woman and she turned savage as the thing with which she fought.

Of superb stature and strength, she was a match for the man, and two pairs of hands searched for a throat, two bodies strained and struggled for the mastery. It seemed that the noise of the conflict, the snapping of dry dead wood, the swish and crash of leafy brush, must draw attention from the camp, but it was too engrossed in its own mad hilarity to heed so small a sound.

Over and over strained the strangely-met foes in silence, and presently they struggled up, barehanded, face to face, for Maren had dropped her rifle when she fell. As they whirled into a more open space the light from the fire struck through the foliage and glistened on a tuft of white hair on the swarthy temple before her.

"Hola! DesCaut!" gasped the girl.

"Oho! I win!"

For, with the sudden illumination, she forgot for a moment the present and DesCaut; for it was the turncoat awaked from a drunken sleep apart, who pushed swiftly forward, took the moment's advantage of her hesitation, and pinioned her arms to her sides.

She might still have had a chance, for she was as strong as he, but that he raised his voice in a call for help.

Thus it was that, in less time than the telling, Maren Le Moyne, rescuer, leader of the long trail, was dragged, fast bound by a dozen gripping hands, into the firelit space in the great circle, a captive under the eyes of the man she had come to save.

Stumbling, jerked this way and that, one white shoulder gleaming against the brown stain of throat and face where the doeskin garment was pulled awry, she came into the central space before the great fire.

Every inch an Indian woman she looked, with the no-wak-wa berries darkening her bright cheeks, her moccasins and beaded garment belted with wampum got from the Indians by Henri, save for one thing, no Indian woman in all the wilderness wrapped her braids around her head and pinned them with whittled pegs. There alone had she blundered.

As the renegades loosed her and dropped away, leaving her alone in the appalling light, for one instant she flung her hands over her face.

The quick disaster stunned her.

There was no longer hope within her for the moment. But, with the rise of the roar of triumph, that part of her nature which joyed in the facing of odds snatched down her hands, lifted her head, and set the old fires sparkling in her eyes.

"White! White! White!" was the cry lifting on all sides. "A white woman of the Settlements! Wis-kend-jac has sent the White Doe! A sign! A sign! The Great Spirit would know the slayer of Negansahima!"

"The White Doe shall choose!"

CHAPTER XXIII

THE PAINTED POST

When McElroy's eyes fell upon the woman he loved the breath was stopped in his throat. For a moment it seemed he would suffocate with the surge of emotions that choked him. Then a great sigh filled his lungs and a cry was forced from him which pierced the uproar like an arrow.

"Maren!" he cried, in anguish; "Maren!"

It drew her eyes as the pole the faithful needle, and across the fire they stared wide-eyed at each other.

Then De Courtenay's silver voice cut them apart.

"Again, Ma'amselle!" he cried, with the old magic of his smile. "Do you bring by any chance a red flower to the council of the Nakonkirhirinons?"

But the Indians closed in around her, pulling and plucking at her with eager fingers, and they saw her fighting among them like a man.

McElroy for the first time loosed his tongue in blasphemy and cursed like a madman, tugging at the bonds which

Vingie E. Roe

held him.

"'Tis all in a day's march, M'sieu," said De Courtenay, "and the sweet spirit of Ma'amselle is like to cross the Styx with us."

But for the first time, also, there was in his tone a note of weariness, a breath of sadness that sang under the light words with infinite pathos.

The new attraction drew the crowd, and the old ones were left in solitude, while the Nakonkirhirinons surged and scrambled for a look at the white woman fallen from a clear sky, leagues from where they had seen her. Half-breeds, dissolute renegades, and Indians, they pushed and peered and in many a face was already burning the excitement of her beauty, especially those of the savage Bois-Brules.

McElroy prayed aloud to God for the heavens to fall, for some great disaster.

But soon it became apparent that something of importance was to take place. A hundred headmen gathered in knots and there was dissension and brawling and once near a riot, while the girl stood in a circle of malodorous, leering humans with her back against a tree, warding off hands with man-like blows.

There was no order in the tribe. Negansahima, whose iron hand had ruled with power and justice above the average, was dead. The new chief had not yet come into power with fitting ceremony, and thus the old men of the tribe were for the moment authority, and, as too many cooks spoil the broth, so too many rulers breed dissension.

But finally a conclusion was reached.

A hundred hands scurried into preparation and the shouts were filled with anticipation.

In the open space a post was set up, tall as a man's head and some two feet thick, adzed flat on one side and painted in two sections, perpendicularly, one half in red, the other in black. A medicine man, hideous in adornments of buffalo horns and bearskin, approached De Courtenay and with a feather painted on his bare breast a circle of black with little red flames within.

McElroy was decorated in like manner, save that his circle was red and it enclosed a death-maul, a dozen little arrows, and two knives.

Thus was foreshadowed the manner of their death.

Then arose a babble of voices.

"The White Doe! The White Doe that runs in the forest! Now shall She who Follows decide!"

And into the midst of the vast circle once more Maren Le Moyne was brought. She stood panting as they drew back and left her, and McElroy looked upon her as he had never looked upon living being in all his days.

There was the same high head, shining in the light, the same tall form sweet in its rounded womanhood, the same strong shoulders, and from them hung the white garment that he had carried to her door that day, in spring. He had wondered then if he would ever see it cling to the swelling breast, set up the round throat from its foamy fringe. And thus he saw it again as he had dreamed, though, Holy Mother! in what sad plight!

She had told him she would wear it. She had relied upon it to help her get to De Courtenay! Of what depth and glory must be the love that sent her after the savages! Even in the stress of the moment the old pain came back an hundredfold. But events went forward and he had soon no time to think.

They drew a line upon the earth as they had done before, squabbling over its distance from the painted post; Bois-Brules, their keen eyes gleaming, haggling for a greater stretch, and presently Maren stood upon that line and they had pressed into her hand a bright new hatchet, one of those bought from McElroy himself in the first days of trading.

Then an Indian, naked and painted like a fiend, whose toes turned out, stepped forth and spoke in good English.

"Woman Who Follows," he said distinctly, "one of these two dogs is a murderer,—having killed the Great Chief when his people came in peace to trade at the Fort. Therefore, one of them must die. The Nakonkirhirinons take a skin for a skin,—not two skins for one. So did the Great Chief teach his people. But none know which hand is red with his blood. For two sleeps and a sun have the braves given them the tests,—the Test of the Flying Knives, the Test of the Pine Splinters, the Test of the Little Lines, but neither has shown Colour of the Dog's Blood. Therefore, justice waits. Now has Wiskend-jac, the Great Spirit, sent the White Doe from the forest to decide. Throw, White Woman, and where the tomahawk strikes shall Death sit. Hi-a-wo!"

The renegade stepped back and a silence like death itself fell upon the assembly.

Then did the colour drain out of the soft cheeks under the berry stain and the girl from Grand Portage stand fingering the bright hatchet in her hand. Her eyes went to McElroy's face and then to that of the cavalier leaning forward between his swinging curls, and both men saw the shine that was like light behind black marble, so mystic was it and thrilling, beginning to flicker in them.

"Bravo!" cried De Courtenay, his brilliant face aglow with the splendid hazard. "Bravo! We are akin, Ma'amselle,—both venturers, and my blood leaps to your spirit! Throw, Sweetheart, throw! And may the gods of Chance guide your hand!"

"Think not of me, Maren!" cried McElroy, in deadly earnest. "You owe me naught! Throw for M'sieu, whose peril is my doing!"

For many moments she stood so, fingering the white handle of the weapon, and there was no sound in all the vast assemblage save the crackle of the flames. Then they saw her muscles tauten throughout her whole young body, saw her draw herself up to her full height, and again for a second's space she stood still. In that moment she had deliberately put herself back in the surging turmoil of Grand Portage, was listening to the words of old Pierre Vernaise: "Well done, Little Maid! Again now! Into the cleft! Into the cleft! Ah-a! Little One, well done! Alas, but you beat your old teacher!"—was feeling again the surge of a childhood triumph which scorned to bring nearer that wilderness of her dreams.

With a swift motion her arm shot up and forward and the tomahawk left her hand, flying straight as an arrow for the target. It struck with a clean impact and stood, the handle a little raised and the point well set in the green wood. There was a rush of the medicine men, who seemed to act as judges, and then a silence. Peering, bending near to look closer, they gathered with confusion of voices and presently stepped back, that all might see.

Neither in black nor red, but directly between the two, the blade cleaved cleanly down the dividing-line.

They surged forward, gathering round like flies with buzzing and excitement, examining it from all sides, while the girl stood upon the line with her hands shut hard beside her.

She did not glance again at the two men beside the fire.

A sachem pulled out the hatchet and carried it back to her, while the circle formed and widened again.

Again she stood at poise, again they saw the tension of her body, again the little wait, while the two men held their breath and De Courtenay's eyes were shining like stars.

"A fitting close!" he was saying to himself, in that joy which was of his venturer's soul and knew not time or place. "Heart of my Life! What a close to a merry span!"

Again the swift, sure motion, unmeasured of the brain, coming out of habit and pure instinct, again the "thud" of the strike, again the rush, and again the wondering buzz of talk.

Once more the hatchet stood upon the line between the black and the red, directly in its own cleft!

There was wondering comment, gesticulation, and swarthy faces turned upon the woman on the line.

Once more the sachem in his waving feathers and tinkling ornaments drew the blade from the post and gravely carried it back to her.

Excitement was riding high in the eager faces bending forward on all sides, and everywhere a growing admiration.

A tribe of prowess themselves, the Nakonikirhirinons knew a clever feat when they saw it.

For the third time the tall woman in the beaded garment took the hatchet and squared her shoulders.

"What does it mean?" McElroy was thinking wildly; "why does she not save him while there is time?" And, even as the words went through his brain, something snapped therein and he was conscious of the circle of faces in the forest edge waving in grotesque undulations, of the arm of Maren as it straightened forward, of the flash of the hatchet as it flew for the painted post, and then of great darkness sewn with a thousand stars.

As Maren had raised her hand for the throw, from somewhere out of the darkness behind the fire a stone death-maul had hurtled, aimed at her wrist, but he who threw was sorry of sight as a drunken man, for it struck the head of McElroy instead and he sagged down against the moosehide thongs, even as the hatchet once more clicked snugly in its former cleft.

Then from all the concourse there went up a shout, half in anger and half in wild applause.

"Nik-o-men-wa!" they cried; "the Thrower of the Seven Tribes! But the White Doe plays with the decree of Gitche Manitou! Bring the spear! Fetch forth the spears, oh, Men of Wisdom!"

But in the midst of the excitement a figure walked slowly forth in the light and held up a hand for silence.

It was Edmonton Ridgar.

Reluctantly they obeyed, sullenly, as if bound by a bond against their will.

In the sudden hush he spoke.

"What do ye here, my brothers?" he asked, and waited.

There was no reply from the mass before him.

"Wherefore is the spirit of my Father vexed that it disturbs my watch inside the death-lodge?"

The small rustling of the excited crowd ceased in every quarter.

They stilled themselves in a peculiar manner.

"Oh, ye sachems and Men of Wisdom," he said, turning to the headmen gathered together, "come ye to the tepee of Negansahima and behold what ye have done!"

Slowly, as he had come, the chief trader of De Seviere turned about and passed out of the light. One by one, in utter silence, their faces changed in a moment into masks of uneasiness, the sachems and medicine men rose and followed. In the wavering shadows thrown by the central fire the big tepee stood in awesome majesty. Ridgar raised the flap and entered, dropping it as the savages filed in to the number of all it would hold.

"See!" he said dramatically.

Over the bier of piled skins which held the wrapped and smoke-dried figure of the dead chief there danced upon the darkness, eerie in pale-green living fire, the ghost of the crested and sweeping head-dress that he had worn in life.

There was never a word among them, but, with one accord, after one awe-struck look at the ghostly thing, they fled the lodge in a mass.

For several moments Ridgar stood in the darkness as those outside peered fearfully in, and, when the last moccasin had slipped silently away, he reached up and took down the fearsome thing, folding it beside the chief.

"We were wise together, old friend," he said sadly; "would I had your knowledge and your power."

Outside the word was spreading wildly.

"The spirit of Negansahima rests not in the lodge! The medicine men have not dreamed true! Silence in the camp while They who Dream repair to the forest fastnesses and seek true wisdom!"

And while the sachems and the headmen, the beaters of the tom-toms, and those who tended the Sacred fires of the Dreamers formed into procession and slowly filed out into the forest, Edmonton Ridgar drew a long breath of relief. Maren had postponed the sure culmination of the tests by her clever feat, he had postponed it a little longer by his own. Full well he knew that the girl could not go on forever after the manner of her beginning. She knew the hatchet, but would she know the spear, the arrow, and the Test of the Flaming Ring? .Sooner or later she would fail, and then would come the last orgy of the rites of a Skin for a Skin. He thought of the whimsical fate which so oddly gave the "Pro pelle cutem" of the H. B. C. to this unknown tribe of the North, and flayed one with the other.

This night was the last wherein there lay one chance of help for the two men and this woman who had so strangely followed from the post, and he lay in the darkness of the death-lodge watching the hushing of the camp, the loosing of the captives, the carrying of his factor, a limp figure, to the lodge of captives on the edge, the leading thither of De Courtenay and Maren.

"Fool woman!" he said in his heart; "sweet, brave, loving fool with the woman's heart and the man's simple courage!"

CHAPTER XXIV

THE STONE TO THE FOOT OF LOVE

Long Ridgar lay in the darkness listening to the hushed sounds that came from lodge and dying fire—vague, awed sounds, that presently died into silence as night took toll of humanity and sleep settled among the savages.

Here and there low gutturals droned into the stillness, and at the west there was oath and whispered comment where the Bois-Brules camped together. Not wholly under the spell of mystery were these half-breeds, but restless and suspicious under the conflicting promptings of their mixed blood. Slower than the Indians were they to obey the mandate of silence and peace that the Spirits of Dreams might descend upon the forest, but at last they were quiet, the tires burned down to red heaps of coals, then to white ashes, the great fire in the centre flamed and died and flamed again like some vindictive spirit striving for vengeance in the grip of death, and the utter stillness of the solitude fell thick as a garment on all the wilderness. It seemed to Ridgar that only himself in all the earth was awake and watching, save perhaps the two guards pacing without a sound the lodge of the captives, and those two within, so oddly brought near.

As for McElroy, his friend of friends, an aching fear tugged

Vingie E. Roe

in his heart that he had waited too long for the chance to help, that the patient strength was sapped at last, that the end had come. He had seen the flight of the maul, the sagging of the sturdy figure.

Who had thrown it, if not that brute DesCaut? Who save DesCaut was so keen on the trail of the factor and the girl? True, De Courtenay was his latest master, and his spoiling of Maren's aim might as easily send the blade into the black as the red, but in either case he would cause her to decide the death she was trying so bravely to postpone.

DesCaut, surely.

The stars wheeled in their endless march, the well-known ones of the forenight giving place to strangers of the after hours, and Ridgar had begun to move with the caution of the hunted, inch by inch, out from the shelter of the lodge, when he felt a hand steal from the darkness and touch him with infinite care. He lay still and presently a voice whispered,

"M'sieu Ridgar?"

"Aye?" breathed Ridgar.

"'Tis I,—Marc Dupre from De Seviere."

"Voila! Another! Are there more of you?"

"I would know first, M'sieu,—where is your heart, with savage or Hudson's Bay?"

"Fair question, truly. I but now am started for yonder lodge on quest of their deliverance, though without hope. Your appearance lends me that."

"Sacre! 'Tis done already. Listen, M'sieu, with all your ears. Just beyond earshot, up the river to the south there lies a big canoe, with at its nose for instant action two men of Mowbray's brigade, while a hundred yards inland another waits, armed and ready to cover a hurried flight. There needs but loosing of those yonder, M'sieu, and here are we. Two Indians pace the lodge.... You one, me one. What easier?

"Many things, my young hot-blood. Yet it is our only way. Here are death-mauls,—two. Take you,—they make no sound, provided a practised hand is behind. Strike near and ease the fall, there are those who sleep lightly here. Even the earth has ears to-night."

"Think you Ma'amselle is bound?" whispered Dupre next; "I could not see for the swinging of the factor's body."

"No," replied the trader; "both she and the Nor'wester walked free. But how, for love of Heaven, comes she here?" he added.

Dupre sighed softly in the darkness.

"For love," he said; "for love of a man."

"I had guessed as much,—how how did she pass the many miles of lake and stream and forest? And how overtake us?"

"I brought her. By day and night also, without camp, have we come, aided by canoe-men from Mr. Mowbray's brigade, which we met on the eastern shore of Winnipeg coming down from York, bound for the Assiniboine and Cumberland House."

"But for which man? She is unreadable, that woman, though love lives naked in her face."

But a sudden ache had gripped the throat of the young trapper and he did not answer.

"Let us be off, M'sieu," he whispered; "now is the time."

"Aye,—if ever."

Slowly, inch by inch, lifting their bodies that they might not rustle the loose earth and trampled leaves of the camp, Ridgar and Dupre drew forth into the shadows.

Meantime, within the skin tepee, where all three had been summarily placed, Maren Le Moyne sat with her head upon her arms and her arms crossed on her drawn-up knees. Across the opening, just inside the flap, the body of McElroy lay inert, though she knew that a low breath rose and fell within him, for she had laid a hand upon his breast. Beside her, close in the darkness, De Courtenay sat upright and alert, as if no forty hours of torture had hail their will of him. She could hear his quick breathing.

Anguish rode her soul like a thousand imps and the slow tears were falling, bitter as aloes, the symbol of defeat. Every fibre of her being trembled with love of the man stretched beyond; she longed with all the passion of her nature to gather the tawny head in her arms, to kiss the silent lips, the closed eyes. Through the dim cloud that seemed to envelop him since that night at the factory steps, holding her from him like bars of iron, she heard again the ringing sweetness of his voice:

"From this day forth you are mine! Mine only and against the whole world! I have taken you and you are mine!"

False as Lucifer, but, O bon Dieu! sweet as salvation to the lost

A hundred feelings tore at her heart,—bitterness and unbearable scorn of her own blundering, and wild protest against failure, but chief of all was the love that drew her to this man like running water to the sea.

Now that death was near, so near that even now it might be calling his earnest spirit out of the darkness, she would do more—a thousandfold!—to give him life. Only life, the gentle, strong soul of him safe in the sturdy body!

And she had but hastened the end she had come to avert!

"Jesu mia," she prayed, from the shelter of her arms, "help! Help Thou—Lord of Heaven, give him to be spared!"

And not once did she think of the great quest, broken by a meagre waiting by the way; no thought crossed her mind in this crisis of the Land of the Whispering Hills, of an old man, dreaming his dreams in the wilderness.

Thus had love set aside like a bauble the thing for which her life had been lived, for which she had grown and prepared herself in the attainments of men.

She had felt the magic touch of the great mystery, and henceforth she was captive, servant to its will, and its mandate had been service. And here was the end—

A hand touched her shoulder, a hand infinitely soft of pressure, infinitely gentle.

"Ma'amselle," whispered the cavalier in her ear, "one more turn of the wheel of Fate,—and we take the plunge together. Kin are we, truly; kin of the tribe of Daring Hearts. A lioness are you, oh, maid with the Madonna face! No woman, but a creature of the wild, superb in courage and unknown to fear!

Vingie E. Roe

I saw it in your face that day in De Seviere,—the something alien to the common race, the spark, the light; oh, I know not what it is, save that it is Divine and yet splendidly of the earth! We are matched in heart. Venturers both, and like true venturers we shall take the longest trail with a laugh and our hands together,—and trust to the Aftermath to give us largess of that love which has its beginning in such glorious wise. Pledge me, oh, my Queen of the World!"

With a grace beyond compare he drew her into his arms, silent and velvet soft, light and inimitable in his love way.

In utter astonishment Maren felt his silken curls sweep her cheek, his lips on hers. Her tears were wet on his face. She put up her hands and pushed him loose.

"M'sieu!" she said, "what do you do?"

"Do? Why, bow to the One Woman of my heart," he said; "my Maid of the Red Flower, whom love has led to share my fate."

"In all pity! M'sieu, you do mistake most grievously!"

"What? Was it not confession at the post gate when this painted rabble fell upon us? Or is it still the maiden within fearing the word of love? In such short space, Sweetheart, there is no time for girlish fears. Be strong in that as in the courage of the lone trail. Speak!"

"Speak?" said Maren, with her old calmness; "of a surety, M'sieu. Though I have thrilled at your careless bravery, your laughing daring which, as you say truly, is kin of my heart,—though I have taken your red flowers, yet there is in me no spark of love for you, no thought beyond the admiration of a true son of fortune. That alone, M'sieu."

De Courtenay was staring at her in the blackness of the lodge, his arm fallen loose about her shoulders.

"Name of God!" he whispered wonderingly, "it is not love? Then what, in the living world, has brought you over the waste to this camp of hostile savages?"

"This," said Maren, and she reached a hand to the body of McElroy.

"Sancta Maria! This factor? This heavy-blooded man?.... But he did speak of half-requited—Oh, Saints of Heaven! What a jest of the world! The threads of tragedy are tangled into a farce!"

De Courtenay threw up his head and took a silent laugh at the ways of Fate.

"Three fools together! And the riddle's key too late! At least I can set it straight for one—"

He broke his laughing whisper to listen to new sounds without, a dull blow, muffled and heavy, the slight whisper of garments sliding against garments, the crunch and rustle of a body eased down to earth,—nay, two blows, coming at a little interval, and from either end the beat walked by the two guards, and from the southern end there came a grunt, a cry choked in the throat that uttered it. Instantly the venturer was up and. at the flap, peering outside. A figure loomed against the stars, paced slowly by with an audible step, passed and turned and passed again.

It was Marc Dupre, an eagle feather, snatched from the quivering form of the guard lying in the darkness by the wall of the lodge, slanting from his head against the heavens.

A little way beyond at the ashes of a fire a warrior stirred, lifted a head, and peered toward the tepee of captives; then, satisfied that all was well, lay down again to slumber. Back and forth, back and forth paced the solitary watcher. De Courtenay within was quivering from head to foot with the knowledge that something was happening. As he stood so the pacing figure halted a moment before the opening.

"S-s-t!" it whispered; "warn Ma'amselle!" then walked away.

Swift on the words another figure crept noiselessly to the lodge door.

"M'sieu," said Edmonton Ridgar, beneath his breath, "give me the factor's shoulders. Do you take his feet and follow,—softly, for your life. Bring the maid."

De Courtenay stepped back, groped for Maren, took her head in his hands, and brought her ear up to his lips.

"Rescue!" he breathed; "Ridgar and Dupre. We carry our friend of the fort here. Follow."

He loosed her and bent to lift McElroy.

With all her courage leaping at the turn, Maren quietly raised the flap and in a moment they were all outside among the sleeping camp.

With measured tread Dupre came up to them, walked with them as they moved silently back, and was on the turn when Maren touched his arm.

"This way," she whispered; "straight ahead."

One more step,—two,—the youth took beside her. It seemed

that the heart within him was breaking in his agony. The shadows of the wood were drawing very near, the chances of escape multiplying with every step.

Another sweet moment of nearness and the misty white figure beside him would fade into the darkness forever, pass forever out of his sight.

Dearer than all the joys of Paradise was that black head, that wondrous face with its strength and its tenderness so adoringly mingled. The one supreme thing in all the universe was this woman,—and she was passing. With an involuntary motion he touched her softly and she stopped instantly, even at that great moment. It thrilled through him, that quick perception of his desire.

"Ma'amselle," he whispered, "fare thee well!"

She caught his hand swiftly, pulling him forward. "Eh?" she said. "What mean you?"

There was startled anxiety in her voice and the heart of Dupre leaped exultantly.

"Naught," he lied bravely, "save that I must hang behind for a moment or so to cover any sound with my sentry's step, but I cannot part from you even so small a space without,—God-speed. Hurry now, Ma'amselle! They pass from sight!"

He pushed her gently after, but she turned against his hand.

"Come!" she commanded; "I will not leave you!"

"Nay,—how long, think you, before utter silence awakes that mob? You must be at the water's edge before I follow. Go now,—quick, for love of Heaven!"

He pushed her away and turned back toward the camp, pacing slowly by the huddled heap that attested Ridgar's hand, past the empty lodge, and on to the northern turn, where lay that other figure prone upon the earth, yet still quivering in every muscle. He died hardly, this strong North warrior, and Dupre almost regretted the need, though the trapper of the Pays d'en Haut took without thought whatever of life menaced his own and considered the deed accomplishment.

Back and forth, back and forth he walked the beat of the watcher and a holy joy played over his soul like a light from the beyond. He turned his mind to that hour in the woods, to the memory of the lips of Maren Le Moyne, the warm sweetness of her beaded breast, the tender affection of her embrace, and the present faded into that land of dreams wherein walk those who love greatly.

Meanwhile Ridgar and De Courtenay pushed silently forward with the limp body of McElroy swinging between, while the girl stepped softly in their trail, straining her ears for sounds from the camp, and carrying the only weapon among them, a rifle which Ridgar had taken from the Indian he had killed.

"To the east," she whispered, "down the little defile to the river, then south along the shore,—it is shingled and open,— to the canoe. Walk fast as you can, M'sieu."

It was riskful going through the strip of woods, but when they entered the little canon that cleft a ridge of cliffs, rising impudently out of a level land, they mended their pace. Here was solid, dry rock beneath them, walls of rock on either side, and a narrow strip of star-strewn sky above.

"Thank God!" Ridgar was saying, under his breath, "the

distance widens!"

But no sooner were the words out of his mouth than a cold chill shot through him, and Maren pushed forward with compelling hands on De Courtrnay's shoulders.

"Hurry, M'sieu!" she cried; "they have awakened!"

"Hi! Hi! Hi-a! He-a! Hi!"

Danger was waking in the camp behind, first with one sharp cry, then another and another, until throat after throat took up the sound and the yapping turned into a roar.

They were but half-way through the narrow gorge. The two men broke into a stumbling run. Ridgar was going backwards, half-turned to see ahead, and suddenly his foot struck a loose pebble and he fell headlong. De Courtenay stumbled, and in the scramble to right themselves they lost more time than they could spare. Before they were up and started, a shrill voice came into the gorge, yelling its "Hi! Hi! Hi-a!"

De Courtenay suddenly stopped.

"'Tis useless!" he said breathlessly; "We'll never make it! Here,—do you take my place, Ma'amselle!"

He caught Maren's shoulder and pushed her forward.

"Take his knees,—so! You are strong,—give me the rifle. Make haste, Ridgar,—Ma'amselle!"

He bowed in the darkness.

"The last turn of the wheel, Ma'amselle,—and I take the plunge alone. All in the day's march!"

With the last words he turned back to face the way they had come, shook his long curls back across his shoulder, and lifted the rifle to his cheek.

The footsteps of Ridgar and Maren were echoing down the rocky gap.

It had been a promising escape, a neat plan well carried out, and there was but one thing lacking to its fulfilment,—another step to pace the deserted lodge of captives.

Across in the darkness among the Bois-Brules one ear had lain close to the tell-tale earth, one evil face peered unsleeping among the dusky shapes of the camp, a swarthy face with a white lock on its temple.

Keener than all the rest, Bois DesCaut, driven by personal hate, listened to all the sounds of night.

And he had heard a changing in the steps that passed and repassed, that separated and came together, before that lodge across the sleeping mob,—a change, a little silence, and then the steps again that presently thinned to ONE,—one step that paced evenly, with a measured tread, a moccasined step like that of an Indian, yet somehow alien in its firmness and swing.

One step where there should have been two,—and the half-breed trapper raised himself and gave the first "Hi! Hi!"

Like startled wolves they were up all around him in a moment and down on that empty tepee with its one sentry!

A torch flared redly with the sudden revealing of a slim youth in buckskins and two Nakonkirhirinon warriors deep in the Great Sleep.

What was there for Marc Dupre in that moment of roused fury,—that tense moment of awaking rage, of baffled rights of payment?

What but death too swift and unrestrained for torture?

A dozen weapons reached him from as many crowding hands and he went down on the last earth her feet had trod, the spot where she had last touched his hand.

Her golden voice, sweet with its sliding minors, was in his ears, the sweetness of her lips on his.

"A stone to your foot, Ma'amselle," he whispered, as the darkness broke and the stars began to dance on a sky of blood-red fire; "serve you with my life,—no better fate,—oh, I love you! I—a stone to your foot,—Ma'amselle!"

And at that moment Maren Le Moyne, straining every muscle of her young body to save the man she loved, looked swiftly back, having left the defile to stagger, stumbling, southward to where Mowbray's men waited with the canoe.

She saw the sudden flaming of the torch, the slim, boyish figure in its buckskins, the ring of faces, and the flash of weapons; saw the forms close in and the slim boy go down like a reed in the winter storm, and a cry broke from her lips as De Courtenay's rifle began to sound in the gorge.

With tears on her cheeks and her face drawn hard, she raised her head and gave a panther's far-off call.

Vingie E. Roe

CHAPTER XXV

ANSWERED PRAYERS

Out of the forest at the signal came running Alloybeau and McDonald and Frith, alert, ready for anything, wondering beyond wonder at the call that meant deliverance. Not one of them had thought to see again this strange, intrepid woman who pierced the forbidden places and wound men like Mr. Mowbray around her fingers. It would have been a toss-up for men to attempt what she had done.

She was coming to the canoe, and she was victorious. Yet they knew that death was up and at her heels, from the sound of the shots.

The big canoe was in the water, the men were ready, paddle in hand, with Wilson knee-deep in the stream ready to push off, when along the reach of shore there came that sorry ending to the gallant venture,—Ridgar and the girl, staggering, stumbling, trying to make what haste they could, with swinging roughly between them the apparently lifeless body of the factor of Fort de Seviere.

Breathless and exhausted they reached the boat. Brilliers and Wilson reached for their burden, threw it into the bottom, and hauled Maren on her knees among the thwarts.

There was a shove, a word, a dip of the paddles, and the canoe shot out to the deeper waters, and none aboard her saw the form of Edmonton Ridgar draw back into the shelter of tangled vines on shore.

"Give me a blade!"

From the rocking bottom Maren was reaching for a paddle, got it, thrust by some one into her hands, and was cleaving water with the best of them, deep stroke after deep stroke, the rush and suck of the eddy in her ears.

In the cold blue darkness the stream whispered and warned like some old witch at her cauldron, the night was clammy, and behind the new fires flared against the towering trees.

A babble of voices told of pursuit,—shouts and gutturals that strung out from the camp all through the gorge and were beginning to flow with the river.

"Only a matter of time,—a little time," thought Wilson, at the prow, but never a word was uttered in the canoe.

Exerting every atom of strength, calling on all the will-power aboard, they shot forward into the night and the current.

The noise behind increased, as the tones of a bell blown by the wind increase when the wind sets in one's direction.

"Not now!" Maren was saying to herself. "Not now,—when we are so far toward the winning! Not now,—oh, Friend of my heart! why was that price demanded? Holy Mary rest him, that young Marc Dupre—and send deliverance for this—"

Ahead the river swept around a turn. Keeping close to the

shore they caught shallow water and cut round into a wider opening.

The cries behind veered and deadened, and suddenly Wilson in the prow raised his blade.

Maren leaned behind him and looked into the shadows.

On every side dark shapes covered the face of the stream like water-bugs, from every side there came the "whoo-sh-st-whoo-sh" of dipping paddles, the little plank and rattle of their shafts against gunwales.

They had glided into the midst of a flotilla of canoes travelling at night and in silence.

The maid from Grand Portage threw up her head.

"In among them," she whispered, "quick! Deep as we can!"

"But, Ma'amselle," whispered back Wilson, "they may be Indians."

"What matters? A chance is a chance, and who would not risk its turning?"

Unconsciously she was quoting that kinsman whose dauntless courage and love of venture had found its last thrill in covering her retreat in the gorge.

"In among them! Deep!"

Softly, as one of their number, the fugitive craft crept out to midstream and forward, usurping boldly place and speed.

Leaning low at each stroke the little company strained eye

and ear for sight and sound, but, look as they might, they saw no eagle feathers against the stars, heard no word or whisper.

Barely had they reached their uncertain sanctuary when the light of torches shot southward across the bend and next moment circled, a far-reaching arm, to spread out and illumine the river broadcast as the Nakonkirhirinons swept into view, their savage faces peering under the raised flambeaux, their eyes like fiery points—searching their prey.

It fell on all the river, that light, on the running waters disturbed by myriad blades of white ash, on the banked background of the trees, on the drooping foliage at the stream's edge,—frail triflers of the wilderness, stooping from the sweet winds of Heaven to the water's wanton kiss,—and on a swarm of canoes, each manned by full complement of men, most of whose faces were eagle-featured and dark, blackeyed and high-cheekboned, though here and there were the fair hair and white skin of white men.

Odd, indeed, was the effect of this tableau on the Indians under the torches. They had come for one lone canoe,—to find a horde; for one man and one woman,—to fall upon a brigade.

They halted and the distance widened between.

And then the flotilla parted at a word of command from the darkness ahead and a boat came back among them. It passed close to the fugitives, and Maren saw a tall man with a square chin, who stood up in it.

When it reached the fringe it went on out into the open water toward the halted canoes of the Nakonkirhirinons, on whose eager faces sat a sort of stupid awe.

"What do yez want?" called the tall man sternly, as he swept face to face with the foremost canoe in which stood a headman of the tribe. "Whyfore is all this bally-hoo wid th' lights?"

There was no answer and he roared at them like a lion

"Can yez not shpake, ye haythen?"

Whereat a canoe glided from the back shadows and the voice of Bois DesCaut came in its broken English,

"A boat,—M'sieu,—we seek a boat that but now escaped from camp with a murderer aboard,—one who killed in cold blood the chief Negansahima back at the post of De Seviere. My brothers travel to the Pays d'en Haut that justice may be done. We only seek the murderer."

The tall man stood in silence a moment and glared at the scene, at the excited faces, the gleaming eyes, the shifting glance of the spokesman.

"A likely sthory!" he said presently. "An' who, may I make bould to ask, is this murderer?"

DesCaut squirmed a moment in silence.

"Who,—did ye say?"

"A man, M'sieu,—a-a-trapper."

"One lone man? Troth I commend his valour in evadin' such a rabble o' hell-spawn! An' what from did he escape,—th' sthake an' th' stretchline?"

"Justice, M'sieu,—his life for the chief's."

"Ho-ho! From th' looks o' yer fri'nds, me lad, I'm thinkin' 'twill be justice wid her eyes shut!... But ye may turrn back an' search the forest,—we have no sthrangers in our party."

DesCaut glowered at him a moment and spoke to the headmen around in their speech. There were threatening gutturals and gestures.

The flotilla was small compared to that of the tribe back at the gorge, they would know, at any rate.

"They say, if M'sieu will let one canoe go through his people with the torches, all will be well. Otherwise,—five hundred warriors, M'sieu, can take their will with two hundred."

"Aye?" said the tall man, jerking his head around. He had been scanning the mass of his own craft, packed behind him, fading into the shadows out of the light. There was a peculiar look in his eyes when he faced DesCaut again, a thrust to his square jaw. In that backward look he had caught sight of the brown face of Maren Le Moyne, the white garment, glittering with its beads,—but he had seen, too, the crown of braids, wrapped round her head after the manner of the white woman.

"Go yer ways," he said; "we thravel fast on urgent business,—ye cannot throuble us wid yer lookin' an' pokin'. Tell yer fri'nds—No."

At this there was commotion among the Indians. A hurried consultation took place, with indrawing of canoes under the flambeaux, waving arms, and angry gestures.

"Then, M'sieu,—we come,—make way!" It was DesCaut, important and ugly.

"No, ye don't, me lad. Shwing back The Little Devil, bhoys!"

The leader's canoe shifted sidewise and another craft, heavy, lumbersome, and vastly bigger than the light boats of the rest poked its nose into its place,—and that nose was brass and round with a gaping maw,—a small cannon, scarcely big enough for the name, but a roaring braggart for all that.

"Belch, me darlin', if ye have th' belly-ache!" cried this tall man, and, without more warning, there was a tremendous flash and detonation, a mighty flying of the clear waters just under the bows of the foremost canoes of the Indians.

There was hiss and sputter of the torches, an upward leap of canoe and savage, capsize and panic and fear, and the night screamed with many voices.

"Formation again, lads!" called the sturdy voice of the leader. "We do be wastin' time wid these haythen!"

The canoe rounded, passed up between the others, which closed in behind, and the cannon-boat lumbered into place in the rear.

As he passed the strangers in their midst the tall man looked hard at Maren, the five men, and leaned out a bit to see what lay in the bottom.

"A close shave!" he said; "kape close in the middle an' shpake me at camp in the marnin'."

The mass of dark objects, drawing out of the light, moved forward and, with a rush of intuition, the girl knew that all danger was past and that safety hovered over them like the luminous wings of an angel.

"Holy Master!" she cried within, "Thou didst answer my prayer,—but at what cost! Oh, Lord of Heaven, what cost!"

Then she dropped her blade and, under cover of the darkness, sat back upon her heels, covered her face with her hands, and wept.

In the silence that had fallen deep again, save for the lessening tumult behind, her weeping sounded to the outermost canoe low and awful, hard and terrible as the weeping of a man.

She did not even feel if the breath was still in McElroy.

Friendship was taking its toll of love.

CHAPTER XXVI

SANCTUARY

"'Twas yer leader I meant, lassie, should rayport to me. Is it he I saw yez rollin' out like a bag o' beans?"

"Nay, M'sieu," said Maren Le Moyne, standing before the tall man in the flush of dawn at the morning camp, her eyes red-rimmed and the curling corners of her mouth drooped and sad; "what poor leader there is among us has been myself."

"Eh?"

All along the river bank were little fires, their blue smoke curling up to the blue sky above, the bustle and fuss of preparation for the morning meal. At one place in the centre of camp two women, their appearance that of great fatigue, were languidly directing the work of a couple of Indians. An abundance of truck was everywhere—utensils for cooking, clothing, and blankets out of all reason to one used to the trail.

These things had not escaped Maren as she came through them in search of the leader. They all set his status in her mind, told her much of the history of her rescuers.

"Eh?" he said in surprise again; "you the leader? An' whatlike was the evil hap that placed ye in among that rabble o' painted beauties, may I ask? An' how comes a slip of a lass"—he looked her over from head to heel with his sharp grey eyes; "—well, not so much a slip, still a colleen—like you wid th' command o' men in this part o' th' world?"

"Of a surety you may ask, M'sieu, and it will be my happiness to tell you, since but for you and your quick help, given without knowledge, we should be now in sorry plight."

"The man you saw taken from the canoe is Monsieur Anders McElroy, Factor of Fort de Seviere on the Assiniboine, and of the Hudson's Bay Company."

"Faith of me fathers! Say ye so! A man of our own men!"

"Aye. Then you are also of the Company? Good! Surely have we fallen on the lap of fortune.... Those Indians, Nakonkirhirinons from the far north and strangers in this country, came to De Seviere to trade. For two—three dais, maybe more,—I have lost track of time, M'sieu,—they passed up and down at the trading,—camped on the shoreand all seemed well, though they were wild and shy as partridges. One man among them seemed to wear the cloak of civilisation,—Negansahima the chief.

"Then one day at dusk,—it was a soft day, gold and sweet, M'sieu, and soft, with all the post at the great gate watching the Indians,—there were many,—four or five hundred warriors and as many women and children,—this day there was,—a tragedy. Something happened,—a trifle."

The girl stopped a moment and a sigh caught her breath.

"Just a trifle—but two men fought at the gate, the factor and another—a Nor'wester from the Saskatchewan,—a long-haired venturer,—a man from Montreal, but a brave man, M'sieu, oh, a very brave man! They fought and there was the discharge of a pistol,—and—the shot went wild. It slew the good chief, M'sieu. There was uproar,—they swarmed upon the two and bound them."

Maren's eyes were growing large with the remembered excitement of that moment.

The tall Irishman was watching her keenly.

"They bound them and struck away to the north, taking them along, and the burden of their cry was, 'A skin for a skin!'"

"They brought them so far,—they would have reached their own country but for a band of Bois-Brules, who joined them some suns back with that red liquor whose touch is hell to an Indian. They had gone wild, M'sieu; wild!"

She was very weary and she shuddered a bit at the word.

"And,—so,—that is all,—save that we had done that much toward escaping when you found us."

She ceased and looked gravely into his face.

"Howly Moses! I see,—I see! But ye have left a wide rent in th' tale. Wherefore are yez here yerself, lassie?"

"I?" said Maren, swaying where she stood. "I followed, M'sieu."

"Followed? From the Assiniboine? Alone?"

"Nay. There was one came with me,—a youth,—a trapper,—

my comrade, my friend. He died yonder in that surging purgatory—"

The tears were welling to her weary eyes.

"The Nor'wester, Alfred de Courtenay, also—We only of that venture are escaped alive,—a sorry showing. The five men who man my boat belong to the brigade under Mr. Mowbray, which we met on Winnipeg. Such is our small history, M'sieu, and all we ask is your protection out of the reach of the Nakonkirhirinons. I take him back to De Seviere,—God knows if he will live to reach it. He lies so still. But I must get him back—"

She ceased and passed her hand across her eyes.

"I must get him back,—I must get him back."

"Aye, aye. Ye come with me. Ye need a woman's hand, girl. Ye're well in yerself."

There was a huskiness to the sharp voice and the man took her by the arm, turning her toward the fire and the two women. She stumbled a step or two in the short stretch.

"I must go back to him, M'sieu!" she protested. "He will need—will need—broth—and a wet cloth to his bruised head—"

"We'll see to him, don't ye fret. It's shlape ye need yerself. Sheila, whativer do ye think o' this! Here's a colleen shlipped through the fingers of those bow-legged signboards and fair done wid heroism an' strategy, an' Lord knows what all, an' off her feet wid tire! Do ye take her an' feed her. Put her to bed on th' blankets an' do for her like yerself knows how, darlint! 'Tis an angel unaware, I'm thinkin'—an' her on Deer River!"

Vingie E. Roe

One of the women, a little creature with dark hair and blue eyes, Irish eyes "rubbed in with a smutty finger," came forward and looked up into Maren's stained face, streaked with her tears, her eyes dazed and all but closing with the weariness that had only laid its hand upon her in the last few moments, but whose sudden touch was heavy as lead.

"Say ye so!" she said wonderingly; "a girl! So this was what caused the rumpus in the night! But come, dearie, 'tis rest ye want, sure!"

She laid her and on Maren's arm and there was in its gentle touch something which broke down the last quivering strand of strength within the girl, striving to stand upright.

"Yes, Madame," she said dreamily. "Yes, but he must have —he must have—broth—and a bandage,—wet"

"Sure, sure,—he shall,—but come to the blankets!"

As Maren went down with a long sigh, her limbs shirking the last task of straightening themselves upon the softness of the unwonted couch, the little woman looked up across her at the man with a world of questions in her face.

"Poor darlin'!" she said softly. "Whativer is it, Terence?"

"A heroine, if all she says be thrue, an' as unconscious of it as a new-born babe!"

When Maren awoke the sun was straight overhead and some one had been calling from a distance for a very long time.

"Come, come, asthore! Opin yer eyes! That's it! A little more, now. Wake up, for love av Heaven, or we'll all be overtaken be th' Injuns!"

Ah! Indians! At that she opened her eyes and looked into the pretty blue ones she remembered last.

The little woman was kneeling beside her with an arm about her shoulder, trying to lift her heavy head and falling short in the endeavour.

Maren was too much in her muscled height for the bird-like creature. She sat up at once and looked around. The canoes were in the water, all the miscellaneous luggage had been put aboard, and every one was ready for a new start. Only herself, the blanket bed, and the little woman were unready.

Just below, her own canoe, with Brilliers, Wilson, Frith, McDonald, and Alloybeau in place, waited her presence. She could see, from the elevation of the shore, the stretched form of McElroy in the bottom, a bright blanket beneath him and his fair head pillowed on a roll of leaves. A shelter of boughs hid his face, and for one moment her heart stopped while the river and the woods, the people and the boats whirled together in a senseless blur.

She sprang to her feet.

"Is he—" she faltered thickly, "is he—"

"No, no, dearie! He is like he was, only they have fixed him a bit av a shelther from th' sun. Do ye dhrink this now," she coaxed in her pretty voice; "dhrink it, asthore,—ye'll nade it f'r th' thrip."

She held up a bowl of broth, steaming and sweet as the flesh-pots of Egypt, and Maren took it from her.

"But—did M'sieu—Oh, I have slept when I should have tended him!"

"Ye poor girl. Dhrink,—he has been fed like a babe be me own hands. There!"

There were tears in the little woman's eyes, and Maren took the bowl and drained it clear.

"You are good, Madame," she said, with a long breath. "Merci! How good to those in need! But now am I right as a trivet and shamed that I must fail at the last. Are you ready?"

She picked up the blankets, smiled at the tall man who came for them, and walked with them down to the canoes.

"In th' big boat, lass, wid th' women," said the leader; "'tis more roomy-like."

"I thank you, M'sieu, but I have my place. I cannot leave it." And she stepped in her own canoe.

"Did ye iver behold such a shmile, Terence?" cried the little woman, when the flotilla had strung into shape and the green summer shores were slipping past. "'Tis like the look av th' Virgin in th' little Chapel av St. Joseph beyant Belknap's skirts,—so sad and yet as fair as light!"

And so began with the slipping green shores, the airy summer sky laced with its vanity of fleecy clouds, the backward journey to safety and De Seviere.

The large party travelled at forced time, short camps and long pulls, for, as the little woman told Maren at the next stop, they were hurrying south to Quebec.

"Where th' ships sail out to th' risin' sun, ochone, and Home calls over th' sea,—the little green isle wid its pigs an' its shanties, its fairs an' its frolics, an' the merry face av th'

Father to laugh at its weddin's an' cry over its graves. Home that might make a lass forget such a haythen land as this, though God knew if it would ever get out av th' bad dreams at night!

"An' now will ye be afther tellin' us th' sthory av yer adventures, my dear?"

Maren was cooking a broth of wild hen in the little pail of poor Marc Dupre, across the fire, and the little woman was busy watching a bit of bread baking on a smoothed plank. Her companion, a tall, fair-haired woman with pale eyes, light as the grey-green sheen sometimes seen on the waters before a storm, was reclining in tired idleness beside her. This woman had not spoken to Maren, but her cold eyes followed her now with an odd persistence.

"Or is it too wild and sad? If it gives ye pain, don't say a word,—though, wurra! 'tis woild I am to hear!"

Maren looked up, and once more the smile that was stranger to her features played over them in its old-time beauty.

"Nay,—why should I not tell so good a heart as yours?" said the girl simply, and she began at the beginning and told the sorry tale through to its end.

"And so he died, this young trapper with the soul of pearl, and I alone go back to De Seviere with—with M'sieu the factor," she concluded heavily.

"Mother av Heavin! An' which,—forgive me lass,—which man av the three did ye love? For 'tis only love could be behind such deeds as these!"

The ready tears were swimming in the Irishwoman's blue

eyes, straight from her warm heart, and she was leaning forward in the intensity of her sympathy and excitement.

"Which, Madame? Why, M'sieu the factor, surely."

And Maren looked into the red heart of the fire.

With a sudden impulse this daughter of Erin dropped her plank in the ashes, and coming swiftly forward, fell on her knees with her arms around the girl's neck.

"Saints be praised!" she cried, weeping openly. "Saints be praised, ye have him safe! An' there can nothin' ha'arm ye now, with us goin' yer ways so close! An' there'll be a weddin' av coorse whin th' poor lad comes round! F'r a flip av ale I'd command Terence to turn aside an' go triumphant entry-in' to this blessid fort av yours and witness th' ceremonies!"

Maren smiled sadly and laid her hand on the black head tucked into her neck. It was a caress, that touch, tender and infinitely sweet, for with the quick heart of her she knew the little woman to be of the gold of earth, and she was conscious of a longing to keep her near, who was so soon to sail "into the risin' sun" and who had been so short a time her friend.

Friend, assuredly, for friendship was not a thing of time, but hearts alike, and they had turned together with the first look.

So they sat a while, these two from the ends of the earth, and the warm Irish heart cleared itself of tears, like April weather, to come up laughing in another moment.

"An' to think ye niver told us your name, asthore!" she said, wiping her eyes; "nor yer home place! Were ye raised in this post av haythins?"

"Maren Le Moyne of Grand Portage. My father—was a smith."

"Of Grand Portage! An' ye are so far inland! I am Sheila O'Halloran, av all Oirland, an' wife to Terence th' same,—yer fri'nd for always, asthore, f'r niver will I be forgettin' this time!"

She turned to the fair woman, smiling and alight.

"Did ye iver dhrame av such romance, my dear?" she asked. "An' isn't it just wonderful to find a real live heroine in th' wilderness?"

The woman was toying with a bunch of grass, winding the slim green blades around her pale fingers, and she looked back with peculiar straightness.

"It is all very wonderful, Sheila, and commands admiration, of course; but, for my part, a strange woman alone on the rivers with a party of men must have something beside her own word to vouch for her before I should take her in with open arms. You are too ready to believe anything. How do you know this venturess is not a—Jezebel?"

For a moment an awful silence fell upon the three, and they could hear the myriad sounds of the evening camp round about.

Then Maren, her eyes wide in amaze, said stupidly:

"Eh,—Madame?"

And the Irishwoman cried: "Frances! For shame!"

But the other was very much composed.

"I am right, all the same,—what woman of modesty would follow a man to the wilderness, confessing brazenly her love? You haven't noticed any hysterics on my part over it,— nor will you. I think it all a very open scandal."

The little woman was flying into a rage of tumbled words and hopeless brogue, but Maren Le Moyne, the blood red to her temples, rose silently, took the pot of broth, and walked away, and never in her life did she hold herself so tall and straight.

As she knelt beside the blanket bed of McElroy, and lifted his helpless head, her eyes were burning sombrely.

"This, too?" she was saying dumbly, within herself. "Is this, too, part of the lesson of life?"

And all through the days that followed, long warm days, with the songs of birds from the gliding shores, the ripple of waters beneath the prow of a canoe, she sat beside the unconscious man and looked at him with dumb yearning.

For love of him,—what would she not have done, what would she not do still for love of him,—he who had sold her for a kiss; and for it there came something,—she could not define it,—something that seemed to live in the atmosphere, to taint the glory of the sunshine, to speak under every word and whisper.

Never again did she cook at the fire with the others, but had her own on the outskirts, and Sheila O'Halloran came and cooked with her, talked and comforted and hovered about Anders McElroy where he lay in a silence like death, his fair face flushed with fever and his strong hands plucking at everything within their reach.

"Don't ye worry, dear, he'll not die. 'Twouldn't be accordin' to th' rights av life,—not afther all ye've done f'r him. He'll opin his blessid eyes some day an' know ye, an' Heaven itself will not be like thim f'r glory."

But Maren only looked tragically down upon him.

What would they say, those eyes that she had thought so earnest, so all-deserving in their eager honesty, if they should open to her alone?

Would they lie as they had done before, with the thought of Francette behind their blue clearness?

Ah, well,—it was all in the day's march.

This day at noon camp she came upon, close to a fallen tree, a wee red flower nodding on its slender stalk. She sighed and broke it.

"In memory of a brave man," she said sadly. "Oh, a very brave man!"

CHAPTER XXVII

RETURN

Eastward through the little lakes, across the portages where McElroy was carried by means of pole and blanket swung from sturdy shoulders, they went at hurried pace, and never a man of Maren's small command but watched the sadness of her face, that seemed to grow with the days and to feel an aching counterpart of it within his own heart.

"Take my coat for your head, Ma'amselle," when she rested among the thwarts,—"Let me, Ma'amselle," when she would do some little task. Thus they served her from the old desire that sight of her face had ever stirred in the breasts of men, she who had never played at the game of love, nor knew its simplest trick.

Southward, presently, up the rivers hurrying to the great bay at the north, and at last out upon the broad waters of Winnipeg, and never for an hour had McElroy's wandering soul come back to his suffering body. Day by day Maren tended him, feeding him as one feeds a helpless babe, shielding him from the sun by her own shadow when the branches gathered at morn withered ere noon, wetting the fair head with its waving sunburnt hair with water dipped from overside, and praying constantly for his life.

As they neared the southern end, where Winnipeg narrows like the neck of a bottle, his tongue loosened from its silence and he began to babble and talk in broken sentences, and it was all about De Courtenay and a remorse that ate the troubled soul.

"I owe you apologies, M'sieu,—'tis a sorry plight and I alone am to blame. And yet I have a score,—gladly would I take my will of you for that one fault,—another time,—another place. Still have I no right, save as one man who,—But I have a plan,—one may escape,—listen—when I grapple with this guard, do you make for the river—with all speed—My God! My God! M'sieu! Why did you not run?" And so he muttered and sighed, and Maren bent above with wide eyes.

Something there was between these two, some enmity that followed even into the land of shadows and yet held them gentlemen through it all, offering and rejecting some chance of escape. A weary, weary tangle.

Again he would fancy himself back in De Seviere and always there was De Courtenay with his smiling face and tantalizing beauty.

"Welcome, M'sieu, to our post! Seldom do we meet so gay a guest!"

Often the wandering words would stumble among his accounts at the factory and he would give directions to the clerks, and then Ridgar's name would come, only to carry him instantly to the camp of the savages on Deer River.

"Edmonton,—friend of my heart,—alone! and you pass me without speech! Ah,—that look! That look! I'd stake my soul—"

And once in the cool twilight of an ended day, with the tall trees above and the river lapping below, he cried out her name,

"Maren!" and once again, "Maren!" with a world of change between the two words.

The first plunged the girl's heart to her throat with its passion, the second chilled her like a cool wind.

And all at once he said, after a pause, "What is it, little one?"

So passed the days of the return.

Hour by hour the bright waters of the lake spoke to the girl with voices of regret and sadness. The blue sky above seemed to mirror the dark face of Marc Dupre, the wind from the shores to be his low voice, each passing shadow among the trees his slender figure returning from the hunt for her.

Her heart was sore that Fate had willed it so, and yet, looking down at the face of this man at her feet, she knew it had to be and that she would do again all that she had done.

And ever before her passed the scornful face of the fair woman who had set the little undertone to all the world.

It troubled her, and for hours together she sat in silence reasoning it all out, while Mowbray's men dipped the shining blades and here and there the voyageurs and Indians who wore no feathers sang snatches of song, now a chanson of the trail and rapid, again a wordless monotony of savage notes.

The evening camps were short spaces of blessed quietude

and converse when Sheila O'Halloran sat beside her and they talked of many things,—chiefly the dear little Island whose green sod would soon again receive the feet of "herself an' Terence."

"'Tis thankful I am, me dear, to be out av this forsaken land alive wid me hair on me head instid av on a hoop painted green wid little red arrows on th' stretched shkin inside! 'Tis a sorry counthry an' fit f'r no woman, but whin Terence must come on some mysterious business av th' government,—an' niver, till this minute, accushla, do I know whut it is,—a cryin' shame 'tis, too, wid me, his devoted wife!—I must come along or die. Wurra! Many's th' time I thought I'd do th' thrick here! But now are th' dangers passin' wid ivery mile,—hark to th' men singin'! 'Tis bad business whin men do not sing at th' day's work. 'Tis glad I am f'r safe deliverance from that counthry av nightmares wid its outlandish name,—Athabasca,—where Terence must moon from post to post av th' Hudson's Bay—"

"Athabasca!"

Maren's head was up and she was looking at the little woman with an eager wistfulness.

"The Land of the Whispering Hills!"

"Thrue,—'tis th' Injun word,—but a woild, woild land f'r all that."

"But beautiful, Madame,—oh! it is beautiful, is it not?"

"Fair,—wid high hills an' a great blue lake an' woildness!—Ah!"

But the tall leader was calling and camp was breaking for

another stretch.

And under the travelling stars of that night there awoke in the heart of the maid of the trail something of the old love, the old longing for that goal of her life's ambition.

She had turned aside from it, only to be taught a lesson whose scars would stay deep in her soul so long as life lasted.

At last came an hour when the party under O'Halloran must turn to the east, where the bottle-neck of Winnipeg split in two, going down that well-worn way which led to Lake of the Woods, Rainy River, and at last to the wide lakes, whose sparkling waves would waft them on to the great outside world.

There was a scene at parting, when the warmhearted Irishwoman clung to Maren and wept against her bosom, calling her all the hundred words for "darling" in the Celtic and vowing to remember her always.

The fair woman, wife of a Scotchman who acted as some sort of secretary to O'Halloran, sat apart in cold silence.

"M'sieu," said Maren, at the last, "I have no words to thank you for this that you have done. I but cast it into the balance of God, which must hang heavy with your goodness."

She had given her hand to the leader, and that impulsive son of the ould sod kissed it gallantly.

"'Tis little we did, lass, for you and your poor lad yonder, and 'twas in our hearts to do more. But here's luck to you both,—an early weddin' an' sturdy sons!"

And, as the morning sun glittered on the ripples of the departing boats, Maren stood long looking after them, a mist in her eyes and her full lips quivering.

She looked until the gathering dimness hid the waving kerchief of the only woman friend who had ever truly reached her heart.

Then she sat down and took up a paddle.

"Last lap, Messieurs," she said, above the mutter of McElroy at her feet, and they turned toward where the familiar river came rushing to the lake.

The summer lay heavy on the land when they reached the Assiniboine.

Deep green of the forests, deep green of fern and bush and understuff, told of the full tide of the year. Here and there a leaf trailed in the shallows, yellow as gold in an early death.

She thought of the spring, so long past, when she had first come into this sweet land, and it seemed like another time, another life, another person.

This day at dusk they passed the hidden cove where she had found Marc Dupre waiting to build her fire. The abandoned canoe still lay hidden where he left it.

Cool blue dawn, hushed and wide-reaching, still with that stillness which precedes the sunrise, lay over the river, when the lone canoe rounded the lower bend and Anders McElroy, factor of Fort de Seviere, came back to his own again.

In the prow there knelt a weary figure in a soiled and sun-bleached garment of doeskin, its glittering plastron of bright beads broken here and there, the ragged ends of sinews hanging as they were left by briar and branch, and the haggard eyes went with eager swiftness to the stockade standing in its grim invincibility facing the east.

The row of wonted canoes lay upturned upon the shelving shore at the landing, the half-moon at the right still glowered with its puny cannon which had spoken no word to save their master on that fateful day, and all things looked as if but a day had passed between.

The great gate with its studded breast was closed, the bastions at the corners were empty of watchers, for peace folded its wings above the past.

Without sound the boat cut up to the landing, Brilliers leaped out and steadied it to place, and Maren stepped once more upon the familiar slope.

They lifted McElroy, swinging in his blanket, and the tread of the moccasined feet was hollow on the planks.

Thus there passed up to the gate of De Seviere a triumphal procession of victory, whose heart was heavy within it, and whose leader in her tattered dress was the saddest sight of all.

She raised her hand and beat upon the gate, and a voice cried, "Who comes?"

"Open, my brother," she called, for the voice was that of Henri Baptiste, whose turn at the gate it was.

There was an ejaculation, a swift rattle of chains, and the heavy portal swung back, while the blanched face of young Henri stared into the dawn. Maren motioned to the men and they stepped in with their burden.

"Holy Mary! Maren! Maren! Maren!" cried Henri Baptiste, and took both her arms in a gripping clasp. He looked into her face with fear and wonder, as if the girl had returned from the dead, while joy unspeakable began to lighten his features.

"Sister! Holy Mary!"

And then, when the touch of her in the flesh had dispelled his first horror, when the sight of the factor swinging grotesquely in the blanket had taken on the sense of reality, he raised his voice in a stentorian call.

From every door it brought the populace running, half-dressed and startled, and in scant space a ring of faces stared upon the strangers in stupid awe.

"Ma'amselle Le Moyne!" they whispered, fearfully.

"Mother of Heaven! The factor!"

"Our factor! Out of the hands of Death!"

"Mon Dieu! One of them! And the maid!"

And in the midst of the awed and hushed excitement that was growing with each passing moment, there cut the voice of McElroy, babbling from the blanket.

"Throw! Throw, Ma'amselle,—for M'sieu!"

"Hush!" said Maren; "where is Prix Laroux?"

"Here!"

The big fellow was pushing through the gathering crowd, to stand before the weary girl with burning eyes.

"Maren!" he said simply, and could say no more.

"Take him, Prix," she said quietly; "take him to the factory. Get Rette de Lancy's hand above him for care, and Jack for all things else. Take these my men, and give them all the post affords, but chiefly rest at present. They have—"

Here there came a tumult among the listening populace, and Marie rushed through and flung herself upon Maren and there was time for nothing else, save that, as Maren turned with her hanging like a vice about her throat and Henri's arm across her shoulders, there was a streak of crimson, a flash of ornaments in the sun, but now risen above the forest's rim, and some one threw herself upon the unconscious form of McElroy, kissing his face and his helpless hands and weeping terribly.

It was the little Francette. At her heels the great dog, Loup, halted and glowered at the strangers.

CHAPTER XXVIII

THE OLD DREAM ONCE MORE

They led her through the new day, between the staring, whispering people, this comer from beyond the grave, to the little new cabin beside the northern wall, across its step and into its sweet, fresh cleanliness of home; and when Henri had shut the door they stood together in a group, their arms inwound, and Marie wept helplessly while Maren looked down with moist and weary eyes.

"There! There! Hush, ma cherie! Hush!" she was saying, but Henri was reading with amaze the change in her glorious face.

"It has been a long trail, Prix, but a longer one beckons with ceaseless insistence. No longer can I sit in idleness. Can we, think you, raise the debt to carry us on at once? My heart is sick for the Athabasca."

Maren stood by the factory door conversing earnestly with Laroux.

From every point of the post curious eyes looked upon her. Here and there groups of women whispered in the doorways, and once and again a laugh, quick hushed, broke on the

Vingie E. Roe

evening air.

Somehow they struck upon the girl's ears with an ugly sound, reminding her vaguely of the fair woman who travelled eastward with Sheila O'Halloran, and her voice grew more earnest.

Laroux, who had not spoken with her since that one word of the morning at the gate, was dumb of tongue, aching with the old feeling in his heart which had told him faithfully so long ago that all was not well with her.

"At once, Maren," he said huskily, "I will raise the debt. When would you be gone?"

"Soon, my friend,—soon, soon."

"The word shall go round to-night. All shall be ready in forty-eight hours."

He paused a moment and presently, "Maren, maid," he said.

"Yes?"

"Hold you aught against me for the stand I took that day— the duty I saw first?"

"Against you, Prix?—the truest, bravest friend I own? Nay, man,—you are my staff, my hope, my courage. Would I had had your strength these heavy days."

"Would to the good God you had! It shall not fail you again."

Maren held out her hand and Laroux grasped it in a clasp of faith.

"See!" cried Tessa Bibye, peeping eagerly from among the women, "she holds hands with that blackhaired man of her people who spurs the rest. One man or another,—as Francette says,—little cat!—all are fish who come to Ma'amselle's net! The factor, or the cavalier, or a common voyageur.

"Can they not see, these fool men, that the woman is a venturess, playing with all?"

"You lie, Tessa Bibye!"

Micene Bordoux had passed unnoticed. Now she turned her accusing glance on the loose-tongued girl.

"Because you are so small of soul yourself, are your eyes blinded to the greater heights? Ma'amselle is lost in the clouds above you."

She went on, and Maren at the factory door turned to enter.

"Give the word,—and make all haste. Fix all things as you think best."

The great trading-room, lined with its shelves and circled with counters, was empty, save for a clerk, Gifford, who cast accounts in the big book on the factor's desk, and Maren's footsteps rang heavy to her ears as she passed through it to the little room behind, where she could see Rette passing back and forth at her tasks of mercy.

She stopped at the open door and looked within that little room. Here were the things of McElroy's life,—the plain chairs, the table, the shelf with its books, the chest against the western wall, and on the bed, pulled out to get the breeze, lay the man himself prone in his splendid strength.

The light from the setting sun was on his head with its fair hair and flushed face, rolling restlessly from side to side. There was no reason in the earnest blue eyes, and Maren felt a mighty anguish swell and grip her throat as she stood looking on the pathetic scene.

"Come in, Ma'amselle," whispered Rette from her motherly heart, drawn by sight of her haggard face, but Maren's eyes had fallen on a little figure huddled on the far side of the bed with its face buried against McElroy's left hand.

She knew the small head running over with black curls.

"Nay, Rette," she said quietly, "I would speak a moment with you."

The woman came out and closed the door.

"Poor little fool!" she whispered, "she is worn to a shadow with these weeks of weeping, and, now that he is back, will not give over hanging to his hand like one drowning."

"Heed not. Is it in your heart, Rette, to do a deed of kindness for me, to keep a word of faith?"

"With all my heart, Ma'amselle!"

"Then," whispered Maren, apart from the clerk's listening ears, "take you this letter. Keep it until M'sieu the factor is in his right mind, then give it him with your own hands. If he— if he should—burn it, Rette, unopened."

And she gave into the woman's keeping the only letter she had ever written to a man.

It was in French, and the script was fine and finished.

This was what she had said, alone in the little room with its eastern window at the end of the Baptiste cabin:

"MONSIEUR MCELROY, Factor of Fort de Seviere, ave atque vale." (The tender word of Father Tenau when he blessed her that last time in Grand Portage)

"The time has come when I must take my people out of your post, must break their contract and their word. Forgive them, M'sieu, and lay not the fault to them, for I, and I only, am to blame. But the time I promised is too long.... I can no longer hold back the tide of longing which drives me to that land of which we spoke once...." (Here there was a break in the letter, a smudge on the page, as if the quill had caught the paper or a drop of moisture run into the ink.)

"I must go forward, and at once, to the Athabasca. The great quest is strong at my heartstrings again. I thank you, M'sieu, for all kindness done my people, and I promise that, should fortune favour them and me in that far land to which we journey, they shall send what trade lies with them to De Seviere. For one thing I ask,—if it be possible, M'sieu, give to certain men who will be found by word to Mr. Mowbray of York, such stipend as you can, for they were good and faithful,—namely, Frith and Wilson and McDonald, Brilliers and Alloybeau.... Adieu, M'sieu. God send you health. (Signed)

"MAREN LE MOYNE, of Grand Portage."

Laroux was worth his word.

Forty-eight hours later there stood at the portal of Fort de Seviere, ready for the trail, that small band of wanderers who had come into it in the early spring.

They were fuller of hope, more eager to face the wilderness than on that day, for joy after sorrow sat blithely on their faces, turned to the tall young woman at their head. And they were fully equipped for travel. Three canoes held wealth of supplies, while six huskies whined in leash, nervous under new masters, touched with the knowledge of coming change.

Not a man in De Seviere who had not given gladly, nay, vied with his neighbour to give, to the helping of this woman.

Had they not their factor back from death and its torments?

There was God-speed and hearty handclasp from the men, and Maren smiled into their faces, reading their simple hearts.

With the women it was different. They hung, gazing, on the outskirts, calling farewell to Marie, who wept a little at sight of her deserted cabin, to Anon and Mora and Ninette, but there was no reflection of the feeling of their masters for this girl with her weary beauty, her steady, half-tragic eyes. Nor was there great regret over Micene. Too sharp had been her tongue, too keen her perception of their faults.

True, the autumn was near at hand. Winter would come with its myriad foes before they could hope to be ready for it, and Maren, looking far ahead, saw it and its dangers, and her heart sickened a bit with the thought of her people; but the thing within was stronger than all else.

She must leave De Seviere at once. Therefore, she raised her head with her face to the west.

It was early dawn again. It seemed that it had ever been dawn when fateful things had happened in this post, every log and stone of which was suddenly dear to her.

She stood in the opened gate and looked back upon it, on the cabins, the well where De Courtenay had placed his first red flower in her hair, the storehouses, and the factory.

The factory!

With sight of it once more the wave of anguish swept over her. She saw the small plain room at the back, the figure of a man prone in his helplessness, a fair head with blue eyes, pleading in their honest clearness, and her lips trembled.

"Ready?" she said, and the deep voice slipped unsteadily.

"Aye," answered Prix Laroux, and picked up the last pack of chattels.

At that moment there was a flurry among the pressing men around, a sound above the many voices wishing them luck, and little Francette broke through.

"Ma'amselle!" she cried, looking up into Maren's eyes with conflicting expressions on her small face, misery and solemn joy and hatred that strove to soften itself beneath a better emotion; "Ma'amselle,—I would thank you! Oh, bon Dieu! I am not all bad! Here"

She seized Loup by the ears and dragged him forward, snarling. "Take him, Ma'amselle! I love him! Do you take him,—and—and-understand!"

All her red-rose beauty had gone from the little maid along with her dancing lightness.

These long weeks had turned her into a woman with a woman's heart.

They drew back and looked on with wonder, and then smiles of amusement, but Maren, gazing into the tragic little face, saw deeper.

"Why,—little one," she said gently, unconsciously falling into McElroy's words after a trick she had, "I—I understand. You need not give up the dog,—I know what you would say."

"No!" cried Francette fiercely. "No! Take him! Take him! I will make you take him! I will!"

She was whimpering, and Maren, stooping, laid a hand on the husky's collar.

Without more words she turned and followed her people down to the landing, half-dragging the brute, who hung back and turned his giant head to the little maid, standing with her hands over her face.

He snarled and bit at Maren's wrist, but she picked him up and flung him, half-dragging on the ground, for he was a mighty beast, into the first canoe.

"Push off," she said; and, taking her place in the prow, she raised her face to the cool blue sky, and turned once more to that West whose voice had called from her cradle, but, with some strange perversity of fate, her heart drew back to the squat stockade slowly fading into the distance.

The sweet wind of the Whispering Hills was very faint on her soul.

CHAPTER XXIX

BITTER ALOES

Eight months passed over the country of the Assiniboine, bringing their changes. The short full-tide of the summer seemed to run out with the going of the venturers, and the autumn to come from the north-west in a night.

Great splashes of colour dropped on the land, spilled from the palette of some careless giant,—gold and crimson and purple. Glorious fires burned in the cooling skies and the sweet breath of autumn tingled in the air.

There was comment, and the shaking of heads among the old trappers. The wrong time of year to take the long trail with women,—the wrong time, but, bon Dieu! who was to stop that woman with the sombre eyes? Voila! A woman to thrill the blood in any man who was still warm with life!

"Love awakened in her would be a thing of flame and fury, they had thought, that long past day," thought Pierre Garcon to himself; "he and that friend of his heart, Marc Dupre,—it had been a thing of patient servitude, of transcendent daring, and Marc Dupre; ah! He had been a part of it. But there was much of mystery about it all, and no one knew, nor would any know, all that it had meant."

So the changes came and passed, and when Anders McElroy again opened his eyes to reason, the world was white against the pane of the one window of the little room,—the long snows had arrived. Winter was upon the Northland.

It was on a night when the wind without howled like a lost soul shut out from the universe and the sucking of the chimney-throat roared to heaven.

Edmonton Ridgar sat at the hearth gazing into the leaping flames, and Rette de Lancy passed and repassed among the shifting shadows, busy at some kindly task.

Long he lay, this man returned from the Borderland of the Unknown, and stared weakly at the familiar sights that were yet touched with a puzzling strangeness.

It seemed that this was all as it should be, and yet there was something lacking,—a great gap, whose images and happenings were wiped out as a cloth wipes clean a slate,—a space of darkness, of blankness, whose empty void held prescience of some great sadness. He lay on his side facing the fire, and twice he thought to speak to Ridgar with a question of this strangeness, and each time he was conscious of a vast surprise that the man did not answer.

His lips, so long unused to sane direction, had made no sound in the roar of the night.

And then Ridgar, drawn by that intangible sense of eyes upon him, raised his head; and, as their glances met, that great void flashed suddenly into full panoply of life peopled with a ring of painted faces against the background of a night forest, a leaping fire, and the heroic figure of a tall woman who stood in the dancing light and threw a hatchet at a painted post.

Ridgar's eyes, as he had seen them in the dimness of the outskirts of that massed circle, brought back the lost period of time and all that had passed therein.

He stared wildly at him, and then around the firelit room.

"Ah!" said Ridgar softly, getting slowly to his feet with a smile at once tender and exaggeratedly calm. "You have awakened, have you; eh, lad? Would you sleep the whole night away as well as the day?"

He came to the bed and took McElroy's hand tenderly in his, while he gave Rette a warning glance.

McElroy tried to rise, but only his head obeyed, lifting itself a bit from the pillow to fall helplessly back.

He looked up at Ridgar with a look that cut that good man's heart, so full was it of wild entreaty and piteous grief.

"Maren?" whispered the weak lips. "Maren,—where—?" And they, too, failed him."

"Safe," said Ridgar gently; "all is well. We are at De Seviere and there is no need to think. Do you drink a sip of Rette's good broth and sleep again."

With a sigh of ineffable relief the sick man obeyed like a child, falling back into the shadows, though this time they were the blessed shades of the Vale of Healing Rest.

Rette in a corner was wiping her eyes and saying, over and over, a prayer of thanksgiving for deliverance from death.

With infinite tact Ridgar kept him quiet, promising the tale of what had happened, and, when the flow of returning life could no longer be stemmed, he set himself the task of telling what he knew of those swift days.

It was again night, though a week of nights had passed since that on which the factor had awakened to consciousness, and Ridgar had dismissed Rette.

There was only the roar of the wind without, the whistle of the fire, and the two men alone in the room as they had been many a winter's night.

"Now,—where shall I begin?" said the chief trader, gazing into the fire. "At what point?"

"Maren," said McElroy eagerly, from the bed; "begin with her."

Ridgar shook his head.

"Nay, it goes farther back. Let it begin with the leaving of De Seviere and the coldness of my bearing to you.... Did you never think, lad, that it was but a blind, covering the determination to help you at the first opportunity? Thought you the friendship of years so poor a thing as to be turned in a day? Day by day my heart ached for some word with you, or even a glance that would make all straight; but those painted devils watched my every move, my every look, the very intaking of my breath, as the coyote watches the gopher-hole when the badger is below. Only for sake of the dead chief at my feet was I given such seemingly free leave among them,—for myself, I had been shipped as were poor De Courtenay's Nor'westers at Wenusk Creek. And now is the time when I must go farther back and tell you of the good chief who was my father, indeed, at heart."

Ridgar paused a moment, and his eyes took on a look of

distant things

"Have you not wondered how it was, lad, that a man should live long as I have lived in the wilderness, alone, without ties other than those which bind him to the Great Company, without love of woman, without the joy of children?... I have not always lived so. Time was when I had my own wickiup, when I lay by my own night-fire and played with the braids of a woman's hair,—long black braids, bound with crimson silk and heavy with ornaments, for whose buying I paid my year's catch, when I looked into eyes black as the woods at night and dumb with the great love she could not speak.... She lived it one day,... nay, died it—when I had some words with a young man of the tribe, who drew a spear before I knew what he meant and hurled it at me. She... leaped between. God!"

He ceased again, and McElroy could hear his breathing, see the whitened knuckles of his hands grasping the poker from the hearth where he had absently stirred the leaping fire.

"It went quite through her,—a foot beyond her swelling breast, full for my only child, unborn.... She was Negansahima's daughter.... We mourned together, the old chief and I, and our hearts were bound close as the tree and its bark. In a far high hill of the Pays d'en Haut we put her to sleep with that last look of love on her dark face... and we made a pact to lie beside her when our time should come, he who out-lived the other to see the rites of the Death Feast. He has joined her. I saw his rites. So for this end, reaching far back, I did not return when you came back to De Seviere, going on with that rabble who dared not harm me who am to share the Sleep of Chiefs some day....

"So!"

"Now for the rest. I know no more of Maren Le Moyne than that first tragic sight of her, hauled into the light by the brute DesCaut. I only know that she stood before those savages as fearless as a lioness and threw again and again, her black head up and sane, her young body under her own command in every taut cord and muscle, and that again and again and yet again the flying hatchet landed in its own cleft,—a wonderful performance!—putting off with coolness and skill the death they would see her decide, choosing neither man of you."

"But," cried McElroy, "it was De Courtenay she came to see,—to save,—to die with,—she loved him, man!"

"Aye,—maybe. But I know only that that young trapper, Marc Dupre, gave his life as gallantly as might be to cover our retreat while we, the Nor'wester and I, slipping among the sleepers, carried you to the river; that they woke, those devils, before we had cleared the little gorge, and that M'sieu de Courtenay, brave man and gay cavalier, gave your knees to this woman who helped me get you to the canoe, himself taking the only gun and meeting what fate was his in the narrow seam among the rocks. She had with her men of Mr. Mowbray's brigade, that she had got somewhere on Winnipeg, and we put you in their waiting canoe. She was dragged in among the thwarts,—while I—slipped back among the shadows, circled the camp, and was at my death-watch inside the big tepee when peering eyes looked in. I saw no more of the dashing Nor'wester, save a flash of long gold curls at a headman's belt. What fate was meted out to him was swift and therefore merciful. Peace be to him!

"No more I know, my friend, save that, when I returned to De Seviere, I found you ill with some fever of the brain."

"But, Ridgar, for love of Heaven, what of Maren?"

"She had brought you here, and Rette says the women hung off from her and laughed in corners, whispering and talking, and that her face was worn and greatly changed, as if with some deep sorrow."

McElroy turned his head upon the pillow and weak tears smarted under his lids.

"Me! It was I she saved when it was I who slew her lover! God forgive me, for I cannot forgive myself!"

"Nay, boy, hush! It is all as God wills. We are but shuttles in the web of this tangled life."

"But—tell me,—what does she now? How looks her dear face?"

Ridgar was silent a moment, and McElroy repeated his question, with his face still turned away:

"Does she pass among them,—the vipers? Does she seem to care for life at all now?"

"Lad," said Ridgar gently, "I know not, for she is gone."

"Gone!"

The pale man on the pillow sprang upright, staring at the other with open mouth.

"Aye, softly, boy; softly! She has been gone these many weeks; even while summer was here she gathered her people, outfitted by our men, all of whom were so glad for your deliverance that they gave readily to their debt, and took up again her long trail to the Athabasca. Rette, I believe, has a letter which she left for you.... Would you read it now?"

McElroy nodded dumbly, and Ridgar went out in the night to Rette's cabin for this last link between the factor and the woman he loved.

When he returned, and McElroy had taken it in his shaking hands, he sat down and turned his face to the fire.

There was silence while the flames crackled and the chimney roared, and presently the factor said heavily:

"I cannot! Read..."

So Ridgar, bending in the light, read aloud Maren's letter.

At its end the man on the bed turned his face to the wall and spoke no more.

From that time forth the tide of returning life in him stopped sluggishly, as if the locks were set in some ocean-tapping channel.

The bleakness of the cold north winter was in his heart and life was barren as the eastern meadows.

So passed the days and the weeks, with quip and jest from Ridgar, whose eyes wore a puzzled expression; with such coddling and coaxing from Rette as would have spoiled a well man, and, with not the least to be counted, daily visits to the factory of the little Francette, who defied the populace and came openly.

With returned consciousness to McElroy, there came back to the little maid much of her damask beauty. The pretty cheeks bloomed again and she was like some bright butterfly flitting about the bare room in her red kirtle.

Sometimes McElroy would smile, watching her play with a young bob-cat, which some trapper had brought her from the woods, and whose savage playfulness seemed to be held in leash under her small hands. The creature would mouth and fawn upon her, taking her cuffs and slaps, and follow her about like a dog.

Rette tolerated the two with a bad grace, for, since the day when Maren Le Moyne had stood at the door with her haggard beauty so wistfully sad, her sympathies had been all with the strange girl of Grand Portage.

Light and flitting, sparkling as an elf, full to the brim of laughter and light, little Francette was playing the deepest game of her life.

With the cunning of a woman she was trying to woo this man back to the joy of earth, to wind herself into his heart, and so to fill his hours with her brightness that he would come to need her always.

So she came by day and day, and now it would be some steaming dainty cooked at her father's hearth by her own hands, again a branch of the fir-tree coated with ice and sparkling with a million gems, that she brought into the dull blankness of the room, and with her there always came a fresh sweet breath of the winter world without.

McElroy smiled at her pretty conceits, her babbling talk, her gambols, and her gifts.

"What have you done with Loup, little one?" he asked, one day. "Does he wait on the steps to growl at this usurper purring at your heels?"

The little maid grew pearly white and looked away at Rette fearfully, as if at sudden loss, in danger of some betrayal.

"Nay," she said, "Loup... is an ingrate. He has ceased to care."

And always after she avoided aught that could excite mention of the dog.

But, in spite of all her effort, McElroy lay week after week in the back room, looking for hours together into the red heart of the fire, silent, uncomplaining, in no apparent pain, but shiftless as an Indian in the matter of life.

The business of the factory was brought to him nightly by Ridgar and the young clerk Gifford, and he would look over things and make a few suggestions, dispose of this and that as a matter of course and fall back into his lethargy.

"What think you, M'sieu?" asked Rette anxiously, of Ridgar. "Is there naught to stir him from these hours of dulness?"

"I know not, Rette. Would I did! The surgeon says there is nothing wrong with the man, save lack of desire to live. He has lost the love of life."

And so it seemed. Weeks dragged themselves by and months rolled after them, and still he lay in a great weakness that held his strong limbs as in a vice.

Winter was roaring itself away with tearing winds, with snow that fell and drifted against the stockade wall, and fell again, with vast silences and cold that glazed the surface of the world with ice.

January dragged slowly by, with dances for the young couples in the cabins at nights, and little Francette, for the first time in her life, refused to share in the merry-making of which she had always been the heart and soul.

Instead, she lay awake in the attic of the Moline cabin and cried in her hands, listening to the whirl of the nights without.

Alone in those long vigils instinct was telling her that she had failed. Failed utterly!

The young factor cared no more for her than on that night in spring when he had kissed her and told her to "play in the sunshine and think no more of him."

She had played for a man and failed.

Moreover, she had not played fairly, and for her wickedness he lay now as he had lain so long, drifting slowly but surely toward that land of shadows whence there is no return.

She clinched her small hands in the darkness and wept, and they were woman's tears.

Back to her led all the threads of tragedy, of death and danger and heartbreak, that had so hopelessly tangled themselves in Fort de Seviere.

But for that one hour at the factory steps what time she lay in McElroy's arms and saw Maren Le Moyne pause at the corner, all would be well.

Young Marc, Dupre would be singing his gay French songs with his red cap tilted on his curls, that handsome Nor'wester of the Saskatchewan would be going his merry way, loving here and there,—instead of bleaching their bones in some distant forest, as the whispers said; and, last of all, this man she loved with all the intensity of her soul would be brown and strong with life, not the weary wreck of a man who gazed into the fire and would not get well.

So the long nights took toll of the little Francette and a purpose grew in her chastened heart, a purpose far too big for it.

At last the purpose blossomed into full maturity, hastened by the dark shadows that were beginning to spread beneath McElroy's hopeless eyes, as if the spirit, so little in the body, were already leaving it to its earthly end, and one day at dusk, trembling and afraid, she went to the factory for the last time.

"Rette," she said plaintively, "will you leave me alone with M'sieu the factor for an hour? Think what you will," she added fiercely, as she saw the woman's look; "tell all the populace! I care not! Only give me one hour! Mon Dieu! A little space to pay the debt of life! Leave me, Rette, as you hope for Heaven!"

And Rette, wondering and vaguely touched, complied.

McElroy was looking, after his habit, at the leaping flames and his thin hands played absently and constantly with the covering of the bed, when the door opened and closed and the little maid stood shrinking against it.

He did not look up for long, thinking, if his dull mind could form a thought through his melancholy dreams, that Ridgar had come in.

At last a sigh that was like a gasp pierced his lethargy and he raised his eyes.

She stood with one small hand over her beating heart and her cheeks white in the firelight.

"Ah! little one!" he said gently. "Why did you come through such a night? 'Tis wild as—as—Sit in the big chair," he added kindly.

But Francette, in whose face was an unbearable anguish, came swiftly and fell on her knees beside the bed, raising her eyes to his.

"M'sieu!" she cried, with great labouring breaths. "Oh! M'sieu, I have come to confess! If there is in your good heart pity for one who has sinned beyond pardon, give it me, I pray, for love of the good God!" McElroy stared down at her in wonder.

"Confess? Sinned?" he said. "Why, little one, what can a child like you know of sin? 'Tis only some blunderer like myself who should speak its damnable name."

"Nay, nay! Oh, no! No! No! Not on you is there one lightest touch, M'sieu, but on me,—me—me—does rest the weight of all!"

Her eyes were wide and full of tears, and McElroy laid a weak hand on her head.

"Hush, child!" he said, with some of his old sternness, when condemning wrong; "there is a fever at your brain. You have come too long to this dull room—"

"No! No! Take away your hand! Touch me not, M'sieu, for I am as dust beneath your feet! I alone am at bottom of all that has happened in Fort de Seviere this year past! Through me alone have come death and sorrow and misunderstanding! I

Vingie E. Roe

caused it all, M'sieu, because I—loved you! For love of you and hope to gain your heart I set you apart from that woman of Grand Portage!"

She buried her face on the covering of the bed and her voice came muffled and choking.

"That night at the factory steps,—you recall, M'sieu,—she came to you,—I saw her in the dusk as she turned at the corner, a rod away, saw her and knew with some touch of deviltry the sudden way of keeping you from her, your arms from about her, your lips from hers! Oh, that I could not bear, M'sieu! Not though I died for it! So I threw my own arms about your throat—you remember, M'sieu—and whispered that for one kiss I would go and forget. In the gentleness of your heart you kissed me—and—she saw that kiss. Saw me lying in your arms as if you held me there from love,—saw and turned away. She made no sound in the soft dust, and when I loosed your face from my clasp she was gone! So I broke your faith, M'sieu,—so I dragged forth one by one all the sorry happenings that have followed that evil night."

The muffled voice fell silent, save for the sobs that would no longer be withheld, and there was an awful stillness in the room, broken by a stick falling on the hearth and the added roar in the chimney.

When Francette raised her weeping eyes she saw McElroy's face above her like a mask.

Its lips were open as if breath had suddenly been denied them, its wasted cheeks were blue, and its eyes stared down upon her in horror:

"Oh! O God! Rette!"

She screamed and sprang up, to run back and crouch against the empty chair beside the hearth.

The figure upon the bed, half-risen, worked its lips and then fell back, and the little maid raised her voice and screamed again and again in mortal terror.

It brought Rette running from where she had waited in the trading-room.

She raised him, and her face was red with rage.

"What have you done! You evil cat! What have you done to the man?"

But McElroy's breast had heaved with a great breath, sweet as the wind over a harvest field to a tired man, and he looked up at Rette with eyes that seemed to be suddenly flooded with life.

"Done?" he whispered; "done, Rette? The child has given me salvation!" And then he held out a shaking, thin hand.

"Come here," he said softly; "come here."

Fearful, trembling, tear-stained Francette crept back, and the factor took both her small hands in a tender clasp:

"I thank you, little one," he said, "from my heart I thank you,—there is nothing to forgive. We are all sinners through the only bit of Heaven we possess,—love. Go, little one, and cease this crying. Know that I shall sleep this night in a mighty peace. You have given me—life!"

CHAPTER XXX

THE LAND OF THE WHISPERING HILLS

Springtime once more kissed all the wilderness into tender green. From the depths of the forest, lacing its myriad branches in finest fluff of young leaves, came the old-new sound of birds at the mating, rivers and tiny streams rushed and tumbled to the lakes, and overhead a sky as blue and sweet as the eyes of loved rocked its baby clouds in cradles of fresh winds.

They blew over vast reaches of forest and plain, these winds, wimpling the new grass with playful fingers, and whispering in the ear of bird and bee and flower that spring was come once more.

They came from the west, sweeping over sweet high meadows, over rushing streams, and down from fair plateaus, and their breath was fresh and cool with promise to one who faced them, eager in his hope, for they brought the virgin sweetness of the Land of the Whispering Hills. By streams, clear as crystal, he passed with a swinging stride, this lean young man in the buckskins of the forest traveller, over meadows soft in their green carpets, through woodlands whose flecked sunshine quivered and shook on the young moss beneath, and ever his face was lifted to the west with undying hope, with calmness of faith, and that great joy which is humble in its splendour.

Thus he swung forward all through the pleasant hours of that last day. Before him, raised against the sky, there loomed the magic Hills themselves, fair to the eye of man, clothed in the green of blowing grass and girdled about below with the encroaching forest.

At dusk he set foot upon their swelling slopes, and knew himself to be near the goal of his heart's desire.

Over among them somewhere lay the blue lake. He could already hear the murmur of its whispering shores, the roar of its circling forests, for the trees followed on and over through some low defile as if loath to lose the hills themselves, rising to heaven in virgin smoothness of cloud-shadowed verdure.

The sun had gone behind them in splendid panoply of fire when he came down into the sheltered woods, and through them to a wondrous meadow, beautiful as the fields of Paradise, sloping, to the shore beyond where waters blue as the sky above sent back the pageantry of light.

Here were the signs of tillage and cultivation, and even now a long dark strip attested the spring's new work, sending forth on the evening air the sweet scent of fresh-turned earth.

Beyond, across the field, in the edge of the farther woods, thin blue smoke curled peacefully up from the pointed tops of some forty native lodges, while nearer the lake there stood two cabins, one old and solid with a look of having faced the elements for years, the other staring in its newness. Indian ponies grazed at the clearing's edge or drank of the rippling waters on the pebbly beach, and a plough lay in the last furrow.

Vingie E. Roe

The stranger stood in amaze and gazed on the scene before him.

While he looked women came from the cabins and passed blithely about at evening tasks, and one went to the lake with a vessel for water. He could see its gleam in the reflection of the gorgeous light.

Thin and high came the sound of a voice singing, the ring of an axe somewhere in the wood beyond the cabins, and peace ineffable seemed to lie upon this blessed place. Here truly was Arcadia.

Long he stood in the fringe of the forest and looked eagerly among the distant figures for one, taller than all the rest, clad in plain dark garments, whose regal head should catch the dying glow, but strain as he might, he saw no familiar form, could not detect the free and swinging step.

Now that the goal of his hope was so near, within the very grasp of his hand, a strange timidity fell upon him, and he shrank from crossing the open field.

Rather would he follow the circling wood and come out at the upper end by the lake, going down along the shore to the cabins.

Keeping well within the trees, giants of the wild nursed in this cradle of sun and water, he bore to the north and ever his eager eyes peered between the bolls at the distant habitat.

He had gone but short space when, suddenly, he stopped, drawn up by sight of what lay in his path.

He had pierced a thicket of hanging vines, too eager to go around, and come abruptly upon some pagan shrine, some savage Holy of Holies.

And yet not wholly savage, for the signs of the red man and the white were strangely blended.

In the centre of the open space within the hanging wall of the vines,—perfect sylvan temple,—there lay a mounded grave, covered from head to foot with articles he knew at once to be the gifts of Indians to some great chief gone to the shadowy hunting-grounds. Rich they were, these gifts, in workmanship and carving, though mean and poor in quality, showing that great love had attended their giving, though the givers themselves must be a meagre people.

At the head of the mound towered a gigantic totem pole, carved and painted with scenes of a most minute history, while at the foot of a smaller stake, alike carved and coloured, bore, one upon another, twelve rings of bone, each one of which stood for the circle of a year.

Crossed and shielded with infinite care, in the centre there lay a set of smith's tools, crudely fashioned and well worn, tongs and a heavy hammer and a small anvil.

But beyond all this, a thing that held his wondering gaze and brought the fur cap from his head, there stood an altar, rude as the rest, but still an altar of God, with a black iron crucifix, whose pale ivory Christ glimmered in the gathering evening, upright upon it. Before the crucifix, and at either end, were the burnt-out evidences of tallow candles, while flanking the holy Symbol there stood two wooden crosses, their pieces held together by bindings of thread. Before one there lay a heap of little withered flowers, frail things of the forest and the spring, and every one was snowy white. Across the other hung a solitary blossom, first of its kind to open its passionate eyes to the sun, and it was blood-red, counterpart of that wee star which Alfred de Courtenay had snatched from the stockade wall one day in another spring.

The earnest blue eyes of the man were very grave, touched with a deep tenderness.

"Maren!" he whispered reverently; "maid of the splendid heart!"

So deep was he in contemplation of the things before him and his own holy thoughts that he did not hear a soft sound behind him, the fall of a light step.

A breath that was half a gasp turned him on his heel.

Leaning through the parted curtain of the hanging vines, one hand at her throat, the other holding three candles, and her dark eyes wide above her thinned brown cheeks, she stood herself. At her knee there hung the heavy head of the great dog, Loup.

She, as she had been when first he looked upon her, yet intangibly changed, the same yet not the same.

They stood in silence and looked into each other's eyes as if void of speech, of motion, held by the mighty yearning that must look and look with insatiable intensity, the half unreal reality of the moment.

And then the stopped breath in the girl's throat caught itself with a little sound that broke the spell.

The man sprang forward and took her in his arms, not passionately, strongly, as he had done once before, but with a love so high, so chastened, so humble that it gentled his touch to reverence.

"I have come, Maren," he said brokenly; "I have followed you to the land you sought. Maid of my heart! My soul!"

Without words, without question, she yielded herself to his embrace, lifted her face to him and gave into his keeping that which was his from the beginning.

"Mother Mary! I thank Thee!" he heard her whisper, and when he loosed her to look once more into her level eyes, they were dim with tears.

* * * * * * * * *

Night had fallen on the Athabasca when they passed out of the wood across the field, and they walked together hand in hand.

A great round moon was rising over the eastern forest, silvering the hills with shining crowns.

Peace brooded on the world.

"And here I found him, M'sieu," Maren Le Moyne was saying sadly, "in that low mound, cared for and worshipped by these peaceful beings who till the land and follow his teachings. They were his people. He taught them purity and peace, the use of plough and tool, the creed of love and kindness. Here was his dream of empire, his plan of progress. He of the Good Heart they called him, these Indians who were his people, and mourn him as a chief. That was his castle yonder, the older cabin to the east. Here is the fruit of his labour." She motioned over the new-ploughed land.

"Beyond the trees yonder are bigger fields, a wider holding. And yet they are poor, these people of peace. The tribes despise them and scoff at their worship... He taught them the prayers,—the rosary. I have come after him... Who knows? This is my dream also, my fulfilment. Love, M'sieu," she raised her face to him, and the deep eyes flickering with the old elusive light, "Love shall be my crown!"

"Aye," said Anders McElroy, after the manner of a covenant, "together we shall work and dream yet greater things, trusting in God,—live and love and enter into our heritage.... I have left the Company forever. Together we shall build the empire of your dreams.... Oh, Maid of my Heart, the Long Trail has ended in the harbour of New Homes!"

Choose from Thousands of 1stWorldLibrary Classics By

A. M. Barnard
Ada Leverson
Adolphus William Ward
Aesop
Agatha Christie
Alexander Aaronsohn
Alexander Kielland
Alexandre Dumas
Alfred Gatty
Alfred Ollivant
Alice Duer Miller
Alice Turner Curtis
Alice Dunbar
Allen Chapman
Alleyne Ireland
Ambrose Bierce
Amelia E. Barr
Amory H. Bradford
Andrew Lang
Andrew McFarland Davis
Andy Adams
Angela Brazil
Anna Alice Chapin
Anna Sewell
Annie Besant
Annie Hamilton Donnell
Annie Payson Call
Annie Roe Carr
Annonaymous
Anton Chekhov
Archibald Lee Fletcher
Arnold Bennett
Arthur C. Benson
Arthur Conan Doyle
Arthur M. Winfield
Arthur Ransome
Arthur Schnitzler
Arthur Train
Atticus
B.H. Baden-Powell
B. M. Bower
B. C. Chatterjee
Baroness Emmuska Orczy
Baroness Orczy
Basil King
Bayard Taylor
Ben Macomber
Bertha Muzzy Bower
Bjornstjerne Bjornson

Booth Tarkington
Boyd Cable
Bram Stoker
C. Collodi
C. E. Orr
C. M. Ingleby
Carolyn Wells
Catherine Parr Traill
Charles A. Eastman
Charles Amory Beach
Charles Dickens
Charles Dudley Warner
Charles Farrar Browne
Charles Ives
Charles Kingsley
Charles Klein
Charles Hanson Towne
Charles Lathrop Pack
Charles Romyn Dake
Charles Whibley
Charles Willing Beale
Charlotte M. Braeme
Charlotte M. Yonge
Charlotte Perkins Stetson
Clair W. Hayes
Clarence Day Jr.
Clarence E. Mulford
Clemence Housman
Confucius
Coningsby Dawson
Cornelis DeWitt Wilcox
Cyril Burleigh
D. H. Lawrence
Daniel Defoe
David Garnett
Dinah Craik
Don Carlos Janes
Donald Keyhoe
Dorothy Kilner
Dougan Clark
Douglas Fairbanks
E. Nesbit
E. P. Roe
E. Phillips Oppenheim
E. S. Brooks
Earl Barnes
Edgar Rice Burroughs
Edith Van Dyne
Edith Wharton

Edward Everett Hale
Edward J. O'Biren
Edward S. Ellis
Edwin L. Arnold
Eleanor Atkins
Eleanor Hallowell Abbott
Eliot Gregory
Elizabeth Gaskell
Elizabeth McCracken
Elizabeth Von Arnim
Ellem Key
Emerson Hough
Emilie F. Carlen
Emily Bronte
Emily Dickinson
Enid Bagnold
Enilor Macartney Lane
Erasmus W. Jones
Ernie Howard Pie
Ethel May Dell
Ethel Turner
Ethel Watts Mumford
Eugene Sue
Eugenie Foa
Eugene Wood
Eustace Hale Ball
Evelyn Everett-green
Everard Cotes
F. H. Cheley
F. J. Cross
F. Marion Crawford
Fannie E. Newberry
Federick Austin Ogg
Ferdinand Ossendowski
Fergus Hume
Florence A. Kilpatrick
Fremont B. Deering
Francis Bacon
Francis Darwin
Frances Hodgson Burnett
Frances Parkinson Keyes
Frank Gee Patchin
Frank Harris
Frank Jewett Mather
Frank L. Packard
Frank V. Webster
Frederic Stewart Isham
Frederick Trevor Hill
Frederick Winslow Taylor

Friedrich Kerst	Hayden Carruth	James Branch Cabell
Friedrich Nietzsche	Helent Hunt Jackson	James DeMille
Fyodor Dostoyevsky	Helen Nicolay	James Joyce
G.A. Henty	Hendrik Conscience	James Lane Allen
G.K. Chesterton	Hendy David Thoreau	James Lane Allen
Gabrielle E. Jackson	Henri Barbusse	James Oliver Curwood
Garrett P. Serviss	Henrik Ibsen	James Oppenheim
Gaston Leroux	Henry Adams	James Otis
George A. Warren	Henry Ford	James R. Driscoll
George Ade	Henry Frost	Jane Abbott
Geroge Bernard Shaw	Henry James	Jane Austen
George Cary Eggleston	Henry Jones Ford	Jane L. Stewart
George Durston	Henry Seton Merriman	Janet Aldridge
George Ebers	Henry W Longfellow	Jens Peter Jacobsen
George Eliot	Herbert A. Giles	Jerome K. Jerome
George Gissing	Herbert Carter	Jessie Graham Flower
George MacDonald	Herbert N. Casson	John Buchan
George Meredith	Herman Hesse	John Burroughs
George Orwell	Hildegard G. Frey	John Cournos
George Sylvester Viereck	Homer	John F. Kennedy
George Tucker	Honore De Balzac	John Gay
George W. Cable	Horace B. Day	John Glasworthy
George Wharton James	Horace Walpole	John Habberton
Gertrude Atherton	Horatio Alger Jr.	John Joy Bell
Gordon Casserly	Howard Pyle	John Kendrick Bangs
Grace E. King	Howard R. Garis	John Milton
Grace Gallatin	Hugh Lofting	John Philip Sousa
Grace Greenwood	Hugh Walpole	John Taintor Foote
Grant Allen	Humphry Ward	Jonas Lauritz Idemil Lie
Guillermo A. Sherwell	Ian Maclaren	Jonathan Swift
Gulielma Zollinger	Inez Haynes Gillmore	Joseph A. Altsheler
Gustav Flaubert	Irving Bacheller	Joseph Carey
H. A. Cody	Isabel Cecilia Williams	Joseph Conrad
H. B. Irving	Isabel Hornibrook	Joseph E. Badger Jr
H.C. Bailey	Israel Abrahams	Joseph Hergesheimer
H. G. Wells	Ivan Turgenev	Joseph Jacobs
H. H. Munro	J.G.Austin	Jules Vernes
H. Irving Hancock	J. Henri Fabre	Julian Hawthrone
H. R. Naylor	J. M. Barrie	Julie A Lippmann
H. Rider Haggard	J. M. Walsh	Justin Huntly McCarthy
H. W. C. Davis	J. Macdonald Oxley	Kakuzo Okakura
Haldeman Julius	J. R. Miller	Karle Wilson Baker
Hall Caine	J. S. Fletcher	Kate Chopin
Hamilton Wright Mabie	J. S. Knowles	Kenneth Grahame
Hans Christian Andersen	J. Storer Clouston	Kenneth McGaffey
Harold Avery	J. W. Duffield	Kate Langley Bosher
Harold McGrath	Jack London	Kate Langley Bosher
Harriet Beecher Stowe	Jacob Abbott	Katherine Cecil Thurston
Harry Castlemon	James Allen	Katherine Stokes
Harry Coghill	James Andrews	L. A. Abbot
Harry Houidini	James Baldwin	L. T. Meade

L. Frank Baum	Paul G. Tomlinson	T. S. Arthur
Latta Griswold	Paul Severing	The Princess Der Ling
Laura Dent Crane	Percy Brebner	Thomas A. Janvier
Laura Lee Hope	Percy Keese Fitzhugh	Thomas A Kempis
Laurence Housman	Peter B. Kyne	Thomas Anderton
Lawrence Beasley	Plato	Thomas Bailey Aldrich
Leo Tolstoy	Quincy Allen	Thomas Bulfinch
Leonid Andreyev	R. Derby Holmes	Thomas De Quincey
Lewis Carroll	R. L. Stevenson	Thomas Dixon
Lewis Sperry Chafer	R. S. Ball	Thomas H. Huxley
Lilian Bell	Rabindranath Tagore	Thomas Hardy
Lloyd Osbourne	Rahul Alvares	Thomas More
Louis Hughes	Ralph Bonehill	Thornton W. Burgess
Louis Joseph Vance	Ralph Henry Barbour	U. S. Grant
Louis Tracy	Ralph Victor	Upton Sinclair
Louisa May Alcott	Ralph Waldo Emmerson	Valentine Williams
Lucy Fitch Perkins	Rene Descartes	Various Authors
Lucy Maud Montgomery	Ray Cummings	Vaughan Kester
Luther Benson	Rex Beach	Victor Appleton
Lydia Miller Middleton	Rex E. Beach	Victor G. Durham
Lyndon Orr	Richard Harding Davis	Victoria Cross
M. Corvus	Richard Jefferies	Virginia Woolf
M. H. Adams	Richard Le Gallienne	Wadsworth Camp
Margaret E. Sangster	Robert Barr	Walter Camp
Margret Howth	Robert Frost	Walter Scott
Margaret Vandercook	Robert Gordon Anderson	Washington Irving
Margaret W. Hungerford	Robert L. Drake	Wilbur Lawton
Margret Penrose	Robert Lansing	Wilkie Collins
Maria Edgeworth	Robert Lynd	Willa Cather
Maria Thompson Daviess	Robert Michael Ballantyne	Willard F. Baker
Mariano Azuela	Robert W. Chambers	William Dean Howells
Marion Polk Angellotti	Rosa Nouchette Carey	William le Queux
Mark Overton	Rudyard Kipling	W. Makepeace Thackeray
Mark Twain	Saint Augustine	William W. Walter
Mary Austin	Samuel B. Allison	William Shakespeare
Mary Catherine Crowley	Samuel Hopkins Adams	Winston Churchill
Mary Cole	Sarah Bernhardt	Yei Theodora Ozaki
Mary Hastings Bradley	Sarah C. Hallowell	Yogi Ramacharaka
Mary Roberts Rinehart	Selma Lagerlof	Young E. Allison
Mary Rowlandson	Sherwood Anderson	Zane Grey
M. Wollstonecraft Shelley	Sigmund Freud	
Maud Lindsay	Standish O'Grady	
Max Beerbohm	Stanley Weyman	
Myra Kelly	Stella Benson	
Nathaniel Hawthrone	Stella M. Francis	
Nicolo Machiavelli	Stephen Crane	
O. F. Walton	Stewart Edward White	
Oscar Wilde	Stijn Streuvels	
Owen Johnson	Swami Abhedananda	
P.G. Wodehouse	Swami Parmananda	
Paul and Mabel Thorne	T. S. Ackland